If the Crown Fits

IF THE CROWN FITS

LEANÉ GILIOMEE

The Twisted Crown Trilogy, Book 1

Revised Edition 2024
Joffe Books, London
www.joffebooks.com

First published in Great Britain in 2022

Copyright © Leané Giliomee 2022, 2024

The right of Leané Giliomee to be identified as author of this work has been asserted in accordance with the Copyright, Designs and Patents Act 1988.

This book is a work of fiction. Names, characters, businesses, organisations, places and events are either the product of the author's imagination or are used fictitiously. Any resemblance to actual persons, living or dead, events or locales is entirely coincidental. The spelling used is British English except where fidelity to the author's rendering of accent or dialect supersedes this.

We love to hear from our readers!
Please email any feedback you have to: feedback@joffebooks.com

Cover design by SeventhStar Art

ISBN: 978-1-83526-871-1

To my grandmother, who made me fall in love with books as a little girl. You are still my favourite storyteller.

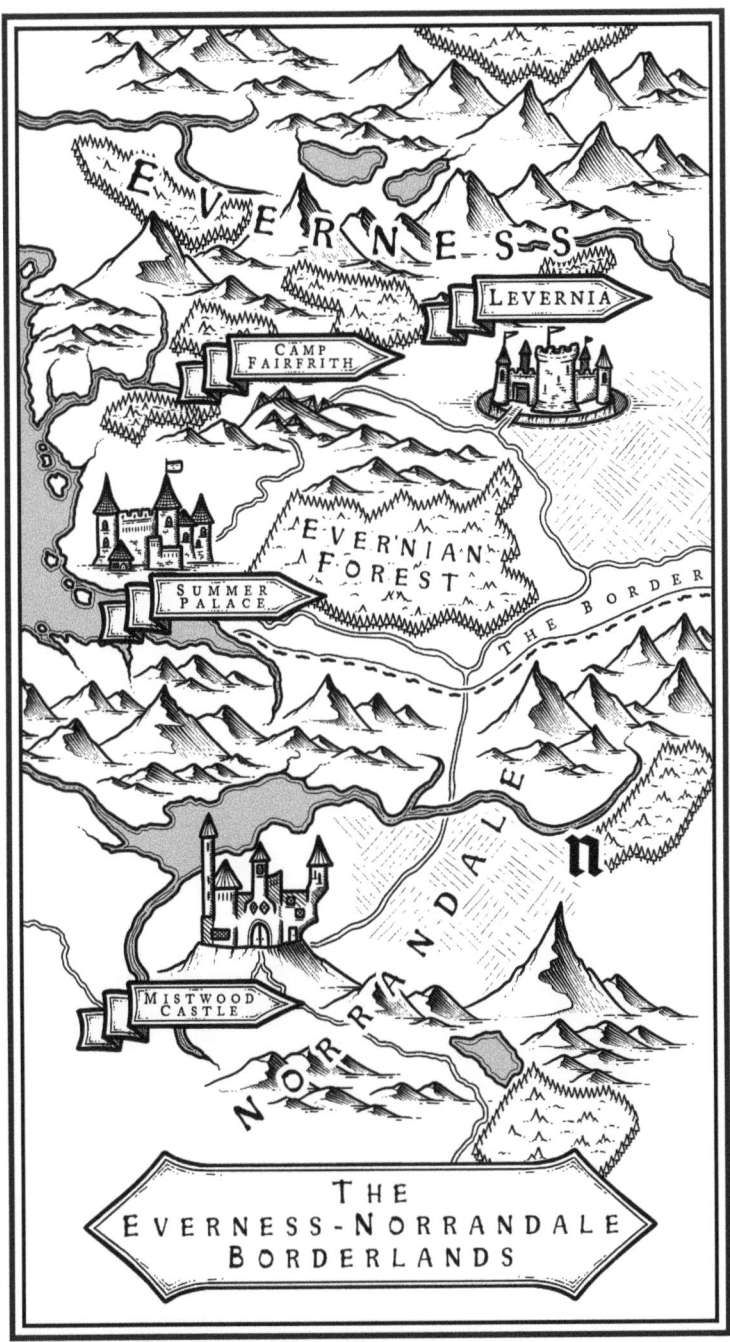

Chapter 1

The Autumn Castle of the Royal Family of Everness

Lara

I was dead.

Well, technically not yet, but I would be if they caught me.

The back door to the castle slammed shut behind me with a heavy thud and I sprinted out into the gardens. My heart beat with such intensity, I was almost sure the royal guards would hear it.

There was shouting behind me, and it pushed my legs to go faster. "Close the gates!" the guards called. "Don't let her get out!"

Fools. Did they honestly believe I was stupid enough to run out through the main gate of the castle? I darted to the right and headed for the small stretch of trees at the end of the gardens. My muscles were burning now, as if scaling the stone walls to steal the necklace in the first place wasn't enough.

I reached a tree near one of the castle walls and proceeded to swiftly climb up. The guards were only a few feet behind me. I lowered myself from one of the branches onto the stone wall. *Here goes nothing.* I jumped.

My knees buckled as I hit the ground hard, causing me to fall and roll into the street on the other side of the wall.

I got up, trying to figure out where to go next. If I were to avoid being caught, my escape would need to be quick and coordinated. Some concerned-looking people stepped out of the way of the masked figure who had just rolled into the street before their feet. My elbows and palms stung where the path had scraped my skin.

I pulled my hood over my head in the hope I would disappear among the sea of faces. My prize was heavy in the pocket of my breeches and I risked a glance back at the royal family's autumn chateau to see if the guards were still behind me. Dressed in their bright uniforms, they stood out from the crowd, eyes scanning the surrounding area.

I dipped my head, pushing through the people. Soon enough, I reached the vendors market and, thinking I'd lost them, I smiled. The market formed the centre of the town, surrounded by houses with tiled roofs and smoking chimneys. There was the scent of fresh bread and yeast in the air, which could only mean a bakery was nearby. Had I not been in a rush, I might have stopped to grab something to eat. The streets were colourfully decorated with banners and flags as the summer solstice was coming up and the people loved to celebrate with large feasts and festivals every year. It was perhaps the one occasion that both the poor and the rich looked forward to, but I suspected this was only because the solstice was an excuse to get hammering drunk.

Merchants offered me things to purchase, but I didn't have the time or the money for distractions. The border was more than a day's ride away and I would have to hurry if I didn't want the guards catching up to me. Getting across was going to be difficult enough as it was, considering the price on my head. My only advantage was that they didn't know exactly what I looked like.

Some part of me wondered if I was making a rash decision, running away from everything I knew. But things back home were getting messy, and I didn't know how much longer I would be able to hold out. I needed a fresh start, away from this life.

So, I would cross into the kingdom of Norrandale, have my freedom, and the Masked Bandit would be nothing more than myth. It wasn't exactly the most original name the monarchy could come up with. I was a bandit who wore a mask. But operating under a name that was well known within the kingdom? Well, I would be lying if I said I didn't feel the smallest sense of pride.

"End the monarchy! Fight for the freedom of the Everneans!" The man on the other side of the market caught my attention. He was standing on top of a wine barrel, preaching to the crowd about how we were taxed too much and that the royal family didn't offer us enough protection from enemy kingdoms or growing crime in the cities. A rebel, and a stupid one at that. His words could easily be seen as treason, for which they could hang him. But I couldn't blame him. The people were suffering, still not recovered from the famine a few years ago. Times were hard. But while some of the poor were dying on the streets, the rich were still rolling in money. Especially the royal family. Perhaps bravery and stupidity weren't all that different.

Turning left into an alley, I started running, but before I could reach the end, a guard stepped around the corner. He was young, his face still the picture of innocence.

His eyes widened suddenly — he wasn't expecting to see me. Well, that made two of us.

"She's here!" he called out. I only had a few seconds to react. I unsheathed the two daggers at my thighs and sped towards the poor kid. He pulled out a sword of his own but he was too slow, too clumsy.

I kicked at his wrist, causing him to drop the sword. It slid across the cobbled path, away from us. Panic formed in his expression and I almost felt sorry for him before I knocked his feet out from under him and jabbed my dagger into his thigh when he hit the ground. He screamed in pain and I quickly pulled out the knife, wiping it clean on his trousers.

"Sorry," I apologised half-heartedly. "It's nothing personal." I got up and looked around the corner to see the guards running towards us. "You'll be fine." His wide eyes met mine in disbelief as he breathed hard, lying on the ground and reaching for his wounded leg.

I turned back, running in the opposite direction and making a quick left into the street. The sound of the approaching guards was thunderous behind me — a wicked melody, as their steps were almost in unison — and a harsh reminder of what would happen if I were to get caught. I was vexed with myself. Everything had been going perfectly according to plan, until a guard had burst into the room like he'd known I was there. I forced myself to concentrate on the task at hand and not consider the possibility of a set-up.

Having nowhere else to go, I barged into the nearest house, and to my luck (which had not been treating me well today) it was empty. I hurried up the stairs of the small home until I reached the hatch that would lead to the roof.

The cool breeze struck me as I pulled myself up and closed the hatch.

I had two choices — I could go left and run across the rooftops or I could go right … and run across the rooftops. I groaned loudly. This was not what I signed up for when I had agreed to this deal.

I walked over to the edge and, sure enough, the guards were below, running about in search of me. I caught one of the guards turning his head and my courage deserted me, knowing he had seen me. Shaking my head, I approached the right edge of the roof. I had never been afraid of heights. I used to fall out of trees soon after I could walk. This, however, didn't stop my stomach from lurching the moment I was mid-air, my arms and legs flailing slightly.

I hit the next-door roof with a thud and my shoulder protested in pain. But I had to get up. Had to keep running. The sky had become grey, a dark cloud pulling over the blue like a woollen blanket. I got up, checking my pocket to make sure the necklace was still inside. Relieved, I couldn't help pulling it out and taking another look. The piece of jewellery was made from a chain of gold with a leafy pattern. Small diamonds formed flowers in between. It also had a larger jewel of a rosy-golden colour that I'd never seen before. It must have come from a faraway kingdom, and it was certainly the most expensive thing I'd ever held in my hand. I frowned, looking up. Even with the slightly overcast sky, the gemstones glinted like they were reflecting the sunlight. I didn't have time to consider it because the hatch on the other roof opened and the head of a guard appeared. His eyes, dark and determined, met mine. I started running again. The roofs from here on were connected to each other. I sprinted as fast as my feet would carry me, trying hard not to slip on the moss-covered bricks and tiles.

The guards were still behind me. I could hear their boots a few roofs back, but this only motivated me to go faster. It would, after all, be no fun if there weren't some sort of chase involved. That was until I saw the rooftops ending and no possible direction to go in …

except maybe down. I stopped at the edge, peering over. It was too high. A jump like that would kill me.

"Nowhere to go." It was the guard with the brown eyes. "Just hand yourself over now while you still have the chance." His hands were in the air in a slightly defensive position, as if the fact that they weren't on the hilt of his sword was a promise that no harm would befall me. Not that I would ever believe that. I couldn't trust him. I couldn't trust anyone.

I looked around, weighing my options. I had an idea, but I didn't like it very much.

"Just hand over what we want and come with me." He spoke again, but I was barely listening.

"Come with you?" I asked, still looking around. "And get beheaded by the King? Not today, thank you. Perhaps another time." I smiled slightly.

"You don't have a choice. We can either do this the easy way or the hard way." He slowly took a step closer.

"I hate to ruin your day." The wind was coming up faster, blowing my hair to the side. "But I never do it the easy way." With that I turned, pulled my scarf loose and jumped from the roof. I only had one chance to do this right.

I flailed for a second before grabbing the banner, wrapping my scarf around it and sliding down towards the street. When I was close to the ground, I let go and shuddered before catching my breath. I looked up towards the guard. He was at the edge of the roof, his fellow guards behind him. I gave him my best smirk before strutting away.

Unfortunately, I didn't get very far before walking into a stone-hard body, which grabbed me by my upper arms to prevent me falling to the ground. He was enormous and picked me up with no effort. I struggled to get free.

But the large guard had me in his grasp. A scar travelled from the space between his eyebrows to his cheek. He grinned down at me.

"You're not going anywhere."

Chapter 2

The Border of Everness and Norrandale

Cai

The sun was high above the clouds as we reached the bridge between Norrandale and Everness. I glanced out of my carriage window at the rush of water below the bridge. Norrandale and Everness were situated on a small mass of land isolated from the continents. High mountains and deep gorges created a border between the two kingdoms. Norrandale, in the south, had lush land for prosperous farming, whereas Everness was covered by dark and ancient forests.

An angry river gushed in the ravine as the Evernean guards approached us.

The bridge was wide, with Evernean guards on the left where people entered, and Norrandish guards on the right, on the other side of the bridge. It was a fairly quiet day, with few faces to look up at us as we passed.

"I present the royal prince and heir to the throne of Norrandale," Jack, my front rider, stated.

Our identities were made obvious not only by our uniform colours, but also the luxury in our travel accommodation. That and the ring on my finger, which bore the crest of the royal family.

"Your Highness." The Evernean soldier bowed at us in greeting. I lowered my head to return the gesture. "We have been expecting your arrival. Welcome to Everness. We shall let the King know you're on your way."

Jack nodded and led our party onwards. I leaned back in my seat then, closing my eyes, and listened to the world outside. The sound of water quickly faded as we entered the Evernean Forest that covered most of the kingdom. It was replaced by birdsong and the breeze making its way through the leaves.

Once we were out of sight of the border, we swerved left off the forest road and into the thicker brush. Keeping an eye out for anyone passing by, we quickly got rid of our uniforms. We abandoned the carriage and mounted the horses, heading back to the main road.

"I still don't see why we had to do that," Conner said. He was the youngest of our party of five, barely fifteen. I was concerned about bringing him along, but Jack, who was in charge of his training, assured me the boy would be fine. And Jack wouldn't be my second-in-charge if I didn't trust him and his opinions with my life.

"Haven't you heard stories about the Evernean Forest, boy?" he asked Conner.

"You mean those fairy tales about it being a magic forest or something?"

"Those are no fairy tales." Jack's tone was teasing. "They say these woods are filled with creatures who have been cursed to roam the darkness of the forest for all time."

"And you know what they say about the trees." I couldn't help cutting in and Conner gave me a glance of uncertainty. "Didn't you know that the trees here have eyes? They are believed to be the guardians of the forest, protecting it from those with ill intent." We'd all grown up with stories of the Evernean Forest and how one should never be alone in it at night. But the myths were centuries old, almost as old as the kingdom itself.

Conner looked towards Jack. "I don't believe you and I know you're just trying to scare me."

I glanced at the branches of green surrounding us. If anything, the forest appeared to be sleeping. Calm and serene. Besides, as far as my knowledge went, there were much more realistic things to be frightened of than the possibility of mythical trees.

"Even so," I spoke up, "These woods are filled with bandits. We cannot risk making ourselves a target of any kind."

"I hear rumours that the infamous Masked Bandit has been busy recently."

"How so?" I asked Jack.

"Merchants of Norrandale have been complaining they fear to travel across the border. But the bandit seems more focused on Evernean aristocrats. I heard this bandit is often encountered on the east side of the city of Levernia, so we shouldn't be too concerned. Though it is affecting the Norrandish economy. Perhaps you should take up the matter with your future in-laws."

"Who's the Masked Bandit?" Conner asked.

"People say it's the most infamous and mischievous thief in the history of Everness, but it's all rumour," I replied. Conner seemed intrigued, but asked no more.

Above all, bandits aside, I didn't trust Prince Lance and King Magnus as far as I could throw them. I hadn't been all that surprised when my father announced the alliance between our two kingdoms by my marriage to the princess. After all, the relationship between our nations had been dire for centuries. We'd been at war so many times, I hardly thought anyone knew what the reason was anymore. Perhaps now we could finally heal a wound of the past.

I was, however, suspicious at the odd request by Lance that I come to meet his sister alone. Father trusted that I would safely find my way, but my men and I weren't taking any chances. Prince Lance had a reputation after all — loyalty was not a characteristic known to him. I would be willing to marry a stranger if it meant peace for my kingdom, but I certainly wasn't too eager to walk into a trap.

Loosening my grip on the reins, I nudged my steed forwards with a squeeze of my calf. I sat back in my saddle comfortably once I had caught up to Jack.

"Beautiful day, is it not?" he stated and I nodded in reply. "What is it, my prince?" Jack asked and I raised an eyebrow in question. "You look rather concerned."

I shook my head slightly. "The strangest feeling. Like we are being watched." Jack glanced around at my words, scanning the area and the branches above. Then he met my smiling gaze and both of us looked towards Conner, who appeared to be desperately hiding any hint of fear or concern. I didn't believe the stories about the magic forest myself. So why was a strange feeling of unease swelling in my gut?

"May I suggest you're simply nervous?"

"Nervous about what?" I asked.

"About meeting your future wife." Conner's voice came up from behind.

"Why would I be nervous about meeting the princess?" I dared to ask, somehow knowing that I would soon come to regret it.

"I would be," Conner stated. "Ladies are nothing but trouble, if you're asking me." His words earned a chuckle from the rest of the group.

"Is that so?" I glanced behind to meet his eyes. "And what made you come to that conclusion?"

"You get in trouble even if they were the ones who broke Mother's vase and you had nothing to do with it. And if you don't do as they say, they drag you by the ear."

All of us were smiling now.

"I see," I replied and even felt a hint of remorse for Conner, who had grown up with an annoying younger sister, it would seem.

"Are you, though?"

I turned back to Jack. "Am I nervous?"

He nodded.

"Truth be told, I hadn't given it much thought."

"Of course you haven't," Jack replied and his tone was biting enough to suggest more to his comment.

"What is that supposed to mean, Jack?"

"It means, I don't think you've thought about any girl since the war."

I pretended not to know what he was talking about. In fact, I didn't want to think about that period of my life at all. Much less have a discussion about it.

"I have a kingdom to think about."

He snorted. "It appears you've forgotten the pleasure and the pain that goes along with having a woman in your life."

I didn't give him the satisfaction of a reply.

"All I'm saying is," he continued, "that spending the rest of your days with someone faithfully is life-altering. She can either be the best or worst thing that happens to you."

I raised an eyebrow in his direction. "How is that supposed to be comforting?"

"Who said anything about comforting?" He chuckled. "You don't pay me for that."

I couldn't help smiling at my old friend.

"The marriage is still advantageous in many ways, is it not?" Alastor, our weapon keeper, questioned.

"Yes. We have lots of crops and raw materials such as gold and silver, which could be beneficial to Everness considering how many of the people live in poverty. But Everness has military enforcements that Norrandale's army simply can't compare to. After the war, we have been a meek army at best. There is a reason so few dare to threaten them."

"The only reason King Magnus has such a large army is because most of the people are hungry enough to sell their souls. At least that's what I've heard," Jack said. "He doesn't pay them nearly enough, but threatens their families — which makes them loyal to the monarchy and to them alone."

"Loyalty out of fear isn't real loyalty," Alastor said.

"I agree." I nudged my horse forwards. "But creating an alliance with them is safer than fighting them. There may be peace in Norrandale now, but until we are able to protect ourselves, we stand the risk of being invaded by almost anyone."

"But still." Jack would not give up the conversation and I was beginning to sense that perhaps it had been too long since *he'd* had a lady in his arms. "You must wonder what she'll be like."

"If she's anything like her brother, you're in big trouble."

Alastor's comment was muttered as a joke. Most of the time he didn't have anything to say at all. Alastor was the quiet sort, but deadly. His words, however, did have some merit, which created an even bigger sense of concern in the pit of my stomach. Stories of Lance travelled to Norrandale, but I'd never heard much about Princess Eloisa. Didn't know of her reputation or if she had a mind as devious as her brother's.

"Now you really do look concerned," Jack commented and I frowned.

"You are here for my protection," I reminded him. "Instead, you have made me fear for my life."

Jack laughed. "Don't worry yourself so, Your Highness. It won't change anything."

"You're right, I'm sure she will be perfectly charming." I made an attempt at convincing myself.

"For your sake, I truly hope so."

Chapter 3

The Throne Room of the Palace of Levernia, Everness

Lara

The prince's crown was too big for his head.

Decorated with more jewels than I could count, it sat slightly askew atop his raven hair. The messy locks contributed to the appearance of a boy pretending to be king. He didn't look like he belonged on the throne. He looked like a philandering prince who thought politics was a game and poverty was a decision. I had heard enough stories to know exactly what kind of a prince he was.

I let out a heavy breath, squaring my shoulders to show the arrogant bastard that I was not one of the people he could intimidate — something he was no doubt used to, which was evident by his boyish smirk and the questionable look in his eyes.

I would not be afraid. Even if my life was in his hands.

If I was going to die, then I was not going to die a coward.

"What is this?" He gestured as if bored by me.

"The Masked Bandit, sire," the guard holding on to me said. He pulled off the hood of my cloak and the small group of people gathered in the throne room let out gasps of surprise as my long hair tumbled over my shoulders. The guard was about to reach for my mask — the cloth tied under my eyes — and I pulled away frantically, when a voice echoed through the throne room.

"No!" The prince leaned forwards on his throne more eagerly. "Let's not spoil all the fun just yet. Besides, she could be an imposter." He sat back. "You can release her."

I glanced up at the marble pillars of the throne room, towering and prominent, serpents wrapped around them like a noose around a neck. The thought made my stomach clench. I would prefer my own neck to remain noose-free.

The guards at either side of me seemed wary of the order, as if they expected me to bolt for the nearest door or pluck out a hidden dagger and stab one of them.

Neither was a viable option for me at that moment … as much as I might have enjoyed it. But they obeyed their prince and unlocked the chains around my wrists. I took a second to adjust my sleeves, which had got pulled up during the process of me being dragged here against my will.

I watched His Highness get up from the throne and the whole room went silent in suspense and anticipation.

He approached me slowly, as if he were a hunter and I were the deer.

I took this as my opportunity to size him up. Getting an audience with the Prince of Everness was hardly a task easily done. You would have to steal something very valuable in order to be tried for treason of the highest degree. A personal offence against the royal family, if you will.

If I had got away with it, then I would have been halfway across the kingdom by now with a sack of gold in my pocket and a brand new life ahead of me. But now the necklace would never be sold and I had the nauseating feeling in my stomach that I would never leave this palace.

Instead, I was being intensely observed by a royal prince.

Apparently, our "faithful" King Magnus had become too ill to attend public events. At least that was what I'd heard at the marketplace, not too long ago. I didn't indulge in gossip, but rumour had it that it wouldn't be long before the coronation of a new king took place.

Prince Lance was tall and lean, his body not quite that of a warrior or soldier who'd be willing to fight for his people in battle. Aside from the ridiculous crown, he was wearing rather glamorous attire — boots polished well enough that I could practically see my own reflection in them, and a tunic threaded with silver. Something so expensive would feed a few families for months. And that thought alone, that he lived such a luxurious life while his people starved, made me hate him all the more.

From afar, his eyes appeared darker, but the closer he got to me, the more I realised they were icy blue. Cold and uncanny enough to give one shivers.

He sneered for a moment and I looked away, taking in the vast room. I didn't enjoy being stared at. I didn't enjoy feeling like prey.

"I mean, you honestly expect me to believe this is the most dangerous thief in Levernia?" He gestured to me. His question was directed towards the two guards. "I was told that someone stole a family heirloom from the royal household." He crossed his arms, lifted an eyebrow, and I swore I could hear the guard to my right gulp. The scar-faced one chose to reply.

"This is her. She stole the necklace."

At his words, Prince Lance started to laugh and I contemplated just how offended I should have been. I was under no misconception about what I looked like — a skinny, raggedy, poor girl. But still, I didn't find the thought of me being a thief *that* amusing.

"You're telling me," the prince started, once he'd caught his breath, "that this—" he scanned me up and down — "scrawny little thing broke into my family's guarded residence, stole something out of our personal possessions, managed to get out of the castle, and outran all of my guards without getting caught?" His disbelief in my ability to do just that was rather insulting.

"We did catch her, Your Highness." Scarface pushed me forwards and I tripped over the toe of my boot, falling to my knees. I kept my palms flat on the ground and I clenched my teeth.

"She shouldn't have gotten in, in the first place. And now you dare tell me you got outsmarted by a thieving little girl?"

Little girl. You could feel the tension in the air now that the guards were getting scolded. Punishment was not entirely out of the question for them as well. Our audience, which consisted of a few aristocrats and their social acquaintances, watched in almost excited expectation. This was not what they bargained for when they thought about lounging in the throne room.

If I were any more stupid, I would have rolled my eyes at Prince Lance. He appeared to be only a few years older than me — if not for his title and power there would be no fear in my heart of any kind. But he held my life, my very existence, in his hand like a pomegranate, with the ability to crush it any second. What it must be to have power like that!

So, I refrained from doing anything outspoken and remained kneeling, but I kept my head up high. It was all the defiance I could manage with a question ringing in my head. Was I going to die today?

"Bring in the one responsible." I heard the two doors to the back of the throne room open. My eyes widened when I saw the young guard being pulled forwards on his knees until he was next to me, facing Lance. His leg was still bleeding from where I had stabbed him, though there was some cloth wrapped around it.

"So," Lance said. "You're responsible for letting her get away?"

The boy didn't say anything, though I could hear his heavy breathing and spotted a trickle of sweat running down his forehead.

"You know the price of letting a fugitive escape, don't you?" Lance's glare remained on the boy, who still didn't say anything, his eyes boring into the tiles of the floor. "Well, speak up, you dimwit, or should I cut out your tongue?"

This made the young guard look up.

"I ... I ... I didn't. She is a skilled fighter. I wasn't prepared."

"Well." Lance bent down, hands on knees to be on eye level with him. "You are going to regret not being more prepared."

"It won't happen again, please." He was shaking.

"You're right." Lance stood back up. "It won't." He called over one of the guards. "Have him drawn and quartered." The boy started begging, with tears soon spilling down his face. A shudder went through my body as they dragged him out of the throne room still screaming.

Prince Lance looked back at me as if nothing had happened. If he didn't have trouble torturing and killing one of his own soldiers, I'd bet he wouldn't have any trouble getting rid of me.

"You are well aware that you committed treason by stealing from the royal family of Everness, and therefore you must be punished without a doubt, Masked Bandit or not."

I didn't want to die, of course. But I had made the mistake of getting caught. This was what happened when I got caught.

"Tell me." He stepped closer and grabbed my chin with his slender fingers. They were just as cold as I'd expected. He leaned over me slightly and pulled my mask down though my face was covered in dirt and grime and somewhat unrecognisable. Not that it mattered much now. He lowered his voice before asking, "Was it worth it?"

There was a mocking tone in his voice, a devilish grin on his face, and before I knew what I was doing, my saliva had left my mouth and rested on the smooth skin of his cheek. You could practically hear the intake of every breath in the room, and it was only after my action that I realised what I'd done.

I had spat in the face of the Crown Prince of Everness.

My eyes widened in surprise. I was definitely going to die now. Prince Lance must have seen the unmistakable look of regret written over my face, because his smile was sinister as he wiped his cheek with that beautiful tunic. He stood back.

"You ought to beg for my mercy and instead you insult me further?"

His voice rang through the throne room. My heart was beating in my throat like a lump, or even worse, like the noose that would be around my neck. He stepped forwards and grabbed me by the shoulders, pulling me up. "I should have you killed right here and now. Death is, after all, a mercy to someone like you."

Someone like me? A lowlife thief.

He pushed me back into the hands of the guards. "Well, then?" His facial expression did not match the anger in his voice. "Have you nothing to say for yourself?"

I didn't move. Couldn't move. It was as if every muscle in my body had gone completely stiff. Every person in the room awaited his next words like a hungry lion waiting for its meagre prey. These monsters were actually hoping that it would be my death sentence. They always loved a good show.

"Have it your way, then. I sentence you to spend the remaining years of your hollow life rotting away in a prison cell." He motioned to the guards. "Take her away."

Immediately the crowd started murmuring. I had committed treason — we had established that. So, why on earth would he give me a prison sentence? Did he honestly expect me to believe he was a monarch of mercy, especially after what happened with the young guard?

Did he plan on being the charming sort that would woo the people with his many words, and yet have few actions to accommodate them? As far as my knowledge went, he'd had legislative power alongside his father for more than a few years and he had done nothing to make any of his subjects' lives any better. The crowd continued their low chatter and I clenched a fist as the guards pulled me out of the room.

It didn't make sense. Even he must have known that the people would have preferred a public execution to just another prisoner. An example of what would happen to anyone who tried to wrong the royal family. If he wanted to win their approval, then he would have done just that. So why was it more important to show mercy instead of creating fear? Fear was power after all, was it not?

I was dragged once again, away from the aristocracy and royalty and into the caverns of the palace where few dared to enter and even fewer ever came out alive. We'd heard stories about prisoners at the palace. When I was younger, I used to think they were only tales meant to scare children from getting caught doing something they weren't supposed to do. But walking down the dark stone hallways, I wasn't so sure about that anymore.

The cries from tortured men could be heard from afar and I tried not to gulp. *I will not be afraid*, I repeated in my head, though it did little to ease my angst. I would get out soon. My only concern was that soon wouldn't be soon enough.

I was tossed into an empty cell before a key turned and the guard left me to my solitude. There was a mouse in the corner of the cell that swiftly scurried away upon my arrival.

"Sorry for the intrusion," I muttered.

I scooted back until I could lean my head against the wall, knowing that by tomorrow morning my whole body would ache from sleeping on a stone floor. I could smell the breeze coming in through the barred window and I imagined what it would be like, had I been near the border now, instead of in a cold, musty prison cell.

Dinner was not a three-course meal … as was to be expected. I could only glare at the cold mush in the bowl before moving it away.

I could only hope that things were better back home. While rumour often got out of hand with my reputation as the Masked Bandit, I was good at thieving, and over the years it had become a responsibility of mine to ensure that my family stayed alive.

I thought about Uncle Arthur and how he was probably sitting at his table, with his hands in his hair, like he'd been doing most days for the past few months. And Ray. My childhood friend who taught me how to pick pockets. What would he say if he knew the trouble I'd got myself into? He'd probably just got back from hunting. Or maybe he was sitting in a tavern somewhere, listening to drunkards overshare valuable information. Ray had a special talent for spotting the perfect target when it came to thieving. And none of them knew I was in a prison cell. They were still expecting me to be home in a few days. And I had left them, had left my responsibility to take care of all of them. Not because I didn't care, but because I cared too much. I had decided to run away, and look where it had got me.

There was a sound echoing through the prison passageways. Another scream. I cringed.

I had eyed everything on my way to the cell — the exits, the guards, the keys. Escaping would not be easy, but certainly not impossible.

It grew dark swiftly and I lay down on the cold tiles to attempt sleep, my cloak covering me, in the corner of the cell.

There wasn't anything better to do ... for now.

The sound of metal clanging woke me up with a start. I heard the cell door open, but it was dark and my head was clouded with sleep. Confused at my location and how long my slumber had lasted, I didn't have time to react before two pairs of strong hands wrapped around my upper arms and I was being pulled out of the cell.

"Hey!" I don't exactly know why I shouted or tried to yank free as they chained my wrists. I knew it was a hopeless effort. But I panicked, thinking Prince Lance had only pretended that he was sentencing me to prison and that I was being dragged out to be privately executed.

"Where are you taking me?"

The guardsman remained silent, staring straight ahead of him, his hands keeping a tight grip on my chained wrists. It was the one from the rooftop again, the one with the dark brown eyes. I was starting to get annoyed with his face. But I had a right to know if I was going to die, didn't I? We followed a guard in front who carried a candle to light our way in the dark.

I kept quiet, realising I was being taken further away from the prison and deeper into the palace. They didn't take people who were about to be executed for a tour of the palace, did they? So it must have been something else. It was pitch-black outside the windows, so I presumed it to be the early hours of the morning.

They marched me through long halls and corridors until I had almost completely lost track of how to get back. Eventually we stopped in front of two large wooden doors. I had a few ideas of what might be behind them. None of them were pleasing. The guard in front knocked twice and another guardsman inside opened the door. With little effort, I was pulled into the candlelit room.

The royal chambers.

The prince's royal chambers, to be more specific.

Evident by the fact that there were the kinds of furnishings you would see in a sleeping chamber. The prince himself was lounging on a chair with his feet on the table, drinking a cup of what must have been wine. And though he had shed his tunic and only his white linen shirt was now visible, that darned crown still sat atop his head.

I wondered for a moment if perhaps he was drunk and then I wondered if I could use that to my advantage.

"You may leave." He gestured to all of the guards.

"But, sire—" the one holding me protested.

"I thank you for wanting to protect me, Rhen, but you are dismissed."

The prince repeated himself, half annoyed, and reluctantly the few guards left. Rhen unchained me and then closed the door behind him.

I stood frozen, unsure of what to do next, waiting for him to say something, to perhaps explain why I was there. He stared at my face and I knew my identity had already been revealed to at least half a dozen people. A character I had spent years creating … gone in a moment. But there would be no use in sulking about it. I tried to comfort myself with the thought that, should anyone start spreading stories about it, no one was likely to believe them anyway.

"Would you like something to drink?"

I glanced at the wine and shook my head. "No, thank you."

"How was prison?" He asked casually, as if asking me about the weather.

I crossed my arms. "Not quite the luxury service I was expecting, but certainly a royal-quality stay."

He chuckled, putting his feet down, and proceeded to get up from his comfortable seat.

I eyed him as he walked around the table, taking off his crown. Based on his mannerisms, I could definitely confirm that he was not drunk and I might even admit that I was slightly disappointed at this fact. To escape from a drunken prince would be much easier than from a sober one. My eyes scanned for the windows, my mind in the habit of looking for the quickest way out. Lance caught me doing this, but he didn't say anything about it.

"So, you do talk? Tell me," he started. The knot in my stomach tightened. My life was still in his hands. "Why did you try and steal that necklace?"

I wanted to grin, just a little. He might have had the upper hand in power, but I was a trained thief. Of course, I had a few tricks up my sleeve. I had to remind myself that even though I'd made a mistake, even though I'd got caught, I was still the best bandit in the business and that I would not be belittled by a spoiled prince any longer than I had to be. He could always have me hanged, but not if I escaped first.

"Tell me something first." I tested the waters. Lance was unpredictable but I might still be able to talk my way out of this. It was worth a try. I had nothing to lose ... Except maybe my head.

He tilted his chin up, his expression intrigued. "You want to ask *me* questions?"

"Why am I here?" I quickly replied, trying not to sound nervous or afraid.

Lance squinted a little. "I don't think you're in a position to be interrogating me." His tone suggested a strange form of familiarity, as if we were old acquaintances. Before I could think of how to respond, he asked, "What is your name?" Not the question I was expecting, but one innocent enough that I might just be able to keep him distracted while I figured out my plan to get out of there.

"I have many names," I replied somewhat truthfully. "Thief, rogue—"

"Masked Bandit." He finished my sentence.

"You said I was an imposter."

"But we both know you're not."

I started walking around the large oak table he'd clearly dined at earlier, each step calculated like a move on a chessboard. I slid into one of the chairs. What he failed to notice was the knife that was on the table, which I slid into my sleeve.

"I'm talking about your real name."

I settled back comfortably as if I owned the room and all its luxurious décor. Even though my heartbeat pulsed in my ears, I couldn't allow him to sense my fear. "I see," I said, as if thinking it over. "And why is that of importance?"

"I like to be on a first-name basis with everyone who steals from me," he replied, sounding almost bored. I once again found myself wishing he was drunk. Maybe he would be less of a prick.

He approached me slowly.

"I can't imagine you would care about the identity of a pathetic little pickpocket."

He came across as the kind of person who'd feel insulted if he had to breathe the same air as someone who didn't have a title.

"Pickpockets don't steal from the royal family."

I stood and grabbed him by the collar with my left hand and pointed the knife at his throat with my right. His eyes went wide in momentary surprise.

Yes, little rich prince. I may never be your equal. But you should be afraid of me.

"You don't want to do that." Lance didn't sound quite as desperate or afraid as I would have liked, but at least there was more uncertainty in his voice than before. "I have half a dozen guards waiting outside who'd be more than happy to escort you to your death."

"Isn't that why I'm here? So you can kill me yourself?" I spat out.

Lance gulped, the apple of his throat bobbing under the knife. "I have no intention of killing you."

It was my turn to be surprised. "You don't?"

"If I wanted to kill you, you'd already be dead." Maybe he did have a point. But that didn't mean I was going to trust him.

"Then why am I here?" I remained unmoved, with one hand clutching his collar and the other holding the knife.

Lance tilted his head towards the table. "Maybe you'd like to put the knife down first." I wouldn't like to, but I didn't want to risk him calling his guards.

"Fine." I jammed the knife into the wooden table.

"What is it with you peasants always resorting to violence?" He rubbed his throat but I knew for a fact I'd caused no damage to his skin.

"Violence is an unfortunate consequence," I answered. "Sometimes we must do unpleasant things to stay alive."

"That's the first thing you've said that we can agree on," Lance admitted.

I wasn't sure what he meant. What did he know about surviving? "You may call me Lara." He looked almost disappointed for a moment and I suspected my name was neither as grand nor as sinister as he'd hoped it would be. But it was gone as quickly as it came. To my displeasure, he pressed his lips into some resemblance of a smile before saying, "Lance. My name is Lance."

"I know that," I replied. Obviously.

"An introduction is still considered polite manners from a prince."

"You threw me into a prison cell — I think we are way past polite manners." Never mind the knife I'd just held to his throat.

"You stole my family's jewellery. Did you expect me to invite you in for tea?"

My jaw clenched in dissatisfaction. "Why am I here?"

"I'm afraid I'm not quite finished with *my* questions, yet," he said. What kind of interrogation was this?

"So, tell me why you tried to steal that necklace?"

I looked around the room and spotted the family portraits that decorated the walls. They were beautiful, but clearly done a long time ago as the living successors were still young children. One of them was a painting of King Magnus and his first wife, Queen Estella, holding a baby boy with black hair that could only be Lance. The next one had the Queen with two baby girls in her arms. Princess Eloisa and her stillborn sister. The story goes that Queen Estella died after giving birth to the stillborn sister. I assumed the painting was an artistic impression, something the King wished could have been. The kingdom mourned for months, but that was before my time, so

I have no memory of it. And the last one was a painting of the King, Lance a little older, and Queen Rivana. Rumour had it that King Magnus married her on a whim to save some alliance. The marriage didn't last very long before it got annulled.

"I like the paintings," I said, just to annoy him.

"Why did you try and steal that necklace, Lara?" His tone was firmer this time, dressed with a hint of annoyance.

I couldn't help but let out a small sigh. "Try is an awful word."

"What?"

"Try sounds as if you attempted to do something only to fail at it. At least, in the context you're giving it."

He frowned. "What are you insinuating?"

"I'm saying that I didn't *try* to steal the necklace." I reached into the hidden pocket in the back of my bodice before pulling out the string of fine-cut jewels and tossing it to him.

"I'm saying I did steal it."

It could have been a stupid move, giving him the necklace, but I was slowly running out of options and bargaining chips. Jumping out of the window didn't even seem like such a good idea anymore. I walked to the other side of the table.

His jaw slackened a little, to my satisfaction. "How did you … ?"

"Steal it?" I allowed myself a small smirk. "Well, that's my favourite part. You see, I was mid-escape when your guards caught up to me and took the necklace. One of them — what did you say his name was again? Rhen, I believe — placed it in his pocket.

"I should tell you that your guards are not immune to pickpocketing and that even an eight-year-old boy could have stolen that necklace back and replaced it with a fake, without being noticed — all before we reached the court. I'd originally planned to replace the necklace with a fake to buy me some time but then the whole plan went up in shambles when the guards discovered me.

"You might want to consider improving your security, Your Highness." Of course they took any weapons I had, checking all the visible places, but thinking they had the real necklace, no one thought to inspect any further. "Now will you tell me why I'm here?"

He surveyed me for another moment before looking at the necklace in his hands and, after some inspection, realising that it was in fact his sister's. His sister who was halfway across the kingdom, staying at the family's Autumn Castle. I eyed him, expecting an answer to my question.

Instead I got another question. "Why?"

Why? I withheld a grunt of discontent. "I already answered your questions. Now answer mine." Never mind stealing from him. I could be hanged simply for the way I was talking to the prince. Although his face didn't tell me he was grossly offended.

"Yes, I'm afraid you're not very good at bargaining."

"You want to know why I stole it?" I asked. "Because there is good money in it, even you could have guessed that. That's why people steal things … to get what they don't have or can't afford."

Lance shook his head. "You're not that stupid. There are a lot of things you could steal that would make you rich, none of which would be treason. This—" he held the necklace up, letting the string of jewels dangle between his fingers — "has a bigger purpose."

Maybe he wasn't as dumb as I thought. Not that it really mattered. He was still a prince. He was still the enemy. Perhaps I did have another bargaining chip after all.

"I have two conditions before telling you."

There was that bored expression again. He let out a heavy sigh. "I'm listening."

"After I tell you why I stole the necklace, you tell me why I am here."

"And your second condition?"

My gaze shifted to the necklace. "My second condition is that I get to keep the necklace." I was in so deep over my head, I didn't think I'd be able to dig my grave any deeper. But I was too far gone to stop now. To my surprise, he tossed me the necklace, which I barely caught. Maybe he only did so because he still planned to kill me. But I had plans of my own.

"Deal."

I stared at him, flabbergasted for a moment.

"Very well." I tried to sound casual, but it would do little to aid me now.

"I want you to tell me everything, from the beginning," he requested, and I took a deep breath.

"I was hired to steal the necklace."

"By whom?"

"I don't know," I answered truthfully. "The person wanted to remain anonymous. I received a letter, with a sum of money, saying that if I stole the necklace, I could keep it. They gave me the location of the necklace and everything. I assumed this person had bad blood with the Crown, perhaps an ex-lover of Eloisa who didn't want her to have it anymore, but didn't want it himself either, you know ... that sort of thing."

"And none of this seemed even slightly suspicious to you?"

I placed my palms flat on the table. "Look, your people out there are starving. It doesn't matter who asks you to do what, or if it is treason.

If the money is good enough, most of us would do anything." Lance didn't come across as the caring sort of prince. No matter how much he might pretend to be one to the court.

"Besides, it's just a stupid necklace — Eloisa has lots of jewellery, and I doubted she was going to miss one of her necklaces."

Lance pressed his lips together, and my concern grew.

If I couldn't jump out the window and I couldn't talk my way out of there, I didn't have many options left. His guards must still have been waiting outside the door. I couldn't exactly just knock him unconscious and make a run for it.

"I'm afraid stealing this necklace isn't as harmless an act as you thought."

He walked over and took the necklace from me again. "This necklace being stolen could lead to war."

My eyes widened. My anonymous benefactor had failed to mention this. Then again, why would they?

"My sister is engaged to the prince and future king of our neighbouring kingdom, Norrandale. This necklace was an engagement gift from Prince Cai to her."

I frowned. "What does that have to do with anything?"

Lance rubbed his chin in a moment of thought. "I was really hoping we would be honest with each other, Lara."

Where was he going with this?

"You see, I know you didn't tell me the whole story. Because you weren't just asked to steal the necklace, you were asked to leave something in its place. Weren't you?"

The letters. How could he possibly know about the letters?

"Did you know the contents of those letters when you left them in my sister's possession?"

"No, I didn't care. I'm not exactly opposed to committing treason, in case you haven't noticed."

"So you did know that you were possibly committing plotted treason."

I felt my breaths getting shorter. "Of course I did. The question remains, how do *you* know?"

"They were fake romantic letters from a made-up secret lover, telling her how he loves the necklace she sent him as a token of affection."

Maybe I should have taken the time or the care to read those letters before I placed them.

"You see, Prince Cai will be visiting the kingdom and my sister in a few days and he will expect her to wear the necklace at their engagement celebration. When it is discovered that she no longer has it, combined with the letters, Prince Cai and Norrandale will be furious to have been betrayed, and will wage war on Everness. King Eric's army may be weak, but he has too much pride to let something like this go."

He pulled up one of the chairs and sat down again. "I know all this, because I'm the one who hired you to steal the necklace."

My mouth fell open, and my palms began to sweat.

"It was you? But why?"

"A few reasons actually. I needed the necklace without my sister getting suspicious, and I needed a thief. You have quite a reputation around here."

"But you're willingly putting your sister's life and your kingdom in danger! And for what?" "We don't have to do any of that." I didn't like him using the word *we* in a sentence when it meant *the two of us*.

"What are you talking about?"

He placed the crown atop his head again, still slightly askew. "As well as testing you, I needed to get you and the necklace in the same place at the same time. This was the easiest and most efficient way to do so. Now, I know about your loyalties and your skills. You are most welcome to applaud me anytime you wish." At least now I knew why the guards were upon me so quickly. It was a set-up. By the royal heir, of all people.

I swallowed hard. I was wrong — he wasn't a philandering, partying prince. No, he was a scheming, conniving liar. "What do you want from me?" What was all this for?

He took a sip of wine. "I need you to steal something for me." I could hardly believe what I was hearing. All of this, everything, so I could steal something for him?

"And what is it that you want me to steal?" The question made him chuckle and I felt a pang in my stomach.

"I need you to steal from a prince."

Chapter 4

The Evernean Forest

Cai

The morning had become afternoon and I rolled my shoulders to release an ache in the muscles of my back.

"We will soon have to find a place to stop for the night," Jack suggested. After our earlier conversation had ended, we spent most of the journey in silence. And for some reason, I was rather thankful for it. Though the quiet did allow my mind to wander to unpleasant places, which wasn't much better.

I heard a bird screech in the trees above and looked up. In that moment I felt a hand on my leg, and I drew my hunting knife before my eyes even landed on the person belonging to the hand. At my action, my guards followed by drawing their own weapons. I was surprised to find myself looking down at an old woman with grey tassels of hair hanging over her shoulders and a large coat wrapped around her small body. She appeared to have come out of thin air. I forced my heartbeat to calm down with a breathing technique we'd learned during the war. Why was she dressed for winter in the middle of a hot day?

"Do you have water for an old woman, please? I need water."

I sighed in relief and gestured to Brutus, who carried our food and drink. He took out a flask of water and handed it to her.

"Thank you, sir."

Brutus nodded in response. I often wondered if he wished he could speak. And if so what would he have to say? I couldn't imagine being in that position.

The woman drank thirstily. What was she doing so deep into the forest? There wasn't a village for miles.

"Do you need help?" I asked, concerned.

"No, thank you, Your Highness," she replied, and I sat back in my saddle in surprise.

"How do you know who I am?" She wiped the sweat from her brow, suddenly appearing much better.

"I know a great many things," she said, and Jack's gaze met mine.

She opened her coat and the insides appeared to be lined with lots of little things, from jewellery to trinkets to small weapons. "Would you like to buy something?" A strand of grey hair fell down her wrinkled forehead but she didn't brush it away.

"No, thank you," Jack replied for me.

"Very well." She shrugged, unfazed, and closed her coat.

Then she looked at me, the gaze in her crystal-like eyes intensifying. "You want to go that way." She pointed to the path that went right at the fork ahead.

"But we are travelling to the coast," Jack said. "We must be heading west, I'm afraid."

The woman shook her head. "You must go east." Her gaze didn't waver from mine. "Soon you will find a pool where you and your men can rest. You must swim in the water, Your Highness, for if one of royal blood enters the water, it will show you images of your future and what you must do in order to preserve it."

Jack chuckled. "Your Highness, surely you don't believe this."

The rest of my men remained quiet and Conner's face had gone slightly pale.

"Do I look like I'm talking to you, young man?" This shut Jack up. Turning back to me, she continued, "Go to the pool as I tell you. From there proceed to your destination. You must have courage, Your Highness. The journey will not be full of ease. But perhaps you will find what you didn't know you were looking for."

She pulled a dagger from one of her coat pockets, the hilt crested with patterns of gold. "You're going to need this." She held it out to me. "And thank you for the water."

Not wanting to seem rude, I took the dagger and thanked her politely.

"Remember my words, Highness," she said in a serious tone. "Be careful please, these woods aren't safe." She smiled and patted my horse's neck before walking off as if nothing had happened at all.

The lot of us looked at each other in confusion.

"Which road are we to take?" Conner asked. His eyes were on the woman, who was quite a distance behind us now.

I took a deep breath, looking at and contemplating the two pathways. "We go right." I couldn't explain the feeling even if I'd tried, but the path that led east seemed to pull me in, like a moth drawn to a flame. There was a sense of warning that came with the feeling, a sense of danger. But I was a soldier, a prince ... there was always danger.

"But, Your Highness," Jack protested. "We have to reach the royal summer chateau in less than five days. And as she just stated, these woods aren't safe."

"Come now, Jack." I grinned. "Don't tell me you're afraid."

"Not afraid, merely concerned for your safety."

I kicked my horse forwards. "That's exactly why you're here, to protect me if harm should befall us."

"I think you misunderstand—"

"It will be an adventure." I urged, looking back. But the old woman was gone, like she had never been there at all.

We veered right and it was only a few seconds later that Conner's voice piped up from behind. "Am I the only one who thinks that was a little peculiar?"

"She was a delusional old woman who'd been walking in the woods for too long, there's nothing peculiar about that."

I watched Jack's expression as he replied to Conner, but he looked like he didn't believe himself. Something about the air around us had changed — we were all on edge, unnerved. I had never given the myths of Everness's magical forest much thought. Their folklore had been around for centuries. People believed that the two kingdoms used to be full of magic. That the old kings and queens used to rule with great power. But the magic seemed to have died, leaving only the stories to tell.

"Well, something wasn't right with her."

I couldn't help but want to agree with Conner. Something was off about the whole encounter. I pulled out the dagger as we continued on our new path. The weapon was small but sharp, easily concealable. It looked a bit old and worn with some marks on the blade. The hilt was decorated with a small jewel. It was quite rare and beautiful. I'd seen the same kind of gemstone in a few of the jewellery pieces in my family's collection. Where did the old woman get something like that?

My horse suddenly twitched beneath me, as if sensing danger.

I glanced up at the sky. Jack, noticing my change in manner, asked "What?"

"Shhh." I held up a finger.

We stopped the horses and they stood nervously, throwing their heads. We were all listening intently, and despite the quiet, something deep inside my gut told me that it wasn't my imagination. I'd heard something.

Jack and Alastor slowly drew their swords, readying themselves.

We waited in tense silence for what felt like forever but could only have been a few seconds when out of nowhere, a loud screech erupted from deeper within the forest.

We all turned to face where the noise was coming from.

"Your Highness" was the only thing Jack managed to get out when the largest flock of birds I'd ever seen broke through the leaves and branches.

It happened so abruptly that my horse got a fright and reared, throwing me to the ground. The birds could have been mistaken for crows, but they were so dark in colour, they looked like shadows as they flew over our riding party. I quickly stood up but my horse had run off.

"Your Highness," Jack said again but I could barely hear him as they continued to screech, horrifyingly loud. Just when I thought there couldn't possibly be more of them, the shadowlike birds dived down to fly between us. They clawed and pecked, and I worried they would scratch my eyes out. We swatted at them, and I pulled out the dagger, randomly slicing through the air. The sheer volume of them cast a darkness over us but I got a few of the birds with my knife. After a few more agonising minutes, the birds flew upwards, disappearing above the canopy.

I huffed out a breath, my heart pumping so loud I could feel it in my ears.

"Are you all right, Your Highness?"

I nodded, swallowing hard.

"What was that?" Conner had the bravery to ask. His skin was as pale as a sheet.

"Just some angry birds." Jack tried to brush it off but I could tell he was shaken. He jumped off his horse and held out the reins. "Here, Your Highness."

I waved him off. "Let's just go find the horse."

I turned the dagger in my hand, eyeing it suspiciously as we rode. We'd finally found my horse grazing nearby, his previous fright forgotten. I was strangely unsurprised when we came to the pool the woman had spoken of.

The pond lay nestled in a small clearing. We stopped, letting the horses rest and drink water. I was busy taking off my boots when Alastor spoke up. "You're going swimming?"

"It's hot. Cooling down would be nice."

"As long as that is the reason and not because you believe a word out of that woman's mouth."

I pulled off my shirt. "Don't be ridiculous. She had been travelling in the heat all morning. She was just telling stories," I lied, not wanting to admit that her words still rang inside my head. I placed the dagger she had given me inside my satchel.

"Mmhhh," Jack responded, not quite believing me. "So why did we go right instead of left?"

"Well, we're not in a rush, are we? It would be nice to see some of the countryside before we meet the wicked siblings."

Jack let out a chuckle. "Is that what you're calling them now?"

"Well, I suppose we hope at least one of them isn't wicked." I glanced at him. "I hardly know anything about Princess Eloisa. Surely your spies must have some information?"

"As far as I know, she keeps to the castle grounds. Visits the harbour town at their summer home often, though. She keeps the company of her ladies' maids mostly, which I suppose could be a little odd. Other than that she doesn't engage with other aristocratic women or society."

"So you presume she's the quiet, shy sort?" Shy was better than scandalously wild.

Jack grinned. "Could be. Maybe she's just mean and nobody wants to be friends with her."

I shoved his shoulder as we walked to the pond's edge.

"I haven't heard anything scandalous," he said. "Then again, I don't hear everything." He spotted my bleeding arm. "You're hurt?"

"It's just a scratch," I said. "It will heal quickly."

The pool was the perfect place to stop for the night and the water felt refreshing after a whole day of travelling through the woods. I didn't know whether or not to believe what the old woman had said, but I was curious. I emerged through the surface and wiped the hair out of my face, taking a deep breath. Brutus had started a fire in order to prepare our next meal while Conner was setting up camp. Jack plopped down on the grass with an apple in his mouth, with Alastor next to him, sharpening his sword.

I noticed the movement of a fish in the water below and looked down only to see it wasn't a fish at all. It was like a painting, flowing with the ripples of the water. I blinked in confusion at the silhouette of the unfamiliar young woman. Maybe the old woman wasn't a liar, or I was hallucinating from a whole day of riding through the woods.

The image faded into that of a bow and arrow, and I rubbed my eyes to make sure what I was seeing was real, but as quickly as it appeared, the rippling image was gone. I looked around to the others but none of them had noticed anything.

My eyes scanned the rippling water. *I am starting to imagine things.* All our joking about the magical forest had gone to my head. I dipped my head beneath the water once more before making my way out of the pond. Jack tossed me an apple as I walked past him.

"Thanks," I muttered, on my way to get my clothes. When I was dressed, I took a seat next to them on the grass, not saying a word about the fact that the scar on my arm had mysteriously healed.

I was in a field. The sky was grey and I shivered from a cold breeze that owned the surrounding air. The field was long and wide and I was surrounded by soldiers in battle uniform. All at once, the silence around me shattered like glass and all I heard was the combination of screams and the wind. I tried to step forwards, but my feet were stuck in the sucking mud that pulled me down the more I tried to move.

Air escaped my lungs quicker than it would return.

I was on the battlefield and I needed to fight or I would die. I grabbed for my sword, but it slipped out of my grasp and I found my hands soaked in blood. They were shaking and I couldn't stop them. Was it my blood?

I heard metal clashing and looked behind me to an Argonian guard driving his sword through the torso of one of my youngest soldiers. I screamed in protest, but no sound came out. I turned and ran for the soldier, fighting the burning in my legs, fighting against the mud. But before I could reach him, I lost my balance and toppled to the ground. I fell over a dead body, his lifeless eyes staring into my own.

I awoke with a start, my breathing ragged and my body covered in sweat.

I tried to shake away the familiar image in my head, but like all the times before, it was no use. A peaceful night's sleep was something I rarely experienced. But it would do me no good to run the images through my mind over and over again. I had to think about something else, anything else.

Perhaps about the fact that in a few weeks I was going to marry a woman I'd never met before. It wasn't that the idea scared me. Forming alliances for the good of my kingdom was my duty as heir to the throne. It was only my intuition that kept telling me that something about the whole arrangement didn't seem right. Perhaps I was simply paranoid. Either way, I was going to find out sooner or later.

Chapter 5

Prince Lance's Chambers

Lara

At first I thought he might be joking. But there wasn't a hint of amusement on his face. "Pour the wine." I gestured with my head to the empty cup. Lance appeared somewhat pleased and handed me some wine. Considering the fact that it had been served to a royal prince, I had an expectation that it would taste better than the wine back home. I was wrong.

"War can be such an unfortunate consequence of these sorts of circumstances. But once your work is done, Everness won't ever have to worry about war again."

I frowned. "You're saying that stealing from Prince Cai is the key to everlasting peace for Everness? I must beg to differ, Your Highness."

"Cai has something that belongs to my family and I want it back." So, it was a specific object he wanted to steal.

"If he's on his way here, it would be easiest to strike while he is travelling. I'll attack the carriage and …"

"You will do no such thing, I'm afraid," He interrupted me. "Though that was the original plan, upon meeting you I believe I have a much better idea. As this matter is of a more delicate kind than your usual scores. And besides, do you honestly believe me to be that stupid? You and I both know that once you get that object, you will run."

He wasn't entirely wrong. "So what is it that you have planned?"

"You're not going to attack Prince Cai. You're going to deceive him by pretending to be a princess."

I almost choked on my wine. "Come again?"

"As previously mentioned, Prince Cai is already on his way to visit my sister at our summer manor. You will go in her place under the close observation of my guards and—"

"I'm sorry," I said. "So you're not yet going to tell me what I have to steal, then?"

"I can't very well tell you if I don't know what it is myself."

I blinked at him in confusion.

"Cai has a family heirloom of sorts. It used to belong to the royal family of Everness, but it was stolen from us quite some time ago. If you can grow close to Prince Cai, close enough that he trusts you, I'm sure eventually the object will reveal itself."

"You're going through all this trouble to take back a family heirloom that you don't even ... know what it is?"

"I wouldn't if it wasn't important." He bared his teeth in annoyance.

"As fantastic as your offer sounds—" I started to make my way towards the door. I was sure the guards were outside, waiting to take me back. In any case, I preferred my chances of escaping prison to this — "I'm fairly sure Prince Cai will recognise that I'm not his fiancée."

"My sister and Cai have an arranged marriage. It is an alliance between our two kingdoms. They have never met before. Prince Cai hasn't the faintest idea what my sister looks like. The only thing to recognise her by is …" He held up the string of jewels.

"The necklace," I finished, and he nodded.

"If I do this, what do I get in return?"

Lance took a moment to respond. "You will get what you desire most. There's a small stretch of land on the far western side of the kingdom. It borders some of the forest, but the title would be in your name. And then, of course, your freedom."

I looked into his eyes. Looked for any signs of deception, but found none.

"You will be compensated for your cooperation and go where you please. A royal pardon."

I dared to question him. "And if I don't?"

"Then you will be hanged for treason. At dawn," he said without any hesitation. "And that is nothing compared to what I will do to your little bandit family."

I swallowed hard.

"I know all about your uncle and his band of traitors." Lance took a sip from his wine. "Unfortunately, I have more important things to worry about than a few petty thieves, but don't underestimate me, Lara. If you betray me, you will bring my wrath upon your family."

I had been right. Prison was a trick. All of this was some messed-up scheme based on a royal feud. "Is this the King's wish? That we are to betray our allies?" I wouldn't put it past King Magnus, but no one knew the state of his illness.

"My father doesn't know anything. Nor does he need to." He tilted his head to the side. "It will be our little secret."

"And if Cai finds out I'm lying?"

"The Crown will deny any knowledge of this and hang you as an imposter." The choice was made then. I didn't have one.

I was taken to a room in one of the guest wings and the door was locked behind me. I walked over to one of the open windows and peered down. It would take more than a few bedsheets to reach the bottom and even then I would be stuck in the heavily guarded gardens. The forest was a better idea if I wanted to escape.

I remained standing at the window, watching the sun's rays leak over the horizon, when keys jangled and the bedroom door swung open. Rhen stood in the doorway with a young woman, around my age, by his side.

"This is my sister, Cordelia," he said, and she smiled at me, her dark eyes piercing.

"Nice to meet you." She placed a tray full of breakfast in front of me.

Proper food. The bread was warm enough that it melted the butter on top. There were fruits of various kinds, some of which I'd never even seen before, and a selection of jams and tarts. I didn't have to be asked twice before stuffing my face.

"She will be your lady-in-waiting and aid me in your training."

"My training?" I said with a mouth full of strawberry jam.

"You are to be presented to the heir of the throne of Norrandale and he needs to be convinced you're a princess. Prince Lance has placed me and Cordelia in charge of dressing you for the part, but also educating you on the history of Everness, as well as the mannerisms of a lady at court."

"Excellent," I muttered. "As you can see, I'm bursting with excitement."

"Rule number one." Rhen didn't seem very amused. "A woman of royal blood does not use sarcasm." I rolled my eyes and Rhen looked towards his sister.

"Get her dressed. We leave in less than an hour."

"I'm still eating." I held up my plate.

But I was beginning to understand why Lance had appointed Rhen for this specific task, as he wouldn't take no for an answer. I was hauled towards the bathing chamber adjacent to the bedroom, and before I could so much as protest, Cordelia had stripped me of my clothes and dumped me into a bath of warm water. She was surprisingly strong for such a skinny girl.

The more I tried to explain to her that I was perfectly capable of bathing myself, the harder she scrubbed the sponge down my arms. However, I did eventually manage to take possession of the sponge while she worked soap through my hair.

Despite the lack of privacy and the fact that I was being blackmailed, it was nice to be clean again. Cordelia pinned my hair up with pearls and painted my lips red after placing me in a very uncomfortable dress. The material was pale pink with a few too many frills for my taste. Cordelia laced the bodice up tight and the silky skirts were a lot heavier than I had expected. As a final touch, she added the necklace, hanging cold against my skin. I could hardly recognise myself in the reflection that stared back at me.

"Won't the servants be suspicious of what's going on?"

"There's a passage that the servants don't use this time of day. We'll go through there. My brother and I, along with a few guards, will be travelling with you. Those are the only people that know."

"And Lance trusts all of you with his little secret plan?"

"The prince has his ways of getting what he wants." Her words suggested more than she was telling me, but I didn't know her well enough to ask further questions.

A carriage with four white horses stood outside in the courtyard. The early morning air was deadly quiet and filled with slumber. Lance waited by the door of the carriage and I gathered all my courage as I approached him, head held high.

"Good morning, dear sister. I trust you slept well."

I gave his acting a disgusted expression before our heads turned as Rhen came running down the steps towards us.

"Rhen, you're late."

"I have news, Your Highness. We've found Prince Cai's carriage and his guards' uniforms abandoned near the border."

Lance clenched his teeth. "The horses?"

"Gone, Your Highness."

"Bodies?"

"None," Rhen replied. Lance slammed his fist on the side of the carriage.

"That bastard. I knew he was up to no good."

"What about the plan?" I asked.

Lance turned his gaze to me. "It stays the same until we find Cai and his men. I will send out a search party. And I'm having Captain Rhen accompany you. He knows the land better than anyone."

I almost snorted, because if anyone knew the terrain of the kingdom, it was my uncle and his band of thieves. It was the reason they had remained undiscovered for so long. Lance helped me into the carriage and Cordelia followed behind.

The carriage ride was bumpy and unstable on the rocky road leading away from the castle and suddenly I missed riding on horseback. Cordelia eyed me from the opposite bench.

"You don't sound like a peasant when you talk. At least not entirely. Your vocabulary could use some work."

I snorted. "You're very honest."

"You know what I mean. Your pronunciation is decent at least. Since Prince Cai is unfamiliar with our accents, I'm sure it will help in disguising your identity."

"Just because I'm a thief, I'm supposed to be illiterate?"

She shrugged. "Most of them are."

Cordelia was clearly the sort of lady who wasn't afraid to offend people, and though her honesty could make her unpopular at court, it made sense why Lance had chosen her for this, and I thought, just perhaps, she and I might get along. At least until I figured out how I was going to get out of this. If I ran now, I risked the lives of my family and being hunted by Lance for the rest of my life. If I didn't run, I risked discovery and a hanging.

I sighed. "I was taught how to read and speak from a young age. My uncle always told me it was a valuable skill."

"Your uncle isn't wrong. But just because you don't speak entirely like a peasant doesn't mean you don't eat and act like one."

I scowled, knowing fully she was right. And to my very horror, Cordelia proceeded to read lessons from a book titled *The Art of Being a Lady*, with all the rules about dining-table manners and what conversation to make with gentlemen at a ball. I was bored to death, though attempted to pay attention half-heartedly, as perhaps Cordelia didn't want to be there any more than I did.

That was until we stopped for water and she made me walk while trying to balance a book on my head. Something about posture, she said. And then she continued with things I had to do and say when I met Prince Cai. Apparently there were a lot of rules when it came to royalty, and it was unfortunate that my life depended on it.

Once dusk began to settle, we set up camp for the night. I watched all the guards carefully and, in turn, they watched me. The scar-faced one, who I came to know as Damon, was there too, and something in his eyes made me very uncomfortable. Before going to bed, Cordelia brushed and braided my hair.

I heard a noise in the distance, which caused me to jump.

"Don't worry, there shouldn't be any wolves in this part of the forest."

"It's not the wolves I'm afraid of. It's the bandits."

"Do you think your uncle's men would attack us in the middle of the night?"

I shook my head. "Not my uncle's men."

Uncle and his men weren't the only bandits in the woods, and through the years he had managed to make more than enough enemies. I knew them, knew what they did to the people they robbed.

"Our clan steals for survival. Others are only after blood." I heard her swallow hard. My uncle didn't even know where I was and my hope was that they wouldn't send anyone looking for me, or this whole thing could fall apart.

Worst of all, I had no way of defending myself. Lance could have at least provided me with a dagger or something. But I assumed he didn't trust me with a weapon of any kind. I could always try my luck and ask one of the guards, though I seriously doubted this would be a success. If I wanted a weapon, I might have to steal it.

I would never forget the first time I stole something.

I must have been around ten years old. Uncle Arthur had some business to take care of in the nearest town, and for some reason, Ray and I had gone with him.

"Now you two wait out here," Uncle told us outside a small tavern. "I have to meet someone inside, but I won't be long." He didn't appear tremendously excited at the prospect of seeing whoever this person was and I wondered who'd dragged him all the way out here. Uncle didn't make a habit of leaving camp unless it was necessary.

I watched as he concealed most of his face in the shadows of the hood he was wearing.

"We'll be fine," Ray reassured him.

We will? I couldn't remember the last time I'd left the camp. The buildings surrounding us felt tall and intimidating, unlike the trees of the forest.

Uncle Arthur nodded in response, letting out a small grunt. He walked into the tavern, leaving me and Ray outside. I looked around at the strangers passing by, not entirely comfortable with the prospect of waiting out here in the street.

"I don't understand," I said to Ray. "Why did he bring us along if he's not taking us with him?"

"Because I'd asked him to," Ray responded, almost cheerfully.

"What?" I looked up at him with slight surprise. Three years older than me, he was growing up to be quite tall.

"I asked your uncle to bring us along so that we could see what the town was like," Ray said.

"But why?"

"Because, little Lara—" he turned my shoulders so that I faced the street full of people — "while the forest provides us with many of the things we need to survive, the towns are full of people ready to be robbed."

My eyes widened. "What are you going to do?"

"You'll see," he said smugly.

Ray, with his scruffy hair and dirt-stained clothes, stood out in the sea of people. I called after him in panic, not wanting to be left alone, but he sent a reassuring smile over his shoulder.

Ray walked to the top of the street, turned around and walked back nonchalantly. When he returned, I looked at him with confusion.

"What was that for?"

"Did you see that man I bumped into?"

I nodded.

"Well, his pockets were quite full." Ray pulled out a small leather bag and opened it for me. Inside I could see the shimmer of gold coins. I gasped.

"Ray, that's quite a bit of money."

"Exactly."

"Aren't you afraid you'll get caught?"

"You know I can run pretty fast." He looked over the crowded street. "Do you see that stand filled with bread outside the bakery?"

"Yes." The freshly baked breads did look pretty good. I could almost imagine they were still warm, and the thought of having a slice of bread practically made my stomach rumble.

"Take one of the loaves lying near the edge of the table."

"But you just got all that money. We can buy it."

"That's not the point. It's your turn."

"My turn? I don't know how to steal that."

"It will be fine. I'll distract the baker and you just casually grab the bread as you're walking by."

"But why do you want me to do it?"

"Because, Lara," Ray replied, "this world is full of people who have much more than they deserve. And if you're going to make it, you need to learn to fend for yourself. Someday, it might save your life."

I wasn't entirely convinced but I also didn't want to feel like I was disappointing Ray.

"Okay, you distract him." I sighed.

Ray looked pleased, walking over to the baker, bag of gold in hand. I kept my eye on the two of them as Ray struck up a conversation with the man. I neared the table and the delicious smell of the breads filled my nose. Ray moved a little so that the man's back would be turned to me.

I didn't think about it for too long and wrapped two dirty little hands around the nearest loaf. My heart raced. I hurried away, slipping between the two nearest buildings. It wasn't long before Ray fell into step beside me.

"Now what?" I asked, a hint of excitement in my voice. There was something thrilling about the whole experience.

"Now," Ray said, grabbing my hand with a grin, "we run."

We were up early the next morning and I yawned loudly as Cordelia helped me tighten my stays.

"If you yawn in public, I would advise you to cover your mouth. Prince Cai doesn't need a view of all your teeth."

I ignored her comment because it was too early to start quarrelling. Once fully dressed, we got into the carriage and I eyed the guards with suspicion. All of them had swords but I couldn't spot anything small enough that I would be able to hide on myself.

"Are you listening?" Cordelia asked when we had stopped again a few hours later.

"This is ridiculous," I muttered. "How is needlework going to help me grow close to Prince Cai so that I can steal something off him?"

"Princess Eloisa is very skilled in needlework." She took one look at the mess I was creating. "You clearly are not."

I sighed. "Can't I just challenge him to a bow-and-arrow competition or something? That would be much more fun." Even if archery was not my best skill.

"You will not challenge the prince to anything. Besides, Princess Eloisa can't shoot with a bow and arrow."

"Princess Eloisa can't shoot with a bow and arrow," I mimicked and shifted uncomfortably in my seat. The frills and laces of my dress were itchy and I was tired of sitting up straight for so long.

"Take a break, then. We'll continue when we're back on the road."

Quite thankful for the respite, I got out of the carriage, slid past the snake eyes of Damon and approached Rhen, who was standing near his horse, drinking water from a flask.

"Your Highness," he said with fake politeness.

"Can I talk to you for a moment?"

"A princess would more likely say, 'May I have a word with you?'" he responded.

"Well actually that was one of the things I wanted to discuss with you." I gestured away from the group and Rhen nodded in understanding. We started walking beside the stream.

"I have no experience in the world of royals and I'm afraid I'll say the wrong thing and be discovered."

"A fair concern," Rhen said. "But what does this have to do with me? Cordelia is already educating you on this matter."

"Well, yes ..." I said. "But—"

"But?" he repeated. We were out of hearing distance of everyone else.

"Well, you're a man, right?"

"Last time I checked." His face was full of confusion.

"So Lance needs me to get close to Cai, needs him to trust me. What would make you trust a woman above all else?"

He thought about it for a moment. "I suppose I would trust her only as much as she trusted me. Based on her words and her actions."

"So you're saying I should pretend to trust Prince Cai?"

"Something along those lines. Surely you have some experience in gaining the trust of men, you know, just before you rob them blind?"

"In some cases," I admitted. "But that's only for a few minutes. Most men will trust you for a few minutes if you pretend to be sweet enough."

Rhen stopped walking. "Would that be all? We need to get back on the road."

"Not quite."

Rhen let out a sigh before we continued.

"I know Lance trusts you and everything, but I'm not sure you know what you're up against in this part of the woods."

"I take it you're referring to the rumours of bandits that have been going around for some time."

I grabbed him by the arm, making him stop. "They're not rumours, Rhen, believe me. I know these people and they will slaughter you if they have to, and not even just if they have to, sometimes just for fun."

He pulled free and kept walking. "What exactly are you trying to tell me?"

I squared my shoulders and followed him. "I'm asking you to give me a weapon so I can defend myself if we were to run into them."

Rhen actually laughed. "You don't seriously expect me to fall for that? For all I know, you'll kill me in my sleep with my own knife."

I frowned. "So you just expect me to sit there and get butchered by them?"

"Nobody is getting butchered, trust me."

"Trust you? You threw me in a prison cell!"

"Because I had orders to follow, and now I have orders to get you to Woodsbrook Manor so you can follow through on Prince Lance's plans. Do you honestly think I would risk my own head? You and I both know the prince will kill my company and me if something happens to you. So you can rest assured you will be safe. Now get back in your carriage and focus on your lessons with Cordelia."

"Okay, fine." I pretended to give up. "I suppose you're right. You have a lot riding on this as well and I'm sure you know what you're doing."

"Thank you. Now let's go." With that, he walked past me, heading for the others. I waited a few seconds before taking the knife I had stolen off him out from behind my back. I smiled and tucked it away. He was right. Men will trust you if you pretend to trust them.

With that being said, he was also wrong ... very, very wrong. It must have been only about an hour after I had fallen asleep that night when the screaming started. It was pitch-black, and just as I managed to grab the handle of Rhen's knife, I was dragged out of the tent.

Outside was chaos, with horses running about and soldiers fighting off the bandits. I had known this would happen, had warned Rhen about it. Cordelia screamed as she tried to get away from one of the men. I ran towards her, knife in hand, but I was pulled from the forest floor and onto a horse. "Got one!" the rider shouted. "You can be sold for a pretty penny with a face like that." The man's breath was foul, and he had the unmistakable paint of the Baruk clan on his arms.

I tried to fight the rider, but managed to dig my heel into the horse's ribs, sending him surging forwards. He fought to hold onto my wrists and even got a blow to my face. But after much struggle, I jabbed his side with the knife and he let out a shout of pain.

Before I could push off the man, a branch hit my neck and shoulders, causing me to lose my balance. I hit the ground hard and groaned as I saw the horse running away into the distance.

I slowly stood up and the forest became quiet once more. The horse, the bandit and my knife were gone and I could only hear the sound of crickets. I turned abruptly, trying to remember from which direction we had come, but the adrenaline and the loud beating of my heart made it difficult to think clearly. That was close, too close.

And there it was, faintly in the distance: firelight. Not from our camp, but someone else's. In my long white shift, I started walking through the woods, focusing on the light and listening for any danger that might surround me.

I stalked as quietly as possible on my bare feet.

Without warning, a screeching bird emerged from the trees, wings flapping wildly. A shriek escaped me and I flailed my arms around for a moment. Once I was certain the bird was gone, I swallowed hard, breathed even harder. And then I scowled for letting myself get scared by a stupid bird. The surprise of it had me on edge as I continued.

The campfire had been much further than I thought. By the time I reached it, roots and branches had cut me. My bare feet were covered in dirt, not that I minded this as much. But there was a cool breeze sailing around the air, a true characteristic of a dark night in the forest. The whisper of it against my skin formed goosebumps and my mind took me back to other stories I had heard growing up. Not ones of rival clans, but of other things lurking in the night.

Things that the mere thought of kept me awake as a young girl.

I eyed the small crowd sleeping around the fire. They were all men, but nothing about them stood out to tell me what kind of men they were, exactly. One of the horses, tied to the tree behind me, stirred. I motioned for it to keep quiet with my finger, as if it could understand me.

I scanned the group again. The one closest to me was snoring and, despite my moving closer, didn't show any signs of waking up. I spotted a small dagger sticking out from the satchel his head rested on, like on a pillow.

Without much thought, I crouched down and reached towards the blade with my fingertips. I smiled at my accomplishment once I stood back up with the dagger in my hands. At least now I had a weapon again. It was one of the most important rules of being a thief, after all — never be unarmed. This way, I could observe them from the shelter of the trees until morning and see if they could help me. Or I could start finding my way back.

After weighing my options, I decided it would be best to try to find what was left of our travelling party as soon as possible. If they were all dead, I hoped for Lance's sake he had a plan B, because I had no idea where I was going. I had never entered this part of the forest. And the events of tonight only served to prove why I'd been warned as a child about the dangers of these woods.

Clutching the dagger, I started to creep away. I entered the thick brush, believing my escape was successful until a voice came from behind me.

"Where do you think you're going?"

Chapter 6

The Evernean Forest

Cai

She froze, her back towards me, and I sensed she was deciding what to do next.

"I don't believe that is any of your business."

Her reply surprised me and so did the tone of her voice. The woman standing in front of me, dressed only in a night shift, with my knife in her hand, was truly very young.

She spun around, her eyes blazing fiercely despite the darkness of the night. Dark hair woven into a messy braid rested on her shoulder, and as I was still taking in the rest of her features, she swung the dagger at my face. But having been trained the way I was since childhood, I had no problem grabbing her arm and holding it in the air.

"Well, it's my dagger you are trying to steal there, so I do believe that it is, in fact, my business."

It had been my turn to keep watch for the night and I had grown tired of sitting on the ground. Deciding to stretch my limbs, I had taken a short walk. I hadn't been far from the camp when I heard her through the bushes. At first, I'd thought her to be something more dangerous, like a wild animal. But upon spotting her figure in a nightdress, I couldn't help but watch intrigued as she approached my guards. What on earth was a woman in her night shift doing here? I thought she might have been in trouble and was going to ask for help, but instead, she stepped closer and took the dagger the old woman had given me out of the satchel Jack was sleeping on.

I expected him to wake, being a light sleeper. But instead, I stared in shock as she took the dagger without having awoken a small sleeping army. It was too suspicious. So when she turned to leave, I had no choice but to question the thief.

And now, she stared up at me with those fire-blazing eyes and I wondered if there could be any sort of innocence under all that wild. She kicked me in the shin, hard enough to hurt, before turning to run. So I grabbed her from behind, pulling the dagger out of her grasp. She struggled against me as I took her back to the firelight.

"Look what we have here, gentlemen," I said, loud enough to wake everybody.

In a moment their eyes were open, hands already reaching for weapons, except for Conner, that is. His hair stood in all directions as he sat up.

"Is that a lady in her shift?" he asked, wiping the sleep from his eyes.

The girl crossed her arms as the lot of them took in her torn hems and dirt-covered feet. She had clearly been running through the woods. The question was ... why?

"She stole this, Jack." I tossed the dagger on the ground before him, partly annoyed that my best man had failed his job so easily. Jack looked half concerned and half impressed at the same time. But

I knew the whole lot of us were thinking the exact same thing ... who on earth was she?

I let go of her arm, pulled out another knife and held it up. "Who exactly are you?" She backed away slowly towards the fire and there was no doubt that genuine concern was written on her face. She hadn't planned on getting caught. That was certain. She appeared to be thinking things over. Perhaps deciding whether or not to tell the truth. "A thief?" I continued. "Thieves don't run about the woods in their nightclothes. So what, then?"

After a moment she squared her shoulders and replied. "My name is Lara. And who might you be?"

"Alcott," I lied, every inch of instinct telling me not to trust her. "Pleasure to make your acquaintance, Miss Lara." My tone was almost mocking. "Sit." I gestured towards one of the logs around the fire, but she crossed her arms, staring straight at me. "Sit," I said more sternly and finally she obeyed, plopping down like a child having a tantrum.

"Now, would you care to enlighten us as to why you were running about the woods in the middle of the night, in nothing but your shift, stealing daggers from strangers?"

She tilted her head to the side for a moment before saying, "Not particularly, no." A few chuckles left my men and I scowled, making them hush.

"Would you care to enlighten me on what exactly *you* are doing in the woods?"

Heads turned in my direction.

"I'm afraid that's private business."

"Well then, I gather we're done here." She stood up, ready to make her escape, but she backed into Jack.

"What makes you think you're going anywhere?" Though she

If the Crown Fits

didn't appear entirely at ease, she hadn't asked for our help, so I wasn't completely convinced that she was in trouble. In fact, something about her face told me she was the trouble herself. "You're going to stay right here with us until you prove that you are innocent. Is that clear?"

She started shaking her head furiously. "No, it is not clear. I didn't do anything wrong. I was robbed. The dagger was just for self-defence."

I approached her before grabbing her wrist with one hand and wrapping my fingers around her neck with the other. "You're lying," I said almost in a whisper. "I was trained to get information from soldiers, and if you were telling the truth, your palms wouldn't be sweating and your heart wouldn't have been beating so fast."

"Careful," Jack said. "She may be an assassin sent to kill you."

I let her go.

"Assassins don't wear shifts," Alastor argued.

"I'm not an assassin!" She threw her arms up in the air dramatically.

"That's exactly what an assassin would say," Conner said.

"This is ridiculous. Why on earth would I want to kill you? I will not allow you to kidnap me simply because you're paranoid," she protested. "You can't take me hostage." Her voice was cracking, an indication of her panic.

She tried to fight off Jack as he was attempting to tie her hands behind her back. Her moves were precise, as if she knew exactly where to strike, but Jack's strength eventually overpowered her own.

"I think we just did," I replied.

Jack insisted we tie her against the tree trunk, but I assumed this was only because it was his turn to keep watch for the night and he didn't feel like running after her if she tried to escape. I lay next to the fire and closed my eyes, but sleep would hardly come.

"Who do you think she is?" Jack asked me the next morning as we saddled up. Conner had just woken her and was carefully untying her, but she looked too tired to run anywhere.

"I don't know." I admitted. "The fact that I can't put my finger on it really bothers me. Part of me thinks she looks way too innocent and fragile to be able to cause any real harm."

"And the other part?" He fastened the girth around his horse, securing his saddle.

"The other part of me thinks she looks like she'll cut your throat while you're sleeping and enjoy watching you bleed to death."

"Those are two very contradictory opinions," Jack replied.

"Why do you think I'm bothered?" I retorted.

He turned his gaze towards her and we watched as she rubbed her wrists. She tossed away the blanket we'd given her for the night and slowly got up while Conner held her arm.

"How far will we take her?" Alastor's voice came from behind us and Jack looked back to me for an answer.

"As far as we have to, until we are certain she isn't a threat."

"Do you think she's alone?" Alastor asked.

"I don't know. But if she is alone and if she isn't dangerous, then perhaps she needs our help. She's clearly hiding something. We'll take her to the next village and see what happens from there."

They packed up the last few things around the campfire. Conner brought Lara to me and handed her over. She offered no struggle and goosebumps formed on the skin of her upper arms.

"You're cold," I said and she shook her head, avoiding my eyes. Her expression indicated that it wasn't out of fear, but pure fiery anger at me for what I'd done.

"Here." I took off my jacket and threw it over her shoulders before leading her to my horse. "You'll have to ride with me."

"Ride where?" she questioned, but I offered no reply. That was when she pulled away, trying to rip her arm from my grasp. "I'm not going anywhere with you."

I held on to her wrist. "Then tell me who you are and what you want and I'll let you go."

It was a dare, though I knew she'd probably stay quiet or lie again.

"I already told you who I am."

I pulled Lara to the horse. "If you needed help, then why didn't you just ask? I don't believe you're the one who needs protection. Even if you look like a damsel in that nightdress."

She didn't respond and I proceeded to lift her by the hips, placing her in the seat of the saddle. I watched in confusion as she threw her right leg over to the other side of the horse and sat astride. All right then.

I got onto the horse myself and sat in front of her in the saddle before nudging the stallion forwards into a walk. We weren't in any rush to reach Woodsbrook Manor where my unknown future awaited me. We rode slowly and stopped often to let the horses rest and drink. Lara didn't say anything, but we all kept a close eye on her.

We made lunch over a fire next to a small stream and left her sitting on the grass by herself. It was a trust that perhaps she hadn't earned yet, but Brutus started unpacking our food and I half grinned as she sat and watched him, not appearing to be making plans to go anywhere. She was hungry, too. Even if she did run now, civilisation was still fairly far off and she would be lucky to make it out of the woods alive without proper food or clothing. I assumed she knew this just as well.

She rested against one of the trees and opened her eyes in surprise when I handed her a plate with some bread and cheese. She offered no thanks, however. And I held back a sigh. All things considered, I didn't see much of a reason for her to complain. She was the one who stole from us in the first place. We weren't planning on keeping her for ever and she was certainly getting much better treatment than any other thief would. Especially if they stole from a prince. Lara did appear to be enjoying the food, though. While she ate, she watched each of us carefully. I pretended not to notice her intense staring and observation. There was no way to know what exactly she was thinking, what conclusions she was coming to.

We didn't rest for long. As soon as she'd finished her last bite, I ordered us back on the horses.

The sun baked my skin and a trickle of sweat rolled down my temple. The forest floor crunched beneath the horses' hooves and I maintained all my focus on keeping my attention away from the female body seated behind me.

"So, Conner."

The blond boy turned his head towards me.

"Yes, Your … yes, Alcott." He quickly corrected himself.

"Jack tells me you're advancing in your training. He says you're particularly excellent with the bow and arrow."

Conner's eyes lit up at my words, though he tried to hide his satisfaction.

"Don't flatter him too much," Jack called out from where he was riding at the back. "Or it will all go to his head and then what will I do with him?"

"You would know better than I," I replied. "You let everything go to your head, after all."

Jack laughed and my eyes landed on Conner again, who was still trying to hide a smile.

"Where are we?" the female voice piped up behind me.

"Should be somewhere close to the centre of the forest," Jack said.

I immediately felt her tense up behind me. "You need to get out of here."

"What?" I asked in confusion.

"We cannot be in the centre of the forest. You need to get as far away from here as possible."

I met a concerned gaze from Alastor. "Why?"

"There's a legend about what lurks in the centre of the forest. During the day there's a mist so dense that if you are caught in it, you will be wandering around, lost, until you die." The more she spoke, the higher her voice got, and I realised she was truly afraid.

"And we're supposed to believe this, based on what?" I asked in disbelief.

Perhaps this was the explanation to it all, her lies, the fact that she was wandering the forest in her shift in the middle of the night and now raved about magical mist that will kill you … she was insane.

"Umm, guys …" Conner was staring behind us, eyes as big and wide as saucers. "I don't think the lady's lying."

I looked back, following his gaze, and there it was, faint and close to the ground, but unquestionably mist, during the middle of the day.

"And you're positive this mist can kill you?" I asked.

"Well, no one ever survived to deny it!" She squirmed behind me.

"Perhaps we should make haste," Jack suggested.

I looked behind us again, and this time the mist was closer and slightly thicker than before.

"Well, I'm not risking my life while the lot of you decide what you want to do." She hit my horse's behind with her flat palm, hard enough to cause him to rear slightly. "Go, go!"

We started into a gallop and the faster we tried to outrun the mist, the closer it started creeping up on us from all sides.

"Do you people live under a rock? Everyone in Everness knows to stay away from the centre of the forest!" she yelled.

I watched the mist reach only a few feet away from us. "How do we escape it?"

"You can't escape it, you fool. Only those with royal blood can find their way through the mist."

I dug my heels into my horse's ribs and it huffed, pushing its legs to go faster.

"We're not going to make it."

I could see it in the distance, a broad clearing, and safety. "We're going to make it."

"No, we're not." She was clinging on to me so tightly, I was sure there would be bruises on my body the following day.

"Yes, we are!"

And then it was there, crawling up my steed's flanks and covering the ground in front of us. It continued advancing, until I couldn't see the field in the distance anymore, until I couldn't see in front of me.

But no sooner did it close in than we broke through it and into the safety of the clearing. The horses heaved and we all looked at each other in pure shock at what had just happened.

"Are you people insane?" Lara jumped off the horse and toppled over into the long grass. "That could have killed us."

"I told you we were going to make it."

"Yes, thank goodness for your arrogance, or how else would we have survived? It almost caught us."

"But it didn't." Jack smiled.

If the Crown Fits

"Whatever." She stood up, still in her shift and my jacket, and dusted off her hands. "I'm not going anywhere with you any longer."

"Then where exactly are you going?" I asked and she proceeded to look left and right before realising that she had no idea where she was.

"You can't walk from here and you know it." I held out my hand towards her. "Just get on and we can take you to the nearest town."

She hesitated, but knew without a doubt that I was right. As she accepted my hand, she made sure we all knew that she was very unhappy about it, then settled into a sullen silence behind me.

She held her tongue until we set up camp for the evening and Jack and Brutus lit a fire.

"You'd better put it out before you go to sleep," she said, her eyes dead serious.

"And why would that be?" Jack asked, twirling the dagger she had tried to steal between his fingers, clearly taunting her.

"Because we're back in bandit territory and they wouldn't think twice about killing you," she responded without hesitation.

"We know there are bandits." I placed my satchel under my head as a makeshift pillow.

"But clearly you don't know how dangerous they are."

"And you do?" Jack asked her, eyebrows raised.

"Yes," she said. "They're the reason I stumbled upon the lot of you."

"You were attacked by bandits?" I asked, and she nodded.

"And instead of asking for help, you decided to steal a weapon?"

"You're all fools if you don't listen to me," she warned.

"We'll be fine," Jack reassured her, taking a bowl of food from Brutus.

"Suit yourself." She lay down next to the fire. "But if they come and murder all of us, you're going to wish you had given me that dagger to protect you." With that, she earned herself a scowl from Jack and chuckles from the rest of us.

I awoke a few hours later at the sound of soft murmuring close to me. I sat up and my eyes landed on Conner, who was fast asleep even though it was his turn to keep watch. Lara's eyes were closed, and she was twisting in her sleep. She let out painful moans, and realising she was having a nightmare, I placed my hand on her shoulder.

Immediately she sat up, gasping for breath.

"You were dreaming," I said, sitting back and folding my hands over my crossed legs. Her hands shook but I didn't mention it. She rubbed the sleep from her eyes and looked around at the lot of us, seeing I was the only one awake.

"What did you dream about?" I don't know why I asked her. The words went flying out of my mouth before I could properly comprehend them.

"It doesn't really matter," she replied, lying back down and closing her eyes, though I knew she wouldn't sleep now. Because I knew what she was going through, knew what it felt like to be scared of closing your eyes at night.

"I dream too," I said softly, trying not to wake the others. She opened her eyes. "All of us—" I gestured with my head towards my men — "have memories that haunt us." She nodded slowly, her mind clearly somewhere else. "You should get some rest," I said, and she nodded again before closing her eyes once more.

Chapter 7

The Evernean Forest

Lara

My eyes opened with the sun shyly peeking out behind the tree branches. I must have eventually fallen asleep again, after my nightmare.

I watched Alcott and his men saddling up their horses, and contemplated who exactly they were, and where they came from. Judging by their accents alone, I doubted they were Evernean, but their clothes bore no symbols or clues as to who they were and they didn't appear to be carrying anything of importance, like merchant goods, to indicate the reason or destination for their journey.

Perhaps my only chance to get away would be to gain some of their trust. I could understand why they were suspicious of me. I'd hardly provided a clear story about who I was and what I was doing when I encountered them. But at that moment I'd been unprepared and taken by surprise and inappropriately dressed. In fact, I still sort of was.

The only thing I knew for certain was that they had managed to cause a lot of trouble in my life in a very short time and that I wanted to get away from them as soon as possible. Lance would explode if he found out I was missing, and that would be only if Rhen or Cordelia or any of them were still alive.

I walked over to where Alcott was returning his sword to its scabbard. For a moment, a jewel at the hilt caught my eye before my gaze shifted back to him. "I have a favour to ask you." My voice came out hoarse and groggy.

"Yes?" He didn't look like he was eager to do me any sort of favour.

"I need clothes."

He looked slightly surprised at my request, but not completely unwilling.

"I hate to tell you, madam, but I'm afraid we don't carry fancy dresses with us."

"I don't need dresses. I'll wear whatever you have."

It wouldn't be the first time I wore men's clothes. Alcott didn't seem entirely convinced.

"I'll see what I can get you."

I stood waiting as he walked over to Conner's mare and pulled a few things out of one of the bags. He made his way back to me and handed over the clothes and shoes. I mumbled a small thank you before turning around and scanning the area for bushes, hoping to find one I could dress behind. There were a few not too far off and I started making my way in that direction, before a voice came up behind me.

"Where are you going?"

I rolled my eyes. Turning around, clothes in my arms, I scowled at him.

"I'm getting dressed," I stated.

"Where?" He crossed his arms.

"Over there." I gestured to where I was heading, and Alcott shook his head.

"I'm coming with you."

My eyes widened. "You most certainly are not!"

But Alcott was already walking. "If you think this is how you're getting away, then you have another think coming."

I didn't have any choice but to follow him, though I did so while stomping my feet as loudly as I could manage, just to show how upset I was with this situation.

I got dressed behind the bush, the morning air forming goosebumps on my skin while my eyes stayed on Alcott, like a bird of prey, making sure he didn't turn around. The clothes were mostly the same as theirs. A loose white shirt, some riding breeches and a pair of riding boots. I pulled the jacket over my shirt and brushed my fingers through my hair. The material hung a little loose, but most of it fitted well enough.

Alcott's eyes widened a little as I reached him, but I ignored his foolish face and walked back to the rest of the group. I tossed the torn shift into the ashes of the fire before noticing everyone's eyes were on me.

"What?" I looked down at my attire before realising most of them had probably never seen a woman prancing around in men's clothes. Where I came from, we didn't have the luxury of choosing what we wanted to wear. A lot of the women wore dresses, but sometimes we had to make do with what we had. Especially in my case. I could hardly rob someone and fight them off in a bunch of skirts. It would be illogical. Feeling more comfortable, I placed my hands on my hips and eyed the lot of them.

"You've never seen a lady in trousers before?" Raising an eyebrow, I took a moment to look each of them in the eye. The fact that I felt a little more like myself again gave me a reassuring confidence.

I heard someone clear their throat before they looked away and went about their business. Relaxing a little, I let my shoulders drop and made my way towards Alcott's horse.

Not having to struggle with the likes of a skimpy sleeping gown, I swung myself up with little effort, meeting the questioning gaze of Alcott. At least I seriously doubted they would even believe me now if I told them I was a princess. So there would be little chance of them keeping me for ransom. Alcott got on behind me before taking the reins.

"Can you at least tell me where we're going?" I asked a while into our ride. Although the clothes were more comfortable, I still had to share a horse with Alcott, which most certainly wasn't.

"I'm afraid not," he replied nonchalantly and I rolled my eyes.

"Well, I'm thirsty. When are we stopping for water?"

"Soon."

I was annoyed with his vagueness and decided that maybe it would be easier to gain the trust of his men first. They seemed important to him. If all of them took a liking to me, perhaps they would simply let me go.

When the afternoon sun was at its peak, we stopped at a small town. I had never been in this part of Everness, but the people appeared to be a middle class of merchants and traders: not wealthy enough to be aristocratic, but not poor enough to be peasants. My stomach rumbled as we dismounted and Alcott's men spread out.

"May I have a look around or would you like to bind me with ropes?" I asked Alcott, who was busy putting on a jacket.

"You may go anywhere you like." My heart dared to leap for a moment. "As long as Brutus keeps an eye on you." My shoulders sagged.

"Fine," I replied, attempting not to show any emotion. "Where are you going?" He was already starting to walk away before he turned around to face me. Holding my hands behind my back, I swayed back and forth a little, smiling ever so charmingly.

"Don't try anything." He disappeared into the small cluster of people in the street.

"Well then." I looked at Brutus, who didn't appear all too eager to babysit me. "I guess it's just you and me, big guy." I slapped him on the shoulder before walking past, knowing he would be following behind. The village wasn't that big and finding the market didn't take me too long. I had an idea — the only problem was I didn't have any money on me.

I started scanning the people who walked past. Their faces, clothes and any belongings they might carry with them. Poverty was easy to spot and therefore so was the lack of it. It took a while and every face I scanned earned a *no* in my mind. But then, my eyes fell on a middle-aged man, clearly a merchant or in business of some sort. His clothes were nice, his hands smooth and his face without a hint of hardship. And a lovely little sack of coins peeked out from his coat pocket.

I looked in front of me to avoid suspicion, though keeping him in my peripheral vision. Brutus continued behind me. When I reached the man, instead of walking around him, I bumped into his shoulder before sliding my hand into his coat pocket and pulling out the small bag of coins.

"Sorry, I'm so sorry." I pretended to apologise, but he barely looked at me and I grinned devilishly. I crossed my arms while clutching the small bag between my fingers. We walked for a few more feet before I turned back to Brutus. "I need you to get me a cloak." I gestured to my attire, which was in dire need of concealing. He hesitated. "People are looking at me suspiciously." Which wasn't even a lie, although Brutus didn't look entirely convinced. I could hardly blame him.

"Please," I begged. I simply needed a few minutes for him to walk to the horses and back. Brutus didn't move. "Come on, what could I possibly do? I can't run far enough without you being able to catch me, but I can start screaming and telling everyone that you kidnapped me."

He swallowed and for a moment my conscience ticked at the thought of me manipulating him. But I pushed it back where all my guilty feelings lay lost and forgotten. Brutus gestured with his head, suggesting I follow him.

"Oh it's all right," I said with my most innocent voice. "I can wait here." I stood with my hands behind my back until the crowd swallowed him, before running back to one of the market stands we had passed.

The man behind the table looked friendly and, as could be expected, very eager for business. He proceeded to show me all the different kinds of daggers and pocketknives he had available. I settled on one with a slightly decorated hilt before paying the man with the coin I had stolen. I thanked the vendor and slid the dagger into my sleeve.

Brutus came back with a cloak, which I wrapped around myself, and we started making our way back.

Alcott and the others were waiting for us when we arrived. "I found a tavern where we could stay for the night," he said. We followed him to a building around the corner with a sign swinging above the door: *Pint Grove.* As if that made any sense.

The chatter from inside the tavern was loud, with a fire in the corner warming up the place. I stood a few feet away as Alcott talked to the owner. "And another room for me and my wife." My eyes widened in their direction. His wife? What exactly did this man think he was up to?

Alcott's men each went in their own direction. Brutus and Alastor were already comfortable at the bar, with a drink or two, and Conner and Jack went outside, I assumed to stable the horses.

Alcott took me by the elbow and led me upstairs. I didn't feel like starting a fight yet, so I followed without hassle. We walked down a small corridor and he opened one of the doors with the key given to him by the owner.

The moment the door closed behind us, I whirled around. "Your wife? What exactly do you think you're doing? I am not sharing a room with you."

"It's for your own protection." He started taking off his weapons and placing them on a small table. I noticed the sword with a jewel at the hilt again. The craftsmanship really was something. And with the thief's mind I possessed, I could only imagine what something like that would be worth. What appeared to be the dagger I tried to steal, and a hunting knife or two, accompanied the sword. The man was well equipped.

"What protection? I don't need you to protect me. After all, I am *your* hostage."

"You're a woman ... actually, a girl, practically. You're not safe in here alone. Even if you locked your door, you might not be the only one with a key. Who knows who might have come to *visit* you!"

I crossed my arms in annoyance. "How dare you insult me like that? And I will have you know that I'm perfectly capable of defending myself." He had no idea just how capable I could be.

There were cups and a bottle of ale on a cabinet. Alcott started pouring himself a cup. "It was not an insult and normally I would have left, but since you're proving to be more stubborn than a mare in heat, I might stay just to annoy you." He sat down on a chair at the small table, grinning like a fool. I merely gawked, flabbergasted. He might just have been the most repulsive male I had ever had the misfortune to meet in my entire life. Which was saying a lot.

"So first you kidnap me and now you want to protect my honour? Well, aren't you just a hero."

Alcott took a sip of his drink and then his emerald eyes met mine, burning with certain intensity.

"My men are soldiers who have been trained their whole lives to protect themselves and others. They are prepared for any kind of attack, and suddenly a woman appears out of nowhere in the middle of the night in only her shift and manages to steal a dagger from one of my most trusted men without him even waking. Do you have any idea what that would take? Seems a bit suspicious, doesn't it?"

"No. It only proves that I don't need you to protect me and that you are simply the most paranoid person in Everness. I am not a threat to you and I demand you let me go at once."

He might have had a point, but I wasn't going to give him the satisfaction of agreeing with him. But he had admitted something — they were soldiers, then. The question was, what kind of soldiers? They could be a team of scouts, sent out to inform Prince Cai. Alcott put his cup down before walking over to me.

"I'm going to ask you one last time: who are you and what were you doing stealing daggers off strangers in the middle of the night?"

I was surprised by how much I wanted to hurt him then. To shove him away from me. Was it because his eyes were boring into my own in a way that almost made my skin crawl? And not in a bad way. I lifted my chin, keeping my plan in mind.

"I've told you once and I will tell you again — I'm nobody important," I stated. "I'm just the daughter of an aristocrat who was travelling through the woods to meet up with her family in their summer home. We were attacked by bandits who tried to kidnap me, but I escaped and got lost. That's when I stumbled upon you and your men."

"So why didn't you ask for help?"

"How was I to know that you weren't just as bad as the bandits? That you wouldn't keep me for ransom? I thought I could watch you for a while to see if I could trust you."

Not my best work, but better than nothing.

"Is that really true?" he asked.

"Yes."

Alcott's smirk was unnerving. "I don't believe you."

My mouth fell slightly open when a knock came at the door. Alcott opened it, said something that resembled thanks and turned towards me. In his hands was a bundle of clothes, which he tossed to me. "Get dressed. I'll be back soon." And then he closed the door behind him. I stood in silence for a few seconds before unfolding the clothes.

Alcott didn't lock the door, but I didn't leave the room.

The windows couldn't open and I had a feeling that I wouldn't be able to get past all of them downstairs. At least not while they were awake or sober. That being said, any good thief knew that patience was more than a virtue. It was a trick all on its own, for the longer you waited, the more rewarding it became.

I pretended to fall asleep on the bed, though I didn't dare get under the covers. I would rather sleep on the forest floor. When Alcott returned he took a blanket and made himself comfortable on the floor, next to the bed. I listened to his breathing until it became even and I knew he had fallen asleep. I reached under the pillow, pulled out the dagger I had got from the market and clutched it tightly.

I placed one foot on the floor and then the other before standing up slowly, though no matter how quiet I tried to be, the bed still made an awful squeaking noise, and I cringed.

Alcott didn't move. I studied him carefully to see if his breathing pattern changed. He had a lock of blond hair resting over his forehead. There were no movements underneath his eyelids. Letting out a small sigh of relief, I stepped over his body. The door was so close, I could smell my freedom.

I was halfway through taking my next step when a hand wrapped around my ankle and pulled me to the floor. A sound of surprise escaped me and I toppled over, my joints protesting at the impact on the wooden floorboards.

I turned, ready to swing a blow, but Alcott was above me, reaching to pin me down.

"What do you think you're doing?"

I kicked at his leg and pulled his wrist, causing him to lose balance and making it all the easier for me to roll him over and press my dagger to his throat.

"Getting out of here, obviously."

He managed to push my arm away and pull us both into a standing position, holding both my hands and my knife behind my back.

"I hardly think so."

"Let me go," I pushed out in a cold voice.

"Or what?" he responded, his eyes daring me.

I tilted my head and smirked, before kneeing him and making a beeline towards the door. The tavern was still busy, despite the late hour. I stumbled down the wooden stairs and turned to see Alcott run out of the room behind me.

I pushed past tables and bodies, and without meaning to, I bumped into someone, causing me to tumble back. "Rhen?" I looked up at him in confusion.

"You're alive?"

"There you are." Alcott's voice came from behind me. He picked me up from the floor while I struggled to get out of his grasp.

"Get your hands off her!" Rhen made his way to Alcott and one or two of my other guards jumped in. He had just managed to pull Alcott away from me when there was a shout from the other side of the tavern.

"Get your hands off him!" And in a moment, Jack and Alastor were upon us. A fight broke out, causing a rise in voices throughout the whole tavern, until something fell out of Rhen's pocket.

Alcott bent down to pick it up and, without thinking twice, I tried to wrench it out of his hands, but his grip was too tight.

"Give it! That's mine."

"Where did you get it?"

"That's none of your business!"

The fight broke off and then it was only Alcott and me pulling the necklace back and forth between us.

"Did you steal it?"

Well ...

"It was a gift."

"From who?" he persisted.

"Why does it matter?" I looked at him like he was insane.

"Because I gave that necklace as an engagement present to the woman I'm supposed to marry!"

At the same time the words left his mouth, both Rhen and Jack said, "Your Highness, please."

Silence fell and we were left gawking at each other.

"Your Highness?" I looked at Alcott, or whatever his name was.

"Cai, actually." He let the necklace go. "Heir to the throne of Norrandale."

I managed to mutter out, "Eloisa, Princess of Everness."

Cai's face turned a fierce shade of red and he swallowed hard. Next to him, Jack and Alastor dipped into a bow.

"Your Highness," Jack said.

My throat had gone dry with shock and I was frozen. Well, who would have seen that coming?

"I—" Forming words would be more difficult than I'd thought.

Cai's eyes slowly took me in. His expression was somewhat horrified as he remembered everything he had done to the woman he now knew he was going to marry.

"Your Highness, I must speak with you." Rhen drew my attention away from the prince.

"Of course," I said, slightly dazed, turning to follow him. "Of course."

"We've been looking for you." Rhen stated the obvious as we stepped outside the tavern.

"Well, congratulations! You found me."

Rhen frowned. "How did you even end up here, with Prince Cai no less?"

I sighed, brushing my fingers through my hair. "Well, after I managed to get away from the bandit, I got a little lost in the woods and I stumbled upon the lot of them. They lied about who they were and I lied about who I was and well, you know, now we're here."

"And you're still lying to him about who you are."

I scowled. "It's not like I have a choice. I'm doing what I have to and it's not like you're doing so very well either. You literally only had one job and that was to guard me. Does Lance even know?"

"Of course Prince Lance doesn't know," he replied. "You've seen how easily he can turn. It wouldn't exactly be difficult for him to convince the kingdom that we lost the real princess and that it was an act of treason. He could have hanged us. So we decided to keep looking until we got to the manor house."

"I can't believe you're all alive. Is Cordelia all right?"

"Yes, she's fine. Just a bit startled. We were really lucky to make it out alive."

"Still, we're going to have to tell Lance something. It would seem rather suspicious for us to arrive at Woodsbrook Manor together."

"We're simply going to tell the prince that our two parties managed to cross paths on our way to Woodsbrook and that will be the end of it."

"Do we stay here for the night?" I asked him.

"It's too dangerous to travel now. Perhaps you can share a room with Cordelia and then we'll leave at dawn."

"That sounds good." I was relieved at the thought of no longer having to share a room with Cai. I wasn't even sure how I was going to look him in the eye again after everything that had happened.

Rhen must have seen my expression because he said, "Don't worry. All will be fine, you'll see."

I wanted to agree but I had a hard time believing it.

Chapter 8

The Pint Grove Tavern

Cai

I didn't know what to make of the truth. We all suspected she was hiding something. Just not the fact that she was the Princess of Everness. Though it did make sense of some things, like her refusal to tell us who she was. She had no way of knowing what we were going to do with that information. It did, however, bring up a lot more questions.

I hurried downstairs the next morning, just in time to see her walking out the tavern door. Without giving it too much thought, I grabbed a cloak and followed her outside. She stood with her arms crossed, indicating she was either cold or frustrated — perhaps both.

"Here." I placed the cloak around her shoulders. She didn't say thank you.

"Can we talk?"

She still didn't say anything, but we started walking down the cobbled street, our guards following very closely behind.

"Perhaps I should start by apologising." I rubbed the back of my neck.

"Perhaps?" she said.

"I should start by apologising."

"For what? Kidnapping me, holding me hostage, tying me to a tree?"

Her tone was teasing, but that didn't stop the guilt crawling under my skin. "Yes, all those things and more."

She shrugged. "I can't exactly blame you. I did attempt to severely injure you … twice."

I looked at her again. Could this girl really be the princess promised to me? The girl who sat astride on a horse and stole a dagger from Jack? She wasn't at all what I'd imagined, to say the least.

"I have a few questions, as you might imagine."

"So do I," she said.

"You first."

"Why on earth are you travelling like a group of hunters or merchants? Where is your carriage, your royal clothes and your crown?" She looked up at me, pulling the cloak tighter over her shoulders.

"We'd heard stories of dangerous bandits in the forest. We thought it safer to travel unlike royalty."

"You're clever." She seemed half impressed. "It was a wise choice. We were attacked by bandits that night — that much of my story was true — that's how I came to stumble upon you. I barely managed to make it out alive."

I looked back at her guards, walking some distance behind us. "It's lucky your guards found you again."

She stared at the ground and I could sense an awkward tension between us.

"So what do you propose we do now, Princess?"

"We'll probably still go to Woodsbrook Manor. We are halfway, are we not? No use in going back now. I could even show you some of my favourite places in the kingdom if you'd like."

"That would be very nice," I admitted. "When are we to meet up with Prince Lance?" He had, after all, for some reason, insisted on taking care of many of the wedding plans and the marital arrangements. I wouldn't exactly feel comfortable until my men and I could keep an eye on him.

"I'm not sure." Eloisa bit her lip. "Soon, I should think."

We left the tavern while dawn was approaching, given that we still had a long ride ahead of us for the day. Eloisa and I rode our horses side by side instead of travelling in her carriage. She appeared much more comfortable than she'd been before.

She wore a dark blue dress and it was the first time I'd seen her in anything royal-looking. I wasn't sure what to make of it. The princess in a gown riding next to me could not be compared to the wild thing that had tried to fight me in her sleeping clothes.

"Are you ever going to tell me where exactly you're taking me?" I loosened the reins on my horse.

"If I told you, then it wouldn't be a surprise, now would it?"

It was different having her act friendly towards me in comparison to her hostile behaviour before. Not that I could exactly blame her … I did tie her to a tree. Still, I hadn't expected her character would be so strong.

We veered off the forest road and followed a small hidden trail until a lake appeared behind a cluster of rocks. My mouth fell agape. The scenery was picturesque if nothing else and I slowly dismounted from my stallion. Trees ringed the lake, which was surrounded by long green grass.

"Are you coming?"

My head turned towards Eloisa and I followed her to the water's edge.

"It's beautiful here," I remarked and she nodded in agreement.

"I think it's one of my favourite places in the world, though I haven't been here in a few years."

"I used to have a secret hiding place as a child," I reminisced. "You see, my great-grandfather rebuilt most of the castle and its gardens when he became king. Made it more modernised and secure against attacks and such. A small part of the garden had been cut off, surrounded by walls and overgrown ivy. It's not as mystical as this, but it was a nice place to be when I needed to think."

"And no one ever found out about it?"

"No, they didn't. Though I haven't been there in ages myself. I should think even *I* would have trouble finding it now."

"Would you show it to me, if I ever come to Norrandale?" I frowned.

"What do you mean, *if* you come to Norrandale? Surely your brother has discussed with you the arrangements of our union?"

"Oh, right." She looked away. "Lance hardly tells me anything. But I suppose it makes the most sense since you are to be king of Norrandale one day."

We started walking along the water's edge. "You will miss your kingdom?"

"Some of it I might miss. Some of it I won't." Her expression suggested there was a lot she wasn't telling me, but I wasn't exactly in the mood to pry. My gaze shifted to the necklace hanging around her neck, which fitted perfectly. When I'd sent her the gift, I was unsure if she would wear it, but the jewels suited her.

We stopped walking when one of her guards, Rhen, ran up to us. "Your Highness, we shall set up camp here tonight and continue our travels in the morning."

"That sounds like a good idea, thank you."

He nodded, but his eyes lingered for a moment too long, as if he were trying to tell her something else. Something I wasn't supposed to see.

"So, when you're not running about the woods and threatening people with their own weapons, what do you do in your free time?"

She chuckled. "I am sorry for that. Why don't we just call it even?"

"Why do I get the feeling you're not quite like any princess I've met before?" I asked jokingly.

"I'm going to take that as a compliment," she responded.

"I never said it wasn't."

"To answer your previous question, I enjoy needlework and listening to piano music."

"Really?" I asked in surprise.

"Not at all."

I watched her laugh.

"I like being outside. It doesn't matter what I'm doing."

"I couldn't agree more." It was nice to know we had at least one thing in common. It was a start.

"What about you?" She brushed a strand of hair away from her eyes. "What do you do when you're not lurking about the woods in disguise?"

"I would hardly call it lurking." I chuckled. "But like you, I prefer being outdoors. Horse-riding, hunting or even if it's just to take a walk outside, breathe in the fresh air. We have the most beautiful beaches in Norrandale, with long stretches of white sand and crystal-clear waters."

"It sounds wonderful. I can't remember the last time I was on a beach."

My forehead creased between my eyebrows. "I thought Woodsbrook Manor was in a coastal town?"

Her head swivelled in my direction. "It is." She cleared her throat. "Of course it is. I go into town sometimes, but for whatever odd reason, I never seem to visit the beach."

Right.

"How do you feel about shooting with a bow?" She quickly changed the subject.

"I haven't had proper target practice in quite some time," I admitted. "But I'm not opposed to it."

"Then would you be up for a little competition some time?" Eloisa smiled.

"You like to shoot with a bow?"

She shrugged. "I must confess, I'm not very good. But perhaps you could teach me?" She tilted her head. "Only if you want to, of course."

I couldn't help the small grin that sneaked up on me. "I should be happy to oblige, Princess Eloisa."

"I'm not sure what to think," Jack said that evening while we were having dinner. The campfire was slowly starting to die out and most of our party were scattered around the camp. "Something's not right about her."

"Maybe she's just cautious of us," I suggested. "We did practically kidnap her, after all."

"It's not just that." Jack shook his head. "Her whole story seems a little strange. She's hiding something, I can tell."

"Well, as the captain of my guard I suppose it would be your job to find out exactly what she's hiding." I smiled.

"Just making sure I have permission, my prince." Jack smiled back. He was the best spy I knew and he loved the task dearly. Jack was an observer and he was very good at it.

"Jack's right," Alastor said. "Something here isn't right."

"I like her," Conner commented as he bit into his chicken.

"Now, now." Jack ruffled Conner's hair and he tried to pull away. "She's already spoken for, lad." We laughed at Conner's expense — the poor boy's cheeks had gone red, though he tried to hide it.

I looked to where she was sitting with her lady-in-waiting. Eloisa didn't seem quite as dangerous as her older brother, but one thing I could be certain of was that looks could be deceiving.

Chapter 9

The Evernean Forest

Lara

"I was so worried about you," Cordelia said the next morning as she did my hair. "I thought they might have killed you or something."

"Well, I actually managed to escape that brute quite quickly," I said, with a hint of arrogance.

"So how did you end up running into Prince Cai?"

"Well, I fell off the horse while fighting the bandit and I saw a campfire in the distance so I followed it until I found Cai and his men."

"What are the odds?" She shook her head in disbelief. "You could have gotten attacked by a wild animal or something."

Not a wild animal, I thought. *Just a prince. Same diffe ence.*

"Thanks for your concern, Cordelia, but I'm quite capable of handling myself." She pinned away a loose strand of hair and I turned to face her. "Really, you needn't be worried about me."

"Oh, I know that," she replied. "The problem is how you've been behaving yourself around the prince." Cordelia narrowed her eyes at me and I felt my cheeks grow warm.

"I may or may not have acted in a way that some would consider inappropriate for a princess," I admitted. "But how was I supposed to know? It could have been anybody."

"Well, let's find out the damage first. What exactly did you do?"

I grimaced. "I may have attacked him several times, including holding weapons with sharp edges to his throat."

Cordelia dropped her hands from my hair. "You did what?"

I covered my face with my hands. "How am I ever going to convince the Norrandish heir that I'm the second child of King Magnus?"

"You're not exactly off to a good start, I'll admit." She handed me a cup of something sweet. "But nothing a few tricks can't fix."

"What do you mean?" I took a sip, eyeing her.

"Well, you're a bandit, aren't you? You should be used to tricking people. However, I do believe this will be quite different from what you've done before."

I took another sip of the warm liquid. "I'm listening."

"Rhen could teach you more about Everness. You would need basic knowledge of the kingdom and what's going on in the royal family. Basic history about Eloisa too."

"And you?" I dared to ask, still not sure that this was actually going to help.

"I'm going to make sure you start acting like a proper princess from now. And then I'm going to help you convince the future king of Norrandale that you are the best thing he's ever had the privilege of laying his eyes on."

"You seem very confident?" I had somehow managed to make an already difficult task an almost impossible one. Pulling this off would be nothing short of a miracle.

"Of course I am. I'm a lady-in-waiting," she replied with a smile.

"Are you really, though? Eloisa's lady-in-waiting, I mean?"

"I'm afraid not." She handed me a small mirror. My hair was elegantly perfect, as always. "One of Eloisa's ladies-in-waiting is with child. I was being trained for the position when my brother informed me that I will have a new duty ... this duty."

I put the mirror down. "You said Lance has his way of getting what he wants?" I didn't say more, prompting her to speak.

"Well, I'm guessing you're not here entirely of your free will?" She looked at me and I pressed my lips together. So Lance wasn't just blackmailing me?

"Is that what you would have wanted, though? To be Eloisa's lady-in-waiting?"

She started putting my things back into the trunk. "There are worse fates for a lady. It's an offer I would be stupid to refuse."

"But?" I encouraged.

"But if you're asking what I really want, I suppose the first answer that comes to mind is a happy marriage."

"Really?" I asked in surprise.

"My parents were very happy. I want a union like theirs. And a house of my own that I can manage, and children eventually. It's a simple dream, but you asked for an honest answer."

"And this future husband of yours, in your mind, is he a duke, a viscount ..."

"A soldier."

I gave her a smile. "Well, when this is over … I hope you find your soldier."

"All right," Rhen said later, as we were seated inside a tent. "Here are the maps of Everness and Norrandale." He spread them out on a small table between us.

I placed my palms flat on the table, inspecting the pieces of paper. I had a fair knowledge of most of the landscape of Everness. It wasn't a very large kingdom. Neither was Norrandale, but I had never seen its full layout before. I tried to pay close attention to the borderlines and landmarks of both kingdoms.

"It is important that you know the history between our nations as well as the history of Everness itself."

"I know the history of Everness," I responded. It was discovered centuries ago by explorers in search of treasure. Surrounded by large masses of water, Everness and Norrandale were mostly separated from the rest of the world. One of the explorers, known as Evrin, claimed the land and built the kingdom of Everness up from the ground. It was common knowledge even among the peasants. He became the first king, and as in every other kingdom, the lineages changed over the centuries up to King Magnus.

"Yes, but do you know of the conflicts between Everness and Norrandale?" He already knew my answer.

"No," I mumbled, looking down at the maps again.

"See these mountain ranges?" Rhen pointed to the north of Norrandale. "They used to be part of Everness a few centuries ago."

"What happened?"

"There was a reason Evrin and the explorers had searched for this land for so long. There were stories about deposits of a valuable type of gemstone hidden somewhere in the mountain ranges. They were so rare that a handful of them could be worth more than a ship full of gold. But no one knows exactly what they look like. The tales had changed too much over time."

"Did they ever find it?"

Rhen shrugged. "No one is certain. Evrin and his friend came into conflict over the land and for many years wars were fought, even by the generations after them. Eventually the land fell into the hands of Norrandale and became part of their kingdom — it has been like that ever since. That's not to say anything is there, though."

"Norrandale hasn't shown any evidence of having the gemstone?"

"No, if it is there then nobody knows of it — it has merely become a legend."

I frowned at him from across the table. "And how do you know all this?"

"I like to read."

I looked at the mountain ranges again. They were vast and stretched between the two countries, surrounded by thick forest on both sides of the border.

"Okay, but if the land now belongs to Norrandale and nobody believes the precious stone to be there, why are we fighting?"

"Two generations ago, Everness was in deep poverty."

"Like we are now?"

"Worse. The king loved spending money and soon his aristocrats turned against him. He knew that he would need to expand onto new land in order to farm more food, and give land to the nobles so he could stay in their good graces. At the time, it was thought that the kingdom of Argon across the sea was weak, and so King Leontius sent armies across the water. But the kingdom of Argon is nothing like we thought.

"They hail from an ancient tribe of warriors, always prepared for battle. The king had been misinformed and so his ships sank before most men even reached the beaches of Argon. King Leontius had almost no money left and, in fear of being taken by Argon, he became desperate. He sent a company into the mountains of Norrandale in the hope they would find the precious stones, enabling him to fund his wars. But the company disappeared and King Leontius reportedly only received a piece of white cloth smeared in blood."

"But they didn't attack Everness in return?"

"Attacking them would prove the stones exist. I think Norrandale was just trying to send a warning. It was ruled by the queen alone, as the king had died some time before, when their child was very young."

"So what happened in the war with Argon?" My eyes travelled over the map to the kingdom across the sea.

"King Leontius lost the war and eventually his council had him removed from the throne."

"So that's when Magnus became king?"

"Yes. Magnus was young, and the dire situation of the kingdom and the famine didn't help."

I thought about the palace with all its luxuries and held back a scoff. "He seems to have done pretty well for himself to me."

"Being king is not as easy as you think. You have less power than you imagine."

The very idea was absurd. "Of course you'd be on their side. They're paying for your loyalty."

Rhen looked at me with an unreadable expression.

"So." I reverted back to the previous subject. "Mine and Cai's marriage ... I mean Cai and Eloisa's marriage," I corrected myself, "is to end the feud of their forefathers and join the two nations once and for all."

"It would seem so," Rhen replied. "It would seem so."

We packed up camp and I spotted Damon leaning against a tree trunk, twiddling a hunting knife between his fingers. As always, his eyes were glued to me. This time, however, instead of just looking away, I gave him a smile and a little wave to accompany it before walking off. Conner was holding Cai's horse as well as mine, ready for us to mount.

Now knowing he was a prince, I couldn't help but notice how close he was with his guards and servant. It hardly seemed appropriate for their relationship to be so intimate, given his stature and theirs. I didn't even know the names of any of Lance's guards, except Rhen and Damon. As far as my knowledge went, it wasn't done. But perhaps things were different in Norrandale.

Our party got on the move and I glanced over at the prince riding his horse a few feet away from me. He didn't seem to notice my stare.

What was Lance after so desperately? He spoke of a family heirloom, but nothing drew my attention enough for me to be convinced that there *was* an heirloom. I would have to observe Cai more closely. The only problem was getting that close to him in the first place, though I hoped Cordelia had a few ideas in mind. Her confidence in my ability to fool the prince was somehow reassuring.

Only the sound of hoofbeats could be heard, with an occasional sigh, or clearing of a throat, from one of the guards. It was quiet ... perhaps even too quiet. We were back in a part of the woods that I recognised. The birds weren't singing the way they should have been. Even the light breeze seemed to have gone to sleep as if listening, waiting for whoever was watching us.

Unfortunately, I had a very good idea of who it was.

I couldn't exactly just halt our whole party and let them know we were about to be ambushed. And even worse, I couldn't tell them the reason I knew this, because it was the work of my uncle and his band of thieves. And they had no idea that they were about to attack me. Had no idea what had happened to me since I left a few days ago on my "mission" to steal the necklace. Last damn time I ever do contract thieving! I could be dead for all they knew. If they recognised me, this whole plan could fall apart. Even if they didn't ... well, no one could be certain how this would turn out.

A slight shadow fell over mine, and without looking up, I knew one of them was in a tree branch above me. I didn't have much time to come up with an easy way out of this situation. I risked a glance back to the body in the tree and to my surprise — and slight relief — it was Ray. He was looking down at one of the guards riding below him. Ray was my oldest friend. And if he could see through my glamour of powder and jewels, perhaps this might not be too bad.

"When I say 'get down', you duck."

I turned my head in surprise at Cai whispering to me.

"What?" I said without thinking. Cai and Jack shared a look. Maybe I hadn't given them enough credit before. Perhaps they were better soldiers than I had thought.

Cai carefully reached for the dagger sheathed at his side. "We are about to be attacked. You need to stay down so you don't get injured in the middle of the fight."

I rolled my eyes before leaning over and grabbing his dagger and swinging around in the saddle. The knife went flying straight into the branch that Ray was sitting on.

One of the guards yelled "Ambush!" and in a moment we were surrounded by bandits ... my bandits. I scanned all the faces, but apart from Ray, most were unfamiliar, and I realised that, in a short time, more men must have joined Uncle. I didn't know whether that was good or bad.

I quickly undid the clasp of my necklace and let it drop into my bodice.

I didn't mind them stealing Eloisa's dresses or whoever's they were, but the necklace was mine.

Suddenly I was being pulled off my horse and tossed into the dirt. I grunted, trying to sit up, when someone held a knife to my neck. I watched Cai fight off two of the men, but he turned, looking for me. Our eyes met and he stared for a moment too long, eyes wide with what I could only describe as some sort of terror.

It cost him, as the two men managed to grab him from behind and toss his sword. It slid to the ground, that jewel still attached to the hilt.

"Don't hurt her."

My expression turned to shock when I heard Cai, a royal prince, begging a bunch of bandits with such desperation in his voice.

"Please." He breathed out the last part.

Upon Cai's words, Ray's eyes settled on me, and recognition instantly set in. I let out a breath and gave a look we'd been sharing since we were children — *it's all part of the plan*. It was impossible to tell what he was thinking, but I would probably be more confused in this situation, had I been in his shoes.

If the Crown Fits

"Look, boys." His voice was laced with arrogance as he gestured to my guards' royal uniforms. We were severely outnumbered. "I think we just got a bunch of nobles." I heard the men laughing. This simple comment indicated enough of their anger and hate for the monarchy ... any monarchy, maybe. This was treason beyond any question — if caught, they would most certainly be killed, and yet they were laughing fearlessly.

Ray approached Cai, both men holding their heads high.

"Now, what is it you were begging for again?" Ray was playing with a knife between his fingers. It was small, but the edge was unimaginably sharp. It was one of his familiar tactics to scare or intimidate people. I gulped. Ray may have been my friend, but he had always been very unpredictable, and he was filled with anger. Not that I couldn't say the same about myself in certain aspects.

"Take anything you want," Cai breathed out. "But let the lady go." Ray turned to me and he didn't have to hide his smile. He was clearly enjoying this. Was this the characteristic of Norrandish men, or princes in general, to sacrifice so much so quickly in order to save the life of a woman? It was unfamiliar to me.

"Well then." He approached me slowly. "Forgive my manners." Ray bowed mockingly. The men laughed again, but the knife didn't move away from my throat. He stepped up to me so closely that I could see my own reflection in his pupils.

"Whatever is going on, you're in way over your head," he whispered under his breath. I couldn't reply, but we both knew that perhaps he was right ... I was pretending to be a princess, for crying out loud! I may have been wearing a dress and expensive accessories, but underneath all that I was still a bandit. However, it was too late to turn back now.

They took our horses and our carriage and anything else they could find lying around, leaving us all with only the clothes we had on us, and a few weapons. But at least we were unharmed. Not that I was too worried about myself.

"Now what?" Jack asked, looking at Cai.

"Now—" without permission, Cai grabbed my waist and pulled me into a standing position with such ease I had to hold on to his shoulders for a moment to avoid falling over — "... we walk."

Yes, *we walk* always seems like a hell of a good idea when you're in breeches and boots. But my layers of skirts and tightly fastened shoes certainly weren't forest-walk-friendly. Eventually I stopped walking and Cai looked at me with concern.

"Are you all right?"

"I think both my attire and prison-torture devices were made by the same guy." I pulled my hair away from my neck, which was covered in a thin layer of sweat.

"Do you want me to carry you?"

Oh, how very princely of him.

"No thank you." Like I would let him carry me. I did, however, place my hand on his shoulder to lean over and start untying my laces.

"Your Highness," Cordelia protested, and the look in her eye was enough to tell me that taking off my shoes in front of *His Norrandish Highness* was a no-go. Good thing I didn't actually give a damn about what she said.

"Oh it's not like he hasn't seen my ankles before." I pulled off my other shoe, and out of the corner of my eye, I caught Cai trying to hide a smile.

"Much better," I said, once my toes were touching the forest floor.

And then I walked onwards as if I hadn't just partly undressed in front of the Prince of Norrandale.

"That was quite a manoeuvre, back there," Cai said a few minutes into our walk.

"What?"

"The dagger." He cleared his throat, as if not entirely sure how to speak to me, not after what had happened. Was he embarrassed that he begged? Did he perhaps regret it? Or was he concerned that the woman he thought was going to be his future wife had good knife-throwing skills?

"It was a lucky throw." I attempted to shrug it off and looked everywhere but towards his eyes in search of a new subject to converse about. Or maybe not to converse at all. Though this was on the list of Cordelia's suggestions in what I had to do to woo the prince. In fact, polite conversation came very highly recommended.

"It was a risky throw. You could have injured someone, had you missed."

"Why does it sound like you're about to lecture me on the safety of knife-throwing?" We'd fallen behind the rest of the group.

"I'm not." He cleared his throat again and I sensed his discomfort. "I'm just curious as to why you seem to be attracted towards knives in general and quite comfortable handling them?"

I'd heard once that in order to tell a successful lie, one must stay as close to the truth as possible. But how was I supposed to do that when I was a bandit pretending to be a princess? Ray's face flickered in my mind.

"When I was young, I had a friend who took an interest in knives. Sometimes when he'd come to visit, he would teach me to throw at a target. It was a pastime to keep boredom at bay." Not entirely a lie.

Ray and I had spent many afternoons throwing knives at tree trunks. Of course, I was the one who taught him, though Ray was much better with a bow.

"Just a friend then?" Cai had a curious expression on his face, as if he were attempting to hide his true emotions.

"Yes," I responded, without hesitation. "Just a friend." But the question got me thinking. Was there a possibility of Cai having someone back home that he would rather marry, instead of Eloisa? For all of the horrors experienced by those of us who lived a life of poverty, at least we mostly got to marry for love.

We walked past a tree with a piece of paper pinned to the trunk. It was a drawing of a hooded figure with the words *Masked Bandit dead or alive. Reward 500 gold pieces.* Just 500? I wanted to snort. It was almost an insult.

"I've heard stories of the Masked Bandit being quite a nuisance in the northern part of the kingdom." Cai motioned towards the drawing.

"I think most of the stories are exaggerated because people are bored," I replied as coolly as possible. "I mean, I've never met anyone who's actually seen the Masked Bandit."

Cai didn't seem entirely convinced.

"I'm surprised your brother or father aren't doing more to get rid of the bandits. They've become a serious problem."

Problem? Was that all we were to them?

Not people who had run out of other options to keep their families alive. Not men and women who had no other choices left in the world, who needed help. No, we were a problem.

"Well, with my father's illness, things have been more difficult to manage."

"You're right. My apologies. I never even asked you how your father was doing." It was a different topic at least, though not exactly a better one.

"Every day brings its challenges." I tried to be vague. "But we won't lose hope."

"No, we won't." He gave me only half a smile, but it was filled with sincerity, nonetheless.

Chapter 10

The Evernean Forest

Cai

We didn't walk very far before spotting smoke in the distance. It turned out to be the estate of one of the wealthy aristocrats. The Duke of Darwick appeared very welcoming and his wife most concerned at our tale of being attacked by bandits in the forest.

We received our own chambers, and our servants and guards got rooms in the maids' quarters.

"What have you discovered?" I found Jack in one of the empty hallways before dinner.

"She's a closed book, I'm afraid, and there isn't much on the cover. Her mother died after she was born, so she was raised by a nursemaid. She spends a lot of time outdoors, reading or horse-riding, and apparently she and her brother aren't very close."

"Well, that seems to correspond with what we've seen of her, at least in some ways," I replied.

"I'll see what else I can find out. I also sent Alastor after that head guard of hers. Rhen, I believe his name is. Something isn't right there. I don't trust him," he whispered.

"Thank you, Jack. I appreciate your efforts."

"My best advice would be to have you grow as close to her as possible. She might trust you."

"I'm the son of one of her father's biggest enemies — why on earth would she trust me?"

"The war between Norrandale and Everness has been cold for years. Your parents are only enemies because their forefathers were."

"Still, the marriage could be a cover-up for something else."

"I'm not disagreeing with you, my prince. All I'm saying is that you should try to befriend her. Apart from the fact that she's suspiciously good with self-defence and stealing small weapons, she's not too bad."

"Not too bad?" I chuckled. "That's what you're going with?"

"Hey, I'm just thanking the heavens she's not my future wife." He held up his hands in defence. "There's something off about her that kind of scares the crap out of me."

"Some friend you are." I snorted.

"Like I said, I just get paid to protect you. So as long as she doesn't try to kill you … again. She's all your problem."

We parted and I made my way to Eloisa's chambers, a small box clutched tightly in my fist. I stopped in front of her door and took a deep breath before knocking.

The door was flung open. "I told you I would be down in a …" She stopped mid-sentence upon seeing that it was me standing at the threshold. I watched her cheeks fill with colour. "My apologies." She took a step back, allowing me to enter the room. "I thought you were … well, never mind. Forgive me, Your Highness."

"Please don't call me that, I much prefer Cai."

"Cai." She tested the name on her lips and I felt a tug inside my stomach. Ignoring it, I stepped forwards, holding out my hand.

"I wanted to give you this." I offered her the small box and she cautiously accepted it. "I was told you would be wearing red tonight."

"Where did you get them?"

She carefully took out an earring and held it up. The rubies, embedded in gold, formed a raindrop of red. They dangled, glinting in the light from the window.

"I have my ways." They were graciously given to me by the duchess, whom I promised to repay as soon as I could.

She smiled at me before turning around and facing the mirror to put them on. After turning her head side to side, she seemed satisfied enough. Eloisa proceeded to pick up her engagement gift from me. "Would you mind? I don't think I can manage the clasp." She held the necklace out to me. It felt strange to think that the last time I was holding it I had no idea who the woman was that would wear it.

"Of course," I said and she turned, facing our reflection in the mirror.

I draped the necklace around her neck and fastened the clasp. I couldn't help but notice the goosebumps form on her skin as my fingers touched her neck. I met her eyes in the mirror and they held an expression that I couldn't quite read.

"Allow me to escort you?" I held out my arm and she placed her hand in the crook of my elbow. Despite the winding hallways and many staircases, we quickly found ourselves in the large dining hall of the Darwick Estate House.

"Your Highness." The duke welcomed us with a bow, offering each of us a cup of wine. The taste of it was quite vile compared to Norrandish wine, but I managed a thankful smile at him.

"It really wasn't necessary to have a feast for us."

"It's our honour, my prince," he replied, but there was a peculiar look in his eyes that provoked a feeling of distrust in my gut.

"Eloisa!"

Her grip tightened on my arm at the sound of her name and we both turned to spot the duchess approaching us.

"I haven't seen you since you were a child. Your mother and I were very close, you know?" Which was probably why she spoke to Eloisa with such familiarity despite the fact that Eloisa had a completely blank look on her face.

"My! You've grown into such a beautiful young woman!"

"Thank you," Eloisa responded, her voice higher than before. She was already taking a step back, pulling me with her, but the duchess was not finished with her conversation.

"You know, I have to say, I was surprised at the announcement of your union with the Prince of Norrandale." She gave me a look up and down. "But seeing the two of you together now, there cannot be a more beautiful couple in the kingdom. Say, do you have dates in mind for the wedding?" No doubt she was hoping to get an invitation.

"Cai has only just arrived in Everness, so we haven't had a chance to discuss anything with my family."

"And such an unfortunate arrival. King Magnus really ought to do something about those bandits and rid us of them once and for all." Eloisa tensed up next to me. "I mean his own daughter could have gotten killed today. I'm so glad you two are safe."

"Yes, your hospitality has been most kind." I answered before Eloisa could say anything. "But I'm afraid we must move on now as there are a few more important people we must see. Or perhaps we will just be looking for a hidden alcove where I can kiss my fiancée." Without waiting for a response from her flabbergasted face, I grabbed Eloisa's hand and pulled her away.

"Are you mad?" She hit my arm, but didn't let go of my hand until we reached the other side of the room. "You can't say things like that."

I let out a laugh. "It was a joke. And if she doesn't have a sense of humour, it most certainly isn't me who is at fault."

She shook her head in what must have been disbelief, but gave me a grin that appeared to be sincere.

The large dining hall of the Duke of Darwick had been filled with guests and food as far as the eye could see. I was surprised by how quickly he'd managed to pull together such a large party. When the orchestra started playing a new song, I held out my hand to Eloisa. "Shall we?"

She appeared hesitant. "I'm afraid I'm not a very good dancer."

I would admit that I was slightly disappointed, but I understood. She was a princess, after all. She didn't have the luxury of embarrassing herself in front of people. Though she must have been the first lady I'd ever met who didn't want to dance. Most of them received lessons soon after they could walk. It was a highly admired skill. But perhaps things were different in Everness. Or perhaps no amount of lessons could teach their princess to dance. I smiled at the thought of this small flaw.

"Very well, then you owe me one. How about we get another cup of something to drink?"

Relief washed over her face and she nodded.

"There must be something you're not good at," she remarked on our way to one of the servants holding a tray full of wine cups.

"I can't whistle," I offered and she started giggling. It was a pleasant sound.

"I'm serious," she replied.

"So am I." I took two cups of wine, handing her one. "If I were in a situation where my life depended on whistling, I would surely be a dead man."

"I doubt you'd ever come into such a situation, though. Perhaps we shall have to find someone who can do it for you."

"You mean someone who follows me around everywhere and whistles at my command?"

"Yes, he shall be the royal whistler. A most esteemed job."

I laughed then and we took a seat at one of the long tables that stretched across the room. "Is there anything else I ought to know about, that you are positively atrocious at?"

"You shall have to wait and see." She crossed her arms, leaning back into the chair. She only held this position for a moment, before suddenly pulling herself up pin-straight as if she had forgotten she was a lady. She met my eyes with an unreadable expression, but I acted nonchalantly. She was certainly unlike any princess I had met before.

We drank and we ate and then we drank some more, and Eloisa clung to my arm for most of the night as we were introduced to the guests, moving from one lord, duke or duchess to another.

"You want to know something?" Eloisa said later in the evening as she was leaning against one of the walls of the dining hall.

"What?" I asked, finishing another cup of wine and realising I'd lost count of how many cups I'd had. Eloisa let out a hiccup and placed her hands over her mouth, eyes wide before bursting out with a laugh. Apparently I wasn't the only one.

"I think that you walk around with those broad shoulders and pretend you're a soldier, always ready to fight but in here—" She placed a finger on my chest. "In here is another person who you won't show to the world because you're afraid of what they might think."

"I'm a prince." I placed my hand next to her head on the wall. "I was brought up to rule a kingdom, to be a soldier, not to have a personality."

"Humph." She tilted her head and looked across the room.

"What about you?" I asked and her eyes met mine again. "You're a princess who pretends to care and act proper all the time, but you'd rather be outside, you clearly hate society and you've got a knack for throwing knives, for crying out loud."

She squinted. "Have you been observing me?" When I didn't answer, she said, "I'm a princess. I was brought up to be married off, not to have a personality."

I was a bit taken aback. "Are you very unhappy about this union?"

She must have sensed a change in my tone because she said, "No, that's not what I meant. I'm just …" She yawned. "I'm just tired, that's all."

"Shall I escort you back to your room?"

"Please."

Truth be told, it was difficult to remember where her chambers were. I'd definitely had too much wine. And I wasn't the only one. We stumbled up the stairs, giggling like little children before stopping in front of her bedroom door. She patted her pockets as if looking for a key and then burst out laughing at the realisation she didn't have a key or pockets … that the door wasn't locked at all.

One of the duke's servants approached us in the hallway and we turned, holding our hands in front of our mouths to keep from laughing, but lost our game faces as soon as he passed.

"You truly did look beautiful tonight." I had no idea where that came from.

"Well, it's only fair I look my best now. Soon, I'll be married and then I won't have all the gentlemen falling at my feet."

"I doubt your marital status will keep them from pursuing you."

"Jealous much?" She raised an eyebrow, swinging back and forth a bit.

"Of course not." I saw the Duke of Darwick's son, Edgar, in my mind once more as he scanned Eloisa up and down while we were in conversation with him and his father.

"Liar." She jabbed a finger at my chest.

I blinked slowly, regretting the fact that I'd had so much to drink and having the sickening feeling that there was nothing to stop my mouth from spilling out my thoughts.

"So what if I was?" I challenged her.

She shook her head. "I've grown up surrounded by men and I will never understand them."

"What do you mean?"

"What's there to be jealous about?" she questioned. "I'm already yours."

I was still processing her words when she turned to open her door, and it must have been the combination of the wine and the long hems of her skirts, but she stumbled and, without thinking, I reached out to catch her around the waist.

She swallowed hard, facing me once more. I didn't drop my arms.

"I hate these stupid dresses. I'm always tripping over everything." She wiped a loose strand of hair away from her face in frustration. Eloisa looked up at me then and I caught myself leaning in without meaning to. She stared at my eyes before her gaze travelled down to my lips and back up to my eyes again.

We were close enough to share a breath when the door behind us flew open.

Chapter 11

Darwick Estate

Lara

Cai and I practically jumped a few feet apart and my eyes met Cordelia's. She was standing on the other side of the threshold, her cheeks flushed a deep red.

"I thought I heard someone," she said, and I turned to Cai.

"Well, goodnight then."

He bowed his head, as princes do, and gave me a small smile. "Good night."

Then he was gone.

I stumbled into the room, where a cold breeze swept across me, and my eyes landed on the open window, curtains blowing around it.

"Good heavens, Cordelia, it's freezing in here. Why on earth is the window open?" I walked over to the other side of the room and quickly closed the latch, rubbing my arms to warm them.

When Cordelia didn't reply, I turned around, and her expression was as guilty as a thief who'd just got caught.

"Why are you looking at me like that?" I asked, slowly putting two and two together. The open window, the door flying open when she heard a noise, her red cheeks.

"Cordelia?" I asked, with a smirk on my face.

She started making herself busy with the brushes and things on the dresser.

"Yes?"

"Was there, perhaps, a gentleman in here?" In a room, without a chaperone, behind a closed door. There really was more to Cordelia than met the eye.

"No, of course not. I came to help you get ready for bed." Those were her words. But I knew a liar when I saw one.

"Well, come on, who was it, then?" I prompted her, my grin as wide as ever.

"No one," she swore and I laughed.

"Well, if you're not going to tell me, Cordelia, then I will just have to find out by myself." She didn't reply, but I could see her smiling to herself in the mirror.

Another nightmare slithered into my subconscious that night. Similar to the one I had a few nights before, it was based on a childhood memory, one I had fought so hard to keep locked away from my thoughts. We'd run out of food in the camp, and in a desperate attempt to avoid starvation, Ray and I had gone hunting. We didn't catch anything for days and all along we got closer to the royal hunting grounds in Levernia. Ray hadn't meant to kill one of the King's prized deer. We didn't even realise that we'd wandered off so far. But that didn't keep the royal guard from punishing Ray for his actions.

I watched helplessly as they whipped his bare back, eventually drawing blood. I could still hear my screams as a villager had to hold me back from running towards him. Anything to make it stop. Anything to keep the guard from ripping open the flesh of my friend's back. A hatred in my heart formed that day, for what the monarchy stood for, for what they'd done to an innocent child, for the life I was forced to live because a king couldn't look after his own kingdom. Ray's hands were tied to a post and he flinched every time the whip hit him. He wanted to scream, I could tell. But he bit his lips so hard that it eventually drew blood. And I couldn't do anything to save him from that pain. But I could spend my time causing as much trouble for the royal family as possible. Being a bandit and a contract thief wouldn't change or make up for what had happened. But it was all I could do then, perhaps until now.

I woke up the next morning with a blinding pain in my head. Someone, I assumed Cordelia, pulled the blankets off my body and I groaned. "Rise and shine, Your Highness." I wanted to smile at her jest, but my head was in too much pain.

"Please stop screaming." Next thing I knew, she was pulling me into a sitting position. I let out a yawn before she splashed some cold water in my face and pulled me out of bed, while I attempted to gather my senses. I squinted from the light coming in through the windows. Cordelia sat me down and started brushing my hair.

"You're a mess," she commented.

"Thank you, I hadn't noticed."

"We're supposed to meet the rest of the party downstairs in a few minutes. The Duke of Darwick has given us a carriage and some horses."

"That's very kind of him." I yawned again. "What happened last night? How much did I have to drink?"

"I wasn't there. But it must have been a lot." She helped me get dressed layer by layer, until she fastened the last button on the back of my dress. "All I know is that Prince Cai escorted you back here and then you fell asleep almost immediately."

We left the room, making our way downstairs as a servant entered the room to retrieve my trunk of new clothes kindly gifted to me by the duchess. "Cai?" I questioned and then the memories started pouring back into my head. "Oh no." I rubbed my temples.

The sharp sun didn't do anything to help my headache. Everyone was already waiting outside by the time we got there, the guards mounting one by one. Rhen brought my horse over, but I caught Cai's eye as he was standing with his soldiers. "You know what, I think I'll take the carriage today."

Rhen nodded, somewhat confused, and pulled open the carriage door, helping me inside. Cordelia frowned and I fell back against the seat in a very unladylike position.

"Mind if I join you?" My resting eyes flew open at the sound of Cai's voice as he got into the seat across from me.

"In that case, I'll just take one of the horses," Cordelia said, and I was about to protest, but she was already out the door. I grimaced, leaning my head against the back of the seat and closing my eyes again.

"Your head too?" Cai asked, and I nodded.

"I don't know what exactly is in your Evernean wine, but I haven't been that drunk since I was a young lad."

"You're still a young lad." I started rubbing my temples with my fingers again.

"No, but this was quite a few years ago. My best friend Thatcher and I snuck into one of my parents' parties and stole a bottle of wine because we'd never had any before, and for some reason thought it was a good idea. My father found us the next morning, passed out on the garden steps. Needless to say we were in big trouble."

"Sounds like your family had their hands full." The carriage pulled away and we were on the move.

"Most certainly. Thatcher and I got ourselves into all kinds of trouble as children and teenagers, but I suppose we grew up eventually."

"I don't think I've ever had as much to drink as I did last night," I admitted.

"I don't even remember anything," he said.

I opened my eyes, looking at him for the first time. The knot in my stomach unclenched a little.

"Tell me more about Norrandale and your childhood?" Rhen said I needed him to trust me. After all the havoc of our initial introduction, perhaps that was a good place to start. A simple question, a safe one.

Cai proceeded with stories about the beautiful landscape and how they would go hunting or simply spend days in the forest so they could sleep under the stars. He told me about the people and the dances and stories about how he and Thatcher often got themselves into interesting situations.

"What about your men here?"

"What do you mean?"

"You seem very close to them. I have never seen a prince address his guards so personally."

"Well, I've known them for so long I suppose you could say they feel like family. Except for Conner, but he's a good kid. Brutus has been working in the kitchens since I was a little boy. I would always steal some of the mince pies, but he would only give me a disapproving look."

"He doesn't say much, does he?"

"Argonian rebels cut out his tongue a long time ago."

I met his gaze in surprise. "That's terrible."

Cai just nodded.

"What about Jack and Alastor?"

"They fought with me in the war."

He looked out of the carriage window as if reminiscing, a dark expression crossing his face. "I owe them so much more than my life." The expression faded as quickly as it had appeared and he looked back at me.

"What about your family? What about Everness?"

"Well, I've already shown you my favourite place in Everness. But I suppose that is where the good things end. The people are poor and unhappy, and I'm not very close to my family."

"I'm sorry." His apology looked sincere.

"It's not your doing."

"Not yours either. You should be able to trust your father and brother to run the kingdom. It isn't your duty to worry about it."

"No, my duty is to be married off to the highest bidder," I spat out, suddenly angry on behalf of a person I had never even met. It was King Magnus and Prince Lance's responsibility to run the kingdom, to look after the people. *And instead they spend and party while Eloisa is to be married to a stranger so Everness can benefit*

Cai's expression looked almost sad. "I know neither of us really have much of a choice in this matter, but I'm not going to force you to …"

I cut him off — his expression alone made me feel guilty. "No, I'm sorry. I didn't mean it like that. I just … I wish that …" I didn't quite know what to say.

"That everything was different?" Cai offered and I nodded. "Me too."

Perhaps he had much less say in this marriage than I realised, and now it was too late to go back. Cai would find out the truth one way or another. And Lance knew that. So what exactly was he planning? Lance was afraid I would take the heirloom for myself, which was why he'd made certain I was under close observation by the guards at all times. But what happened to Cai when it was over and he found out that it was all a lie? Was he going to kill him?

And how could I be certain that Lance wouldn't betray and kill me too, once I'd given him what he wanted? Despite how much I cared for my family, I'd chosen to run away out of fear for the future. I'd chosen to run away from the life I was living, in the hope of a better one, in a different kingdom. But I'd never planned for all of this to happen. For me to be in a position to change things. One thing was certain: Lance could not be trusted, and whatever he had planned, it couldn't be good. I didn't know what exactly to make of Cai, yet. Had my uncle been here, what would he have told me to do? Kill Lance? Would it change anything except make me a sought-after thief and a murderer? The price on my head would increase, that was certain, but it wouldn't change anything for the better.

Trust Cai? They said the enemy of your enemy was your friend. Could that be true? Nevertheless, I was inside enemy lines and Uncle would want me to play the game.

We arrived at the manor house some hours later and Cai got out of the carriage first. He held out his hand to help me out, but clumsy as I was in this costume of a gown, my foot got caught between the two carriage steps and I fell ... straight into Cai's arms. I met his beautiful eyes in embarrassed horror while clinging to his shoulders, which felt even more muscular than they looked. Had he always smelled so nice? The scent of him was earthy. Like the forest on a cool autumn morning. Why hadn't I noticed it before?

"Are you all right?"

My face heated again. This was silly. I quickly pushed myself away from him, finding my footing and brushing a strand of hair away from my eyes. "Quite all right, thank you." I cleared my throat. Cai looked like he was trying to hide a smile. Damn prince.

"This is a beautiful home," he commented, and I caught myself staring at it in awe.

Lance called it a house, but it was more like a small castle, surrounded by vast gardens and a small stretch of woodland. The large stone building had to date back a few hundred years, but no effort had been spared in the upkeep of the estate. Everything seemed perfectly in place, from the pine trees that lined the road to the rose gardens — tranquil and quiet. I could even smell a light sea breeze in the air. And then I remembered I was supposed to be used to all of this.

"Oh, you know. It's modest but comfortable," I said as we walked up the marble steps. The two large wooden doors were opened for us and I had to keep from taking in too large a breath in amazement at the beautiful foyer. Rich people had no idea what they really had. And if they did, they certainly didn't show it.

Maybe I was biased. Maybe I was bitter. Or maybe I was right.

"Eloisa?" A voice came from one of the adjacent rooms.

A very familiar voice.

"Lance?"

He came over, dressed in his formal royal attire, and placed a kiss on each of my cheeks. "Sister, it is so good to see you."

I tried to refrain from looking too surprised or uncomfortable.

Lance turned to Cai. "And it is good to see you too."

"It's been some time." Cai replied with a smile on his face, but it wasn't quite the one I had become familiar with.

"Come, we must get you something to drink." We followed Lance to a parlour and I placed myself in one of the chairs, hands folded neatly. Lance poured us each a drink before taking his own seat.

"I heard you two had quite the journey in getting here. Blasted bandits."

Neither Cai nor I replied. How the news had reached Lance so fast was beyond me. As well as what exactly I was supposed to do now. He'd only revealed up to this part of the plan. Told me to look for a family heirloom, and I had discovered none. I'd barely had any time to get to know Cai.

"I'm very glad you both got here safely." He smiled and I felt a slight shiver run down my spine, but blamed the light breeze making its way through the house.

"Yes, quite so," Cai said, and Lance took a sip of his drink, staring at the two of us intently.

"I trust you two are getting along well, then?" The question came off innocently, but I knew what it meant — knew what he was really asking.

"Yes, we are," I said before taking a sip.

Lance abruptly stood up. "Cai, you don't mind if I borrow my sister for a moment, do you? I'm afraid we have some family business to discuss, you know the sort of thing." He led us back into the foyer. "But your chambers are ready for you, I believe."

Cai nodded in thanks and followed one of the servants upstairs. The moment he was out of sight, Lance grabbed my lower arm and pulled me in the opposite direction. I yanked my arm out of Lance's hand as he closed the study door behind us, and rubbing it a little,

I watched Lance pour himself another drink. In fact, I was trying to think of a time when I hadn't seen him with a drink.

"What was that all about?" My tone came off as offended.

"You're a bandit," he replied as if this was the answer to everything.

"Well yes, but I would be a lot more compliant if you were nicer to me."

Which was half true.

"You'll be as compliant as I want you to be." He took a seat behind the large oak desk, motioning for me to sit opposite. There was an unnerving look in his eyes. "So, the two of you ran into each other?"

"Yes we did." What else was I going to say? The truth wasn't going to help me. "What are you doing here?"

"Does he trust you?" Lance answered my question with a question and I became frustrated.

"I think so."

"You think so, or you know for sure?"

It was clear which answer he wanted to hear from me. "Yes," I said quickly. "Yes, he trusts me."

Lance nodded slowly, almost as if in approval, before folding his hands together. "Rumour has it that some time ago a gift was forged with a very valuable gemstone and it has been passed down by the kings from father to son ever since."

I thought back to my conversation with Rhen in the tent. "So you think a jewel was forged into the heirloom that Cai supposedly carries with him? Let's say it's true, then what?"

"I'm afraid that's where your involvement in this ends." I fell back in my seat, vexed with the prince in front of me. "Is there any object that Cai seems attached to? What have you learned so far?"

I thought back to every moment that we had spent together and only one thing stood out. "His sword. There's a jewel set in the hilt of his sword, but it just looks like an ordinary emerald."

"Excellent."

"You honestly believe this is the precious stone that everyone's been fighting about?"

He took a sip from his drink. "It's more likely than not."

"But what if it's not? Isn't this risking too much?"

"Not if you do your job properly."

"So tell me what you want me to do and I can get out of this stupid dress." I was starting to get tired of the charade. I wanted my reward and I wanted to get away as soon as possible.

"I'll have you know that is a very expensive dress you're wearing."

I internally rolled my eyes. "Well, it's uncomfortable and impractical."

"Steal the sword."

"That's it?" I lifted my chin in distrust.

"That's it," Lance repeated.

"You're really going to risk war and the downfall of your kingdom for an expensive jewel." It probably wasn't my place to be lecturing him on my political concerns, but in all honesty, this was a lot bigger than a stupid little jewel.

"It's not about the money," Lance said.

"Then what is it about? Do you have something personal against Cai? Then take it up with him. It's not worth getting so many innocent people killed."

Lance stood up slowly and placed his palms flat on the desk. "I can't tell you," he said in a low voice and shifted clumsily. I realised that Lance hadn't started drinking upon our arrival, but way before that.

"Why not?" I crossed my arms.

"Because you're a thief," he spat out and silenced me. "Because you're a liar and a cheat and a criminal and you would take it for yourself if you knew the truth."

I assumed the alcohol was making him share more than he intended to.

"Lance." I stood up too. "If you don't tell me what it is, I'm not going to steal it for you." Which was an utter lie. I knew my head was on the table. If I stole the jewel for myself, not only would I never be able to sell it, but also Lance would be after me for the rest of my life. I wasn't that stupid. But Lance was drunk and it was worth a shot.

"Lance!"

"It contains magic," he cried out and I fell back into my seat.

"How much have you had to drink?"

Lance didn't reply.

"You can't be serious," I scoffed.

"It's a Myrgonite stone. It has no equal in the realm."

"Rhen told me that Everness and Norrandale have fallen out over these stones in the past. I understand it has value and the kingdom might need money. But surely there is a better way to go about this?"

"It's not about the money." Lance sighed. "It's about the power it holds."

"I have a really difficult time believing these little gemstones possess magic. I mean, what kind of magic are we even talking about here?" Of all the ridiculous conversations I might have had in my life, this one certainly took first prize.

"It's not the stones themselves. It's the objects they were forged into," he responded, as if I should have known this already. I was no stranger to the myths and folklore of the kingdom, but apart from the Evernean Forest, I believed them to be fairy tales. If this kind of magic ever existed, then it was long gone and dead.

"You're going to have to give me more context." It was as if we'd forgotten he was blackmailing me into stealing from his enemy. But the longer I could keep him distracted and talking, the more important information he would keep revealing.

"It is believed that King Evrin's wife, Queen Riona, took a few of the jewels for herself and had a goldsmith forge them into three objects using an ancient magic."

"All right." I blew out a breath, trying to gather my thoughts. "And what kind of objects were they?"

"That's the problem. Nobody knows."

Growing up in the forest had me experience things for which there was often no logical explanation. I'd practically grown used to the unexplainable noises, or pairs of yellow eyes looking at me through the dark. Even now, it often felt as though the trees were watching me as I went about my business. Living in the forest for most of my life had forced me to respect it, but as I grew older, I blamed anything unusual on my imagination. Although, if the past few days had taught me anything, it was that I didn't know what to believe anymore. Was it truly possible for magic not to be entirely gone?

"I cannot tell if you're actually being serious," I said, almost repeating myself.

"I am." Lance pressed his fingers to his head as if he were in pain. "When I was younger, my father and I went to Norrandale. I overheard King Eric by accident once. I know it's real."

"And you're convinced Cai has a piece of the precious stone?"

"He is the future king of Norrandale. And like I said, the objects are believed to have been passed down from one generation to another after the stones fell into Norrandale's hands."

"And what do you plan to do with it?" Cai possessing that kind of power was one thing ... Lance was another.

"I plan to protect Everness." The words were that of a hero and yet I didn't believe him. Didn't believe he was capable of caring about anything or anyone but himself. Then again, perhaps neither was I.

"So you thought that if your sister married Prince Cai and became queen of Norrandale, she would grant you access to magic? Magic which, by the way, Norrandale have done such a good job of hiding that nobody apart from you seems to know anything about."

"If that were the case, I would have asked Eloisa, not you." Which begs the question, why didn't he ask her?

"So, what happens when this is over and Cai finds out? You break off the alliance? How long do you plan to keep up this ruse?"

"Cai won't find out."

I stared at him, flabbergasted. "What do you mean, he won't find out? Of course he's going to find out."

"Why don't you let me worry about that, and you just worry about your part in this?"

"Are you going to kill him?" I was almost too afraid to ask.

"That could make things a little messy. Unless we make it look like an accident, of course—"

"I won't help you hurt him." This was getting out of hand. I had not agreed to be party to a murder.

"Calm down, would you? Once we have the sword, we'll remove the jewel and place the weapon back where we found it. If Cai notices, he'll think he lost it somewhere."

"It won't be easy to steal. He is always carrying it and he's always surrounded by his guards."

"Well." Lance finished the last drops in his cup. "That would be your problem."

I stood up and made to leave the room, but Lance caught up to me and grabbed my arm.

He pulled a small knife out of his pocket. "And if you even think of betraying me, I will cut you … here." He dragged the knife lightly over my arm. "Here." Across my stomach. "And here." A fine line across my neck.

"And then I will feed you to the wolves so that they can eat you alive. You have three days, dearest sister."

Chapter 12

Woodsbrook Manor

Cai

The servant showed me my chambers and I thanked him before he closed the door behind him. The room was glamorous, with large windows presenting a view of the estate gardens. I made my way over to a basin and filled it with cold water from the jug that had been placed next to it.

The water cooled my face, but did nothing to soothe the gnawing feeling in my stomach. I was filled with unease, though I had no idea why, and perhaps that was what bothered me most of all. Lance was definitely up to something, but Eloisa's involvement was unclear.

Jack appeared to be right about the two of them not getting along, as they acted very coldly towards each other. But I needed to spend more time with Eloisa if I really wanted to know her. I had a feeling that with time, all would reveal itself.

Deciding that waiting around until dinner wasn't going to make me feel better, I started to explore the manor. The entire place possessed large windows and from some of the hallways you could see the ocean in the distance. I didn't see Lance or Eloisa and I contemplated what exactly they could be discussing. It didn't appear to be a very joyous reunion, after all.

I pushed open a white wooden door and found myself standing in a small parlour. Surrounded by books, I paced along the bookshelves, hands behind my back.

The books were all quite old and well-worn. Nothing appeared to be of any interest. I turned to face the fireplace on the other side of the room. But it was the painting above that caught my eye. I stepped closer to observe it more intently. It was clearly an old painting, as the royal children were still young. I glanced over the colours that composed a picture of the young princess. Something caught my attention and I wondered if the artist had purposely forgotten to add Eloisa's small birthmark. I reached out, gently dragging my fingers over the small black lines that formed the names of the royal children on the bottom corner of the painting. And then it hit me. It was like the air had been sucked out of my lungs for a moment, but only a moment. It was shock first, but confusion settled in quickly. It simply didn't make sense.

I burst through the white doors and marched down the hallway to find out if what I thought to be true was, in fact, true. Rounding one of the hallway corners, I ran into Jack.

"Your Highness, is everything all right?" I don't know if it was my shocked expression or ragged breathing that gave me away.

"All is fine, never you mind about me, Jack." I was about to go round him when Jack spoke again.

"I couldn't find out much more about Eloisa, but Alastor has been on Rhen's trail and it turns out he's only been working for the royal family for a few months — and somehow became the prince's most trusted confidant. Something doesn't quite add up there."

"It's all right. You can forget it. Forget all of it."

"But, Your Highness …"

"Forget it!" I spat out, and I walked away abruptly, without giving Jack a chance to reply. It was only a moment later that I felt guilty. I couldn't remember the last time I had spoken to him like that. The poor man was only following orders. I would apologise later. Right now, there was a more important matter at hand.

I asked one of the servants to lead me to Eloisa's chambers. Not bothering to knock, I swung open the door, but it wasn't Eloisa inside. Her lady-in-waiting, who appeared to be in the middle of unpacking her trunk, looked at me with wide eyes.

"Cordelia, is it?" I closed the door behind me.

"Yes, Your Highness?"

I glanced around the room again for some unknown reason, as if my senses couldn't be trusted any longer, but she definitely wasn't there.

"She's not here." Cordelia didn't move, garments still in her hand.

"I must speak to her. It's very important." I didn't know Cordelia at all. Didn't know if I could put any trust in her yet, though my instincts were telling me she wasn't much trouble. But my instincts had been wrong before … clearly.

"If she comes back, would you please tell her that I'm looking for her?"

"Of course, Your Highness," Cordelia said, closing the trunk. I was about to leave when she spoke up again. "I know she seems odd." She hesitated for a moment. "But deep down … she's not a bad person."

"I know," I said and left the room.

* * *

I didn't get a chance to see her again that night, but I was told that a hunt had been arranged for us in the morning. If what I thought to be true was indeed true, maybe this would be my way of finding out.

I met her at the stables, dressed in hunting attire, her hair braided away from her face. It certainly had a way of bringing out those determined eyes.

"Good morning," I said politely while my eyes scanned her guard with the scar on his face. He'd remained very close to her throughout our travels and I couldn't quite put my finger on it. It was as if she would tense up every time he came close to her.

"Good morning," she said and then frowned at the stable boy who handed her a bow and quiver. She looked at them for a moment, as if she weren't quite sure what to do.

"I thought you couldn't shoot with a bow?"

She looked at me sheepishly. "I can't. But you said you'd teach me."

"I did say that, didn't I? Well, I suppose a promise is a promise."

She looked pleased as we mounted. We rode in the middle of our party of guards, all Evernean. I hadn't seen any of my men this morning, though I was more than certain they were occupying themselves with sword duels in the gardens.

"Do you and your family do this often?"

She shook her head. "Not at all. But yesterday you spoke of the good times you had while hunting, and well ..." Her cheeks flushed a little. "I thought you might enjoy this?" she said, looking hopeful, and I smiled in slight disbelief.

"You arranged a hunt for me?" I watched her jaw clench, her eyes looking back and forth between the guards. We weren't exactly riding on top of each other's horses, but I was fairly sure they could hear most of what we said despite the sounds of the forest that stretched behind Woodsbrook.

"Don't look so surprised." She lifted her chin. "I can be a very likeable person."

"This coming from a woman who held a dagger to my throat," I teased and she gawked at me for a moment.

"Hey, you tied me to a tree first!" Her accusation, though true, was made in a humorous tone.

"For which I am profoundly sorry."

She shook her head, but there was a smile on her face and, truth be told, I was starting to grow quite fond of that smile. I bit the inside of my cheek, the truth dripping into my train of thought once again. I couldn't lose focus on the task at hand.

"I can't remember the last time I went hunting, though. These past few years I've been too occupied with other royal duties. I really miss hunting with my younger brother."

My eyes drifted towards her face, seeing if she would take the bait. If not, I would look profoundly silly and suspicious.

"You have a brother?" She didn't meet my stare, as if trying to regain a memory.

"Yes, I told you all about him in that letter I sent a few months ago. Don't you remember?"

Her face fell, and upon realisation of this she tried to pull herself together. But it was too late.

"Yes, of course I remember. It was just so long ago."

Just as I'd assumed she would, she had fallen into my trap and had given herself away. I didn't have a brother and I most surely never sent her any letters. Eloisa and I had never communicated before my arrival in Everness, and now I knew we still hadn't. The biggest problem was figuring out why.

The conversation died down after that, as we carefully listened to the sounds of the forest and hoped for an interruption of the harmonising birdsong by the sound of an animal grazing amid the undergrowth. But luck was not on our side, and after a few hours of riding, we hadn't managed to catch anything. Not that I could really get my mind to focus on the forest or the hunt. I could only think of her next to me.

We turned back, making our way to the manor. "May I ask you something?" She gazed at me from under her lashes, a curious expression on her face.

"You may." I grinned. I had to applaud her pretend interest in me.

Perhaps I should have felt betrayed. But curiosity had always been one of my biggest flaws and I knew I was knee-deep in trouble, because I was intrigued.

"When we first met, you said that dagger was a gift."

"Yes?"

"From whom?"

I chuckled. "It's a peculiar story actually. It was the morning we crossed the border and we stumbled upon this strange old woman in the woods. She appeared to be selling little trinkets and she asked us for water. As a thanks, she gave me that dagger."

"You're right, that is fairly odd," she said sarcastically.

"Mock me all you want, but there was something strange about her."

"Something mystical?" she teased, eyebrows raised.

"Sort of. Regardless, it's a very nice gift."

"Is that story really true?"

I looked at her in confusion. "Yes, it's true. Why would I make that up?"

"I don't know. I just thought that a gift like that would be from a past lover or something."

I snorted. "Delany wasn't very fond of giving gifts."

"Ah." She smirked. "So there is a past lover?"

I sighed, looking towards her and away again. This question wasn't a pretence.

I could tell from her face: she truly wanted to know.

"*Lover* was hardly the word. She was the girl who had been promised to me since I was scarcely a child of four. We were to be married after I turned eighteen. Her family is one of the wealthiest in Norrandale and they had good relations with my family."

"What happened?"

My grip tightened on the reins. "When the time came, she decided that she would rather marry someone else." I remembered, as clear as daylight, when Delany had told me the truth.

"Who?"

"My cousin, the Duke of Orrington," I admitted.

"She gave up being a future queen to be a duchess?"

"She married him because she loved him. I could hardly blame her for choosing love over a title."

She tilted her head to the side. "But you loved her?"

"I used to think so. But I was too young and naive to know what love even meant. I was very fond of her, though. We got along really well."

"And you didn't take another for a wife?"

"The war with Argon happened so soon after. I had to train and leave to go and fight. And when I came back—" I couldn't bring myself to remember. "Well, things were so different."

I could see the manor, indicating that we were close to the gardens.

"Why did you agree to this union?"

No one had asked me that before. "Our kingdoms have been in each other's bad graces for a very long time. As future king it is my job to create alliances and not enemies, so that I can protect my people."

It didn't appear to be the answer she was looking for. It was half of the truth anyway. I wasn't sure if I could admit all of it to anyone.

"So you're going to be the kind of king that makes sacrifices for his people?"

I managed to chuckle at her words. "You think of marriage as a sacrifice?"

"For some people it most definitely is. I suppose it depends on who you end up with." She met my gaze.

"Yes, I suppose it does."

We emerged from the stretch of woods and entered the gardens. "What about you?"

"Oh, I'm just in it for the riches and advancement. I could never be queen of Everness."

I laughed at her joke. "You are second in line to the throne. It is not impossible."

"Yes, let's plot the death of my father and brother, shall we?" she said, and we dismounted near the stables. "Thank you for the ride, it was most pleasant."

She curtsied before walking away, and I realised she hadn't answered my question.

Chapter 13

Woodsbrook Manor

Lara

I ran up the marble steps to my chambers, heat crawling up my neck. I had arranged the hunt for Cai in the hope I might earn more of his trust and his affection. Even if it didn't aid me at the end of play, it certainly wouldn't make things worse. It would be impossible to take the sword with his guards constantly surrounding him. They weren't with us on the ride, but for some reason I hadn't felt like knocking the man off his horse and leaving him unconscious in the woods.

Maybe it's that stupid smile he keeps sending my way.

Even though I hated to admit it, some part of me would feel better if I took it from him without his knowing. Which didn't make sense, because I had no reason to feel guilty. I was one of the best bandits in the kingdom. Bandits didn't feel guilt.

Cordelia was already waiting in my room, ready to help me change. I told her about the hunt and shared my concerns regarding Cai's interrogative questions, but I could tell by the look in her eyes that her mind was somewhere else completely.

"Cordelia?" I asked a few minutes after saying something and still not having received a reply from her. She looked up to meet my gaze in the mirror as she was brushing my hair.

"Yes?"

"What did *you* do today?" I questioned, a smirk on my face and the memory of the night I caught her up to something on my mind.

Cordelia looked abashed and it gave her away. "Oh, you know. I—" She started to fumble for words. "I just went for a little walk and got a book from the library, that sort of thing." She went back to brushing my hair with fierce concentration.

"Where did you go for a walk?"

"Mmhhh?"

I could tell she was avoiding the question.

"You said you went for a little walk. Where did this walk take place?"

"In the rose garden," she replied, too quickly.

"Oh, I see," I said. "And were you alone?"

She looked up again and I grinned. "A gentleman was with you, wasn't he?" Her eyes went wide and she began to shake her head, but I didn't give her a chance to reply before letting out a small gasp. "Oh, Cordelia," I teased. "Is it because he's in fact not a gentleman that you refrain from telling me?"

Her mouth was wide open as she scrambled for something to say. I turned in my seat to face her.

"Is he a servant? Or a pirate or an outlaw that you met up with at the harbour town?"

She looked about ready to jump out of the window if that was what it took to get away from this conversation.

I held her by her wrists. "Or is he married? Or a romancer that your father would disapprove of?"

She said nothing but her face was an open book. "Ah, so that's it."

"Is there anything else I can help you with?" She put the brush down on the dresser.

"Yes, actually." I turned back to face the mirror. "I need a big favour from you. Tonight I'm going to meet Prince Cai in the rose garden."

"Alone?"

We both knew it was inappropriate according to the rules of polite society and the monarchy, but that was exactly what I would be counting on.

"Yes, alone, and then I need you to sneak up to his chambers and steal his sword while I keep him distracted."

"Have you gone mad? I can't do that."

"Please, Cordelia, you have to. Lance is pressuring me and I'm afraid I shall have to suffer consequences if I don't get this over with soon."

She didn't seem convinced, but agreed anyway.

I waited in my chambers for the sun to set before putting on my cloak Pulling the door open, I was a little surprised to find Rhen there, clearly standing guard.

"Don't you have anything better to do?" I asked. "Like an assigned duty?"

"This is my assigned duty. I am to keep watch at your door."

"You say it as if it means keeping someone unwanted from coming in. But you and I both know it's to keep me from going out." I smirked.

"Where exactly are you going?"

"For a walk." I shrugged. "I need some fresh air."

"Lara."

I turned to face him.

"Princesses don't sneak out of their rooms at night," he warned, as if he could read my mind.

I squared my shoulders. "Well, it's a good thing I'm not a real princess, then."

The evening air created a chill down my spine as I stepped into the garden and I pulled my cloak closer to my neck. I rushed down the steps that led into the large gardens of the manor house. Cordelia had informed me that Cai's chamber windows looked over the west side of the garden. Hiding my head beneath the hood, I strode past the large hedges and berry bushes.

I hoped that this absurd plan would work out. There was no guarantee that anything would go the way I wanted. In fact this whole plan was based on my gut instinct about Cai's character. And I'd been wrong about character before.

I walked slowly, in the shimmer of the moonlight, my figure visible between the splashes of flowery colour hidden in the night shadows. Cordelia had pulled out a beautiful dress. It was simpler than my other gowns but just as elegant. The material was white and light blue, my sleeves long and flowing. Every fibre of my being yearned to look back and up at his window to see if he was looking outside, if he had noticed my movement. But it was too risky. He shouldn't for one second consider this was planned.

I allowed my fingers to run over the nearby leaves when I heard footsteps on the marble steps of the back porch. A rhythm I had become all too familiar with.

I smiled, although pretending I had heard nothing, and stalked among the tall thorny rose hedges until I could no longer hear his steps. But I knew he would find me still.

This part of the garden was a maze, turning to the left and right.

With only the moonlight as a guide, you could barely see where you were going. The green hedges allowed for plenty of dark, secluded corners. It was a good thing I wasn't a real princess with an actual reputation to be concerned about. This would be considered positively scandalous.

"You're out late, Your Highness." The sound of Cai's voice forced me to stop at the entrance to the maze.

"So are you." I picked one of the white roses and held it up to my nose, still not having turned to face him. I feared my expression would give me away.

"Well, I am a gentleman, if nothing else. It wouldn't be right to leave a lady wandering outside alone at night."

I faked surprise in my voice. "You followed me?"

"The more important question is what are you doing out here alone at this hour?"

I looked at him over my shoulder for a moment, pretending to hide a grin.

"I needed some fresh air," I stated nonchalantly as Cai fell into step beside me. I couldn't help but feel a certain tension between us. Something I'd only felt that night at the Darwick estate when we'd had too much wine. I used to think it was my strong dislike for him. Now I was no longer sure.

"And an open window wouldn't suffice?"

I stopped again, forcing him to face me. There was a hint of a sparkle in his eyes, and I wasn't sure if it was the starlight or the fact that he knew exactly what I was trying to do. Cai was a prince. He'd be no stranger to women trying to flirt with him. I simply wished I was more of an expert at the skill, but despite Cordelia's advice, the mere way he looked at me caused my stomach to tighten.

"Are you accusing me of something?"

Cai surprised me by leaning in so that the space between us became minimal. "Is there something to be accused of?"

A lump formed in my throat. A thought that perhaps I hadn't given Prince Cai enough credit all along, that maybe, just maybe, he had figured it all out. There were, after all, a great many things to be accused of.

"Whatever can you mean?" I attempted to keep up the act. I had to distract him at all costs, and if I were lucky, Cordelia would be successful in her task and I wouldn't have to spend another minute in this place. But this meant I had to keep him busy for a while.

"Who is to say you weren't meeting a man here in the garden at night? A secret lover whom you can't marry because you're promised to the Prince of Norrandale."

I let out a chuckle. "You think I have the time and the will for secret lovers too?" We hadn't moved from our proximity.

"I think you have the will for a great many things."

I wasn't sure what to make of his words. And I believed him. So I gave the Prince of Norrandale my best attempt at a seductive smile and turned away before taking the first left turn in the maze. He was quick to catch up with me.

"So are you going to tell me what you're actually doing out here in the gardens?"

"I told you." I twirled the rose I'd picked earlier between my fingers. "I needed some fresh air."

"Liar," Cai replied, but he wore a smile.

"Maybe I am planning to meet someone out here, in which case I must ask you to leave," I teased.

"I'll only leave in order to go and retrieve my sword."

His words made me halt.

"What for?" My voice was more strained than I would have liked.

"I must duel with him for your hand, of course."

Of course.

I had to force myself to take a steady breath. "There will be no sword fighting."

"Would you prefer if I used my bare hands?"

"Cai." I couldn't help but let out a laugh until I saw his expression. "What? Why are you looking at me like that?"

"No reason. I just don't think I've ever heard you say my name like that."

I wasn't sure exactly what he meant but it felt personal and borderline intimate. I found myself feeling shy, so before things got awkward, I tucked the rose behind his ear. "I think you're ready for a portrait painting, Your Highness."

Cai adopted a faraway gaze as many royals had in the paintings I'd seen. "Like this?"

"Yes, that looks perfect."

"You reckon?"

I nodded with sincerity.

But his witty smile gave way and he took the rose to place it behind my ear. "I think it is much better suited to you."

I could barely move. *When did he get this close again?* Cai's hand trailed from the rose down my cheek and to my jawline. My breath got caught in my throat. When he pulled his hand away, I could still feel his touch lingering on my skin.

Cai cleared his throat before stepping back. "It's getting quite late, I—"

"I wonder about mazes sometimes," I blurted out. It was a

ridiculous topic but the first thing that came to mind. Pretty soon I was going to run out of things to say.

"You wonder about mazes?" he asked in confusion.

"Yes." I gestured to the hedges around us. "I think one has to be awfully clever to design a maze like this."

Cai scratched the back of his neck. "I suppose."

I started walking backwards. "Do you want to know what else I think?"

"What?"

"I think that if I hide, you won't be able to find me." Before he had a chance to reply, I turned and made a run for it. Unfortunately, I was quick to step on the hems of my dress and nearly toppled over. I grabbed the fabric, thankful not to hear a ripping sound, and veered left and then right. I had no idea which way I was going but I hoped it would keep Cai out here just a little longer. When I reckoned I was far enough from where I'd left him, I stopped to catch my breath.

I listened intently for him calling my name but there were only the sounds of the night. Where could he be? I continued walking, figuring I would reach the end of the maze at some point.

After a few minutes of walking alone in silence, I began to grow worried that perhaps Cai had abandoned our little game. Maybe he'd gone back to his chambers, having had enough of the awkward princess and her strange topics of conversation.

"Cai?" I called out hesitantly, but there was no response.

What if he'd gone back and caught Cordelia red-handed? Lance certainly wasn't going to defend her. She'd find herself in endless trouble and it would be all my fault. *How did I ever think this was a good idea?*

"Cai?" I said again, a little more uncertainty in my voice this time.

I peered around one of the hedges when an arm wrapped around my waist and gently pulled me back.

"Got you," a breathy voice whispered near my ear, causing shivers to run down my spine.

I turned to face the prince with emerald eyes. "You scared me."

"That was not my intention." His voice was low and the hedges hid him from the moonlight, casting a shadow across his face.

I swallowed. We were very close again … and it wasn't entirely unpleasant. In fact, it was kind of nice.

Nice and nerve-wracking and what was happening to my pulse?

Cai's eyes softened as he looked at me and I found myself unable to look away.

"What was your intention?" I dared to ask, wondering where my breath had gone.

Cai's mouth began to form a grin when an owl hooted in the distance and I stepped back.

"Any idea how we get out of here?" I looked left and right but I had no idea which direction I'd come from. It couldn't have been that complicated a maze, but the darkness of the evening certainly didn't help.

"I think I can find my way."

I contemplated holding on to his arm as we continued our walk in the garden but I feared there had been more than enough touching for one evening. I tried to remember all of Cordelia's lessons in flattery and charm. Although I suspected I was the one being charmed.

"Norrandale has a wonderful library, you know? I should think you would take quite a liking to it." Why would he bring up a library? Perhaps neither of us were very good conversationalists when nervous. Could he tell I was nervous? My mind replayed our earlier moment repeatedly.

"And why is that?"

Cai cocked his head to the side. "I was told that you loved to read. Was I misinformed?"

Of course, damn it. Princess Eloisa was very fond of books while I, on the other hand, didn't take very much pleasure in reading. I could read but I wouldn't unless it was a necessity. I'd slipped up, yet again.

"Of course I love to read." I attempted to recover from my blunder. "I only meant, why would you presume your library to be superior to the one I have at home?" Better.

The corner of Cai's mouth jerked, but he pulled a straight face again as if the action was involuntary.

"I never said you would find it superior to your own library. I simply said I think you would *like* it."

"Are you fond of reading?" We'd made our way out of the maze and back around the rose garden.

"Sometimes. Though I haven't had much time for reading at leisure lately." The rose that he had placed behind my ear earlier fell to the ground and I reached down to pick it up. But those bloody hems wouldn't allow me that simple task and I lost my footing. In a moment, Cai was holding my arms, keeping me from falling.

"Careful now."

I was thankful the darkness wouldn't allow him to see the flush in my cheeks.

Cai bent down to his knees, picking up the rose.

"Your Highness." He held it out to me.

"There's no need to get down on one knee." I took the rose and placed it in my hair. "We're already engaged."

My words made Cai smirk.

I hoped that Cordelia had finished her job and that I had managed to keep Cai away from his chambers long enough.

"You were right, you know." We walked up the steps of the porch and he held open the door for me before we entered.

"Right about what?" I asked.

"You're not like any princess I have met before." His words managed to put a smile on my face, though I wasn't entirely sure what I was satisfied about.

"Well, I never lie." And I turned and headed for my room.

"You what?"

Cordelia motioned for me to be quiet. "It wasn't my fault! How was I to know he would be there?"

All my hopes had come crashing down when I stepped into my bedroom and found Cordelia standing empty-handed with a disappointed look on her face.

Apparently Cordelia had run into Jack as she was entering Cai's room.

"What did you do?"

"I told him I got lost and then we walked back to this side of the manor."

I huffed in frustration. "I tell you to steal a sword and you end up strolling with the enemy."

"I didn't have a choice. You know I didn't." Which was true. I hadn't taken Cai's guards into account and, once again, I had not got Lance what he wanted. I fell onto my bed with a groan.

"I'm never going to pull this off." The bed dipped as Cordelia sat beside me.

"You will. You're not thinking straight, that's all." Taking my palms away from my face, I peered at her in confusion.

"What do you mean?"

Cordelia wore the strangest of smiles on her face. "You know exactly what I mean."

"I do not," I replied in earnest.

"Obviously you are completely besotted with Prince Cai."

My eyes grew wide and I flew up into a sitting position. "I am not!"

Cordelia let out a giggle. "I can't very well say I blame you. He is very handsome and charming, is he not?"

I stood up and started pacing in front of her. "Did you hit your head on the way here, or something?"

"You cannot deny it," she persisted. "I see the way you look at him." I met her eyes from across the room. "You've taken a liking to him, haven't you?"

"*Like* is a very strong word."

"But?" She urged me on.

"But I'll admit he isn't quite what I expected him to be."

"You mean he isn't arrogant, selfish and spoiled?"

I didn't reply.

"But you cannot deny he is very handsome." She swooned slightly, repositioning herself more comfortably.

"Then you should have been the one to pretend you were going to marry him." I stopped pacing.

She laughed again. "That would never have worked."

I placed my hands on my hips. "And why ever not?"

The look Cordelia gave me suggested she knew something that I did not. "Because, my dear friend, I see the way he looks at you as well. And he has taken quite a liking to you too." I snorted and she stood up, taking my shoulders from behind and urging me to face the mirror. The reflection looked so unlike the girl I was used to. "Don't be upset. It's what you wanted, isn't it?"

Which was true. With all Cordelia's lessons and my attempted flirting, the goal had been for Cai to like me, but to trust me most of all.

"I understand why you do what you do. I know you see it as justice. And I don't think you're entirely wrong. But this," she said, "this is more personal. You will have to decide if the gold you're being paid is worth his life."

My chest tightened a little. Lance wouldn't kill Cai.

Would he?

I turned to face Cordelia. "What about you? You said Lance had his way of getting what he wanted." She hadn't given me an answer the last time.

She sighed and looked away. "You mean, how did I get myself into this mess?"

I didn't answer.

Cordelia stepped away from me. "My parents, though happily married, didn't always make good choices. They married me off to a terrible man for money."

"I'm sorry." And I did feel some remorse for her.

She slowly paced up and down the room. "When he tried to hurt me, Rhen went at him, but he fought back and, well, Rhen killed him while defending himself. Instead of hanging him as a murderer, Lance gave Rhen a chance to redeem himself by working for him."

"But this also means that he can blackmail you into doing anything he wants?"

She nodded.

I walked over to her and placed my hands on her upper arms. "When this is over, we're going to get you out of this. I'm not sure how, yet, but I'll figure it out."

Her eyes brightened up a little. "You know, if it wasn't for your stubborn attitude, you would have made a good royal."

A laugh erupted from the back of my throat.

I was already in my nightdress, covered by my sleeping gown, when a thought occurred to me. The best bandit in Levernia and I'd failed twice to steal a sword.

Uncle Arthur would be disappointed. I threaded my fingers through my hair. It couldn't be that difficult. It wasn't that difficult. I'd just been approaching the matter wrong. I burst out of my bedroom before I had time to change my mind. Damon was standing guard outside.

There would be no question about Damon's loyalty to Lance. He reminded me of a hawk, always looking for something innocent to prey on.

"What are you looking at?" I mumbled, storming past him down the hall. I had a reputation to uphold and I would not be a failure. I'd already made the mistake of getting caught, and look where it had got me. It was a simple sword.

Yes, it was out of my usual line of work. I went for smaller things, like jewellery or coins, which could easily be hidden, and my targets were never surrounded by their own group of guards. This was unlike anything I'd attempted before. I ran along the manor corridors, my bare feet noisy on the tiled floors. Rhen rounded the corner ahead of me and I stopped, catching my breath.

"Finally decided to run away have you?"

"Where's Cai?" I was heaving, already becoming unfit from not running for the past few days.

"He's in the study with Lance."

"And his men?"

"In their chambers I believe." Perfect. "What are you … ?" I didn't give him time to finish his question.

"Thank you!" And I was running again. I stopped for a second at the door of Cai's bedroom, listening for any movement or voices inside.

Once I was sure there was only silence, I pushed open the door with the palm of my hand. The door creaked and I peeked inside. Empty. I slipped through the opening and carefully shut the door behind me. I quickly scanned the room, looking for the sword. It wasn't lying around in plain sight — that was certain. Did Cai have it on him, perhaps? No, it had to be here. I looked around, under the pillows, inside cabinets.

My eyes landed on the trunk at the foot of his bed. I hurried over and pulled it open. And sure enough, there it was. The sword lay on top of his other weapons and clothes, and I reached to pick it up.

Footsteps echoed from the hallway outside. Someone was coming. Cai was coming. I slammed the trunk shut and looked around the room. Where could I hide? Under the bed? And then what, wait till Cai fell asleep and risk him waking up when I tried to leave? How would I explain that? The footsteps became louder. There was always the window. But it was too high and I didn't have anything to help me on the way down. I didn't have time.

The door opened and I spun around. At first, Cai didn't see me, with the room being dark and him looking at the floor. But when his eyes did land on me, his expression was one of shock, and I could have been wrong but … also intrigue.

Panic. Pure panic rushed through my whole body.

"What are you doing here?"

Nothing. I couldn't think up a single excuse. The silence in the room became awkward and I felt my heart beat inside my throat. Something. I just had to say something.

"I ..." *I came here to steal your family's heirloom.* I doubted the truth would go down well. "I ... uh ... I forgot something." I stuttered. "In the garden. I forgot something in the garden." I wasn't making even the slightest bit of sense. "I forgot to give you something." I rephrased. No, that wasn't any better.

Cai cocked his head sideways as his look of confusion remained. "You forgot to give me something?"

"Yes," I replied, too fast. Why was I out of breath? Why was I so nervous? I rubbed my hands together, glancing around the room to see if I could spot anything to help me talk my way out of this.

"What did you forget?"

I met his eyes again, those wild green eyes.

"I forgot to give you this." I walked over and grabbed his face, pressing my lips to his in a chaste kiss. It lasted only a moment before I pulled away. I didn't give Cai a chance to say anything before I ran out of the room.

What had just happened? I was pretty sure Cai was wondering the exact same thing but thankfully he didn't follow me to ask any questions. The door slammed shut behind me as soon as I entered my chambers. I pressed the back of my hand against my mouth.

What the hell did I just do? I'd just kissed a prince. That ... that was the only solution I could come up with? If it hadn't made me appear less suspicious, he probably thought I was insane. My heart was still hammering when I got under the covers of the plush bed and pulled the blanket over my head. I did nothing to erase the image in my mind. Nor the feeling of his lips, which I could still taste. Maybe what bothered me most of all wasn't the fact that I'd kissed Cai, it was the fact that I wouldn't mind doing it again.

Lance caught me by one of the doors the next morning. "I need to speak with you."

"With regards to what?" I frowned.

"Goodness, you even sound like her." He rolled his eyes and pulled my arm in the direction of the door before letting go. I followed him out on to the porch.

"Like who?"

Lance shook his head. "Nothing, it doesn't matter. When did you start talking like that?"

"Like what?"

"Like you weren't born in a barn."

"I've never talked like I was born in a barn. Cordelia simply helped me improve my vocabulary a little. That and the tone I talk in. Apparently my regular voice is 'too harsh', whatever that means. I'm trying to convince His Royal Highness that I'm a princess, remember?"

"You won't have to worry about that for much longer." We walked past the entrance to the gardens, in the direction of the stables. "Have you made any progress?"

"I took him on a hunt yesterday in the hopes I might be able to take his sword if he were distracted. Maybe even knock him out and leave him in the woods. But we couldn't find anything and he's so bloody attached to that thing." I mentioned nothing about our scandalous meeting in the rose garden.

"That's rather cruel, wouldn't you say? You've probably managed to make him half fall in love with you by now and yet you'd leave him lying cold on the forest floor."

I rolled my eyes. "That's rich, coming from you."

"Me?" He placed a hand on his chest. "Cruel? Never."

"What do you want me to do, ask him to hand it over nicely?"

"You're running out of time. And you are the bandit, not I. Out of everything, this is supposed to be the easiest part for you. I hired you because of your reputation. Don't tell me I've hired the only bandit in the kingdom who can't steal a bloody thing."

I stepped in front of him, making him stop abruptly. "Don't underestimate me," I said in a low voice. "That would be a mistake."

He bent his head slightly. "Then prove me wrong."

Lance made the formal announcement for dinner to be later that evening.

My first destination was the kitchen. I ordered all of the servants to take a long lunch outside. They stared at me with surprise and confusion, but there was no refusal. I started gathering herbs and crushing them before pouring boiling water onto the mixture. Daggers and knives weren't my only skill, but this would be my last attempt at stealing Cai's sword. I couldn't afford the risk of being unsuccessful again. There was simply too much at stake.

I poured the tonic into two small bottles and placed them in the hidden pocket of my dress. I spotted Rhen in one of the hallways on my way to my chambers. "Good, I've found you. I need to ask you a favour."

Rhen snorted. "I don't believe you're in a position to be asking any favours."

"It's not for me, it's for Lance." I took out one of the small bottles. "I need you to get rid of Cai's guards."

His eyes widened. "I can't just kill all of them."

"Not kill." I took his hand and placed the bottle in his palm. "This is a sleeping tonic."

He frowned. "I don't understand."

"Look, I don't have time to explain but please make sure they get it." It was the first time Rhen had heard me say the word *please,* so he knew I was desperate enough.

"Very well," he agreed. I headed in the direction of my chambers.

Cordelia helped me get dressed for dinner a few hours later. I hurried down the stairs, towards the dining room, hoping to arrive before Cai and Lance. Upon entering, I found the room empty, and let out a sigh of relief. The table was beautifully set with lavish cutlery and golden cups. I took out the little bottle and poured some of the tonic into Cai's cup. The healer of our clan, Benette, had taught me how to mix such tonics as a young girl, and with the correct dose, this one could knock a man out cold for hours.

I had barely put the bottle away when Cai entered the dining room.

"There you are. I've been looking for you."

"Well, where else would I be, than at the dinner table, where we'll be having dinner ... at dinner time."

Cai gave me a look of slight confusion before shaking it off. I hadn't meant to stumble over my words, but along with the fear of being caught and his charming face, which I had momentarily forgotten was kind of dashing, I hardly knew what to say.

"I must speak with you most urgently."

"Cai," I started in protest, but he sensed what I was about to say.

"It cannot wait anymore."

"Surely there can be nothing of such importance …" I moved away, but he wrapped his fingers around my upper arm and turned me to face him.

"I know," he said, his face completely expressionless and awaiting a reaction from mine.

"What?" I decided that acting ignorant was my last option until I could buy myself some time.

"I know." He placed so much emphasis on the word *know*, eliminating any conviction in my mind that he was lying. "I know you're not Eloisa."

My mouth opened, but no words came out. It was at that moment the dining-room doors burst open and Cai and I sprang five feet apart. Lance sauntered in with his usual swagger and strutted over to his seat at the head of the table.

"Why the sour faces?" he joked, falling into his seat. "It is a joyous occasion we are celebrating, is it not?" I reached for my chair, but Cai beat me to it, pulling it out and waiting for me to sit.

"What do you mean?" I asked Lance, who had already started pouring himself some more wine, despite the fact that his cup was almost full.

"Well, your wedding, of course."

Cai took a seat across from me, but wouldn't meet my eyes.

"Cai and I had a very pleasant discussion about all the big wedding arrangements, didn't we, Cai?"

Cai nodded, taking a sip of his wine, and my stomach dropped.

I glanced at the two of them nervously. Clearly Cai didn't plan on sharing his newfound knowledge with Lance, yet. I could handle one unpredictable prince, but two was a completely different story.

"And would you mind sharing what you have discussed or am I to be left in the dark?" I took a large gulp of my wine.

"Cai signed the marital agreement that he will marry the eldest daughter of King Magnus and we settled that the wedding would take place in Everness, after which you will travel to Norrandale."

Why was Lance making Cai sign agreements if we weren't going to marry anyway? Did he still plan for Eloisa to marry Cai after this? It didn't make sense. And if Cai knew I wasn't Eloisa, why did he sign the agreement? How did he see all of this ending? Perhaps I had underestimated his character and the boyish charm was all an act, similar to mine.

What if he had planned something far worse? The thought made me slightly nauseous and I took another big gulp of wine.

The courses were carried out on silver platters and served one by one, while we spent the whole dinner in the most unnerving silence. Cai excused himself after we'd eaten, claiming he was tired, which meant the tonic was working. I could see it in the way his eyes started drooping.

"What have you done to the poor prince?" Lance asked once he was out of earshot.

"A sleeping tonic."

"I didn't know you could make tonics."

I shrugged. "It was a last resort."

"You and I aren't all that different, you know."

I laughed. "You and I are different in every way possible."

He leaned forwards, holding my gaze. "You would like to believe that, wouldn't you? But you and I both know we do what we have to do for survival. Even if it makes us cruel sometimes."

I looked at him in dismay. "I'm cruel when I have no other choice. You are cruel because you like to see others suffer."

"You really do think the worst of me, don't you?"

"You have given me nothing to prove otherwise."

"All in good time." He leaned back in his chair again. "Now go." Lance gestured with his cup. "I believe you have work to do."

I left the table without another word.

Chapter 14

The Cellar of Woodsbrook Manor

Cai

I woke up damp and cold, the stone floor beneath me causing aches all over my body. My eyes took a few moments to adjust to the dimly lit room and it was only then I discovered that I wasn't in a room at all, but in a cell.

"Well, well, well." I heard Lance's voice from somewhere in the dark.

Metal clanged and the cell gate swung open before Lance stepped into the light.

"If it isn't the Prince of Norrandale."

I was dressed in my shirt, trousers and boots, as I remember falling asleep in, on my bed. My hand went for the small knife I kept hidden in the inside lining of my riding boots. "Don't bother," Lance said. "My guards have disarmed you. There is no use in fighting anyway." He muttered the last part, but I heard every word clearly.

"Where are my men?" I stood up, my fists clenching.

Lance leaned against the opposite wall. "Look, you and I can do this the easy way or the hard way. I don't know about you, but I much prefer the easy way."

"Where is she?" I took a step towards him and immediately his guards approached the cell, but Lance waved a hand.

"My sister will be completely safe as long as you do exactly as I say."

"I know she's not Princess Eloisa."

He shifted his head slightly, his eyes searching for something. "You're right," he admitted. "How long have you known?" He didn't seem very fazed that I had discovered the truth.

"Since our arrival at the manor."

"Interesting."

"What do you want?" I asked, though I had more than a few ideas what his answer would be.

"You know exactly what I want, Prince of Norrandale." He stood up straight. "I thought I knew where it was, but I underestimated your wit, and as it turns out, I was wrong. Now I want you to tell me exactly where the jewel is."

I scoffed. "Don't tell me you're a believer of mythical stories as well."

"It is not a myth!" He raised his voice. "I know it exists."

Lance didn't give me time to question how he came by this knowledge. . "We visited your family when the two of us were still children, remember? You and I had a pretend sword fight in one of the training rings."

I did remember. We must have been about twelve years old. I gazed at the man who could perhaps have been my friend, had it not been for the feud between our families. That, *and* Lance's more than questionable character.

"I know that precious stone is somewhere in the mountains of Norrandale. I know it contains magic and I know you have one of the jewels with you. So I suggest you tell me where it is, sooner rather than later," he warned.

"Even if it were true ..." I stepped towards him. "What makes you think that I'll ever tell you?"

"The hard way it is, then." And with that, he launched a blow to my face. I didn't wait for another one before I hit back, causing his lip to split and a small stream of blood to pour out.

His guards rushed inside, grabbing my arms and holding them behind my back. Lance touched his lip and smirked at the trace of blood on his finger. "Not bad. But I haven't given you all the rules yet." He wiped the blood from his mouth. "There's a guard in her bedroom, you see. She's fast asleep now, but she won't be for long, and for every blow you strike me with, there will be a blow to her."

"You're lying."

"Perhaps I am." Lance shrugged. "But would you be willing to risk it?"

He punched me again and a guard kicked the back of my leg, forcing me to my knees. Lance let out a sinister laugh. "You were always going to be the man to kneel first, rather than the one being kneeled to." He tilted his head. "I hope you know it's nothing personal, just politics." He sent a fist into my torso. I heaved as the air was forced from my lungs.

"What if I tell you this? If you don't tell me where it is, I will kill every one of your men in cold blood." Another blow to my face.

"Those men signed up to be my personal guard. They would not have done so if they weren't willing to lay down their lives for mine or for their kingdom." It wasn't entirely a lie and I hoped none of my men would get injured because of me. Regardless of their willingness.

"I don't believe you actually care that little for them, but you're right, that would be awfully boring and I doubt very successful." His eyes suddenly lit up in the most devious of ways and I found myself shuddering slightly.

"What about her? Despite knowing the truth, you've grown quite fond of her, haven't you?"

He told a guard to go and fetch her, and I found myself shouting "No!" before Lance hit me in the ribs again.

"Would you like to tell me where it is, then?" He bent down so that we were face to face.

"I don't know what you're talking about." Another punch in the face and I could feel the blood dripping from my brow.

A guard dragged her into the cell and tossed her to Lance. She was only wearing her night shift, looking much like she did on the night we had met, only so much more pale. Lance turned her to face me, and though she struggled, I could tell she wasn't fully conscious. What had they done to her?

"So glad you could join us," Lance said and I watched the blood drain from her face. "Where is it, Cai?"

"I don't have it!" Which was the truth.

"Then where is it?" His shout echoed against the stone walls.

"Leave her out of this." Stars were beginning to form in my vision, but I couldn't risk falling unconscious now, couldn't risk him hurting her.

"I'm afraid it's too late for that," Lance replied. The truth had become a compilation of questions to which I did not have the answer. Perhaps my suspicions hadn't been entirely right. Or perhaps my presumptions about Lance's character were completely right.

"Now." He took a knife out of his pocket. My knife. "You're going to tell me exactly where it is, or I'm going to slit her throat."

"I can't help you." I spat out some blood. He was bluffing. He had to be.

"I'm warning you, Your Highness," he said. "If you don't tell me, I will kill her." My eyes switched between the two of them, Lance's eyes filled with something cold and dark and hers filled with panic and disbelief.

"Don't believe me?" He took the knife and sliced across her upper leg. A red stain bloomed on her shift. She let out a scream of pain and my chest tightened. Even if he was above killing her, he certainly wasn't above hurting her.

Lance moved his hand, going for her other leg, when I heard my voice surging through the cell. "The necklace!"

Silence fell abruptly.

"What?" Lance asked, but his hand moved away from her leg.

"The jewel is in her necklace." He wasn't going to stop. She may have been a liar, but I couldn't watch him hurt her.

"If you're lying ..."

I shook my head, breathing hard. "It's there, I promise."

Lance laughed bitterly and placed the knife in his belt. "You had it in her necklace this whole time. I really have underestimated you. You're much cleverer than I realised, Cai. After all, it's the one place I would never have thought to look."

"Please don't do this."

"You and I are pawns in a wicked game. We do what we have to for our kingdoms. I have no doubt, had you been placed in my position, you would have done the same."

He started pulling her out of the cell and she tried to fight him, but she was weak. "Cai!" she called out my name and I looked up. "Let me go!" She tried to hit Lance, but it was to no avail as he dragged her away. I couldn't move, couldn't stand up, and couldn't help her. I could barely breathe.

Chapter 15

Woodsbrook Manor

Lara

I don't know why I shouted his name. It was instinctive and unplanned and utterly useless. Lance pulled me up the small stone staircase that led out of the cellar. Dark spots filled my vision. "What did you do to me?"

"You think you're the only one who can make tonics?"

My stomach made a knot. I should have known, should have seen it coming and now I barely had the strength to stand up, much less fight back.

"If you're wondering, it wasn't in your wine, but on the rim of your cup."

I let out a moan of pain and clutched my bleeding leg once we reached the top of the stairs. This tonic would need to wear off soon if I ever hoped to get out alive.

"It's in your chambers, correct?" Lance asked, referring to the necklace, and I nodded. Why would Cai tell him?

Why would he give that up, even after knowing that I'm not Eloisa? It didn't make sense, none of this did.

"Where did you put it, Lara?" Lance shoved open the door of my chambers and pushed me inside.

"In the top drawer." I gestured to the dresser, watching the knife in his belt with every step he took. I brushed my hair out of my face as he opened the drawer, and I discovered it was wet with tears.

Lance pulled out the necklace and inspected it. I gathered all my strength and will in that moment and leaned forwards to grab the knife. Before he could turn, I jabbed it into his torso as hard as I could manage.

Lance let out a gasp, and once he realised what I had done, he smirked devilishly before dropping to the bedroom floor. I didn't check to see if he was dying. I pulled open the dresser drawers and grabbed a few things. The world was still blurred, but the adrenaline coursing through my veins was starting to overcome the power of the tonic. I was slowly starting to become more awake, more in control of myself.

I stumbled into the hallway, awkwardly putting on breeches under my shift, but not before I had ripped a piece off to tie around my bleeding upper leg. After tucking my shift into my pants like a shirt, I pulled on a pair of riding boots without caring to fasten the laces.

I was running until it became difficult to breathe and then finally, finally I saw the glass door that led to the gardens and, beyond that, the forest. I stopped suddenly and Cordelia's words sounded in my mind: "You will have to decide if the gold you're being paid is worth his life." I sighed. The gold was completely out of the question now. After all, I might have killed the man who was supposed to pay it to me.

However, Cai's life might still be worth something, and not in the sentimental sort of sense. That, and the fact that he had stopped

Lance from killing or wounding me severely. And I did so hate owing people things.

Clenching my teeth, I ran in the opposite direction, back towards the cellar.

It was dark and cold and smelled of must. I hurried towards the dim light of Cai's cell. He was lying on the floor, barely conscious. I feared we didn't have long before Lance's guards came back.

"Come on." He looked surprised to see me. I probably would have been too, if I were him.

"What—" He groaned as I helped him sit up. "What are you doing here?" I placed his arm around my shoulders to help him stand.

"Making sure you don't die, at least not yet."

We made our way out of the cellar and my leg felt weak.

But complaining about the pain wasn't going to do me any good now. I was just lucky that Lance hadn't cut too deep. It hurt, but it wouldn't kill me. At least now I knew why he was so desperate for Cai not just to trust me, but also to like me. He knew that if his first plan didn't work out, he would be able to use me to get what he wanted from Cai. If only I knew what his plan was after that. Was he really going to let me go, or simply kill us both?

"Where's Lance?" Cai coughed.

"Bleeding on the bedroom floor," I replied curtly.

"You killed him?"

"I don't think so."

I headed for one of the doors, hoping they would lead to a fairly secluded spot outside. If Lance's guards were to see us, neither of us would be able to run away.

"I wouldn't go that way if I were you." A voice came from behind us.

It was Rhen. I swerved slightly in panic. I could feel Cai tensing up next to me. Rhen knew exactly who I was, what I was, and I knew how loyal he was to Lance. Our odds weren't exactly looking good.

"There are guards stationed on the roof that side. Follow me." I met Cai's eyes, his questioning whether or not we could trust Rhen. I didn't think we had much of a choice. He placed Cai's other arm around his shoulder, easing the weight for me, and together we walked to what appeared to be the servants' quarters.

He stopped at a small trapdoor in the floor. "This leads out to the woods behind the manor." He pulled open the trapdoor and helped Cai climb down. I stopped to look at him for a moment as I placed my foot on the ladder.

"Why are you helping us?"

"One day, you'll find out." He eased me down and closed the trapdoor above us. It was pitch-black, but I could feel Cai's heavy breathing next to me.

"Are you okay to walk?" I asked Cai, who muttered "Yes". I dragged my hand over the stone wall as we walked through the dark passage, until a small stream of moonlight leaked in at the end. Cai and I climbed out of the passage and, sure enough, we were in the woods behind the manor, just like Rhen had said.

Cai sat against a tree trunk and I placed my hand against it to keep from swaying. "My men are still back there," Cai said, his voice a combination of sadness and worry.

"I'm sure Rhen will do something to get them out."

"You seem to have a lot of faith in this man." I couldn't sense the tone he was saying it in.

"He did just save both our lives."

"You have a lot of explaining to do," Cai said, and I felt my stomach drop. Straight to the cold hard truth it is, then.

"I just saved your life. A 'thank you' would do as well."

"I'm fairly sure you're the reason it was in danger in the first place." He let out a chuckle and then a sigh. "I cannot believe Lance has the necklace."

"Well, it's your fault you told him where it is."

"I couldn't just sit there and watch him hurt you."

"Why not?" I raised my voice, forgetting for a moment that we couldn't be too loud, or we might be discovered. "You knew I wasn't Eloisa, just some stranger, an imposter. Speaking of which, how did you find out?"

"I saw a portrait of Eloisa in one of the studies at the manor house."

My shoulders fell a little. I hadn't thought Lance would be stupid enough to forget something like that.

"Not that it matters much now. Lance could be dead for all we know, and the necklace is gone."

I proceeded to sigh very loudly.

"That's only if I was silly enough to tell Lance where the real necklace was."

I pulled the string of jewels out of my pocket and Cai's eyes filled with relief.

"I didn't think I'd have to steal it more than once," I said, more to myself than to him.

"What do you mean you stole it?"

"That's what thieves do, they steal things. Even Lance should have known better than to trust a thief."

"A thief?" Cai said in confusion.

"Yes."

"A thief?" he repeated and my brows furrowed.

"I'm pretty sure that's what I just said. Why are you looking at me like that?"

Cai's expression appeared as I imagined it would if I'd told him I was a fairy of some kind.

"Wait, who are you?"

I stuck out my hand towards him. "You may call me Lara. Though some refer to me as the *Masked Bandit*."

Cai didn't shake my hand. In fact, instead, he started laughing.

"There's no way you're the Masked Bandit."

I placed my hands on my hips. "And why ever not?"

"You mean to tell me that the best bandit in Levernia convincingly played the part of a princess?"

"I'm not just the best bandit in Levernia, I'm the best bandit in the kingdom."

"Then why on earth are you working with Lance?"

"It's complicated."

Cai tilted his head questioningly.

"Lance hired me to take the necklace from Eloisa, play dress-up and pretend to be her in order to get you to trust me, so that I could steal the jewel from you — if only we had figured out sooner that it was in the necklace."

"So Eloisa doesn't even know about this?"

"No one knows."

"But why did he hire *you*?"

"I just told you, I'm the best bandit in the kingdom." I held up the necklace. "If I wasn't, I wouldn't be holding the one thing everyone wants. And I'm a woman, so it worked out well for Lance, well … at least until he got stabbed." I looked back to Cai, his face as pale as a sheet. "Wait, who did you think I was?"

He swallowed hard. "Just a court lady, I suppose. I didn't think Lance would go as far as bandits. Guess I was wrong."

I stowed the necklace away in my pocket again. "We can't stay here. It won't be long before they start combing the woods."

"Then what do you suggest?"

"There's only one place we would be safe now," I said.

"And where is that?"

"Home."

Chapter 16

The Evernean Forest

Cai

Our footsteps crunched the leaves as we trudged wearily through the forest.

Every part of my body was aching at this point and if it wasn't fear driving me forwards, I probably would have passed out a long time ago, though I hardly knew how much longer I could keep walking.

"So you're a bandit?" I stated the obvious, once more hoping that she would tell me more about herself. But I only managed to earn a scowl from Lara, or something that appeared to be close to a scowl.

"It's not by choice, so you can stop giving me that judgemental expression, Your Highness." She spat out the last part.

"What judgemental look?"

"That one written all over your face. It's not like I take that much pleasure in it. It's a means to an end."

"You don't seem particularly sad about the fact that you still have my necklace." I managed a chuckle and then cringed at the pain from my ribs.

"First of all, if what Lance says is true, this thing is dangerous and shouldn't be in the hands of someone who would abuse it."

"And secondly?" I raised an eyebrow.

"And secondly, you shouldn't be giving away magic necklaces to women you don't know."

"What can I say? I'm too trusting of people. It's my weakness."

We reached a small stream and Lara stepped into the ankle-deep water, gesturing for me to follow. We walked in the stream and I realised this was her making sure they wouldn't be able to track us easily.

"So why did you do it?"

"Why did I agree to work with Lance?"

"Yes. I assume he held something over your head?"

"It was more than that," she said. "He offered me my freedom."

We stepped over rocks and puddles and brushed past tall grass.

I listened for any strange noises coming through the night air, but all was fairly quiet.

"Your freedom?"

"You see, my parents died when I was just a baby."

"I'm sorry for your loss." I offered my condolences, but Lara brushed it off.

"It's the world we live in. You can't miss somebody you never knew. I was raised by my uncle, who also happens to be the leader of a group of bandits. He raised me to be like him. Raised me to fight for my survival, even if it sometimes meant doing questionable things. But Uncle Arthur has been busy with something else these past few years and I always thought he would never really get far and eventually give up, but I was wrong. He is planning something and I'm not sure I can be part of it.

"He gets messages from people, suggestions as to where a rich party will be travelling, or where something valuable is hidden, like aristocrats' family heirlooms. Sort of like the common folk helping each other out, helping the cause."

"The cause?" I dared to ask.

"It's no secret that many in the kingdom are suffering, all while the nobility sit in their fancy homes and couldn't care about anyone but themselves. My uncle—" She sighed. "My uncle uses some of the money to help those in need. But he's had many things to take care of in the last few years, so I've taken on more responsibility in this area. Especially with the bigger stuff.

"I received a message addressed to the Masked Bandit, saying they would pay a large amount of money if I could steal this particular necklace from the princess. I thought I would take the money and run away. Needless to say, it didn't go as planned."

"Because Lance caught you."

"Because Lance was the one who wrote the letter and hired me," she said and my eyes widened a little. "He wanted to test my skills and get the necklace with little effort." Her story was starting to add up, but it still didn't explain what I thought I had known after seeing the painting in the library. And it was starting to sound like Lara knew even less than me. I kept my mouth shut until I could be certain I was no longer being lied to.

"What does he do with the rest of the money?"

Lara looked at me then, her eyes dead serious. "He's planning a rebellion, Cai."

My fist clenched. This wasn't good. Civil wars were never pretty and it could cause a lot of trouble for Norrandale as well, considering we were trying to make an alliance with Everness. Then again, it could mean something else entirely if the Evernean monarchy was overthrown.

"And you're in favour of the monarchy?" I questioned.

"Not at all. I hate them, for everything they've done to the people of Everness. It's probably why I don't feel bad for driving a knife into Lance's torso. But stealing some earrings isn't the same as a war with blood being shed."

I would know. "Where were you going to go with the money?"

She chuckled. "I was actually planning on going to Norrandale. I heard you have the most exquisite beaches there. I might have bought a cottage and settled down somewhere."

"You don't worry about what will happen to your uncle and the rest of them?"

"It's their decision to fight a war you and I both know they will not win. I cannot change their minds. It's their right to fight. They're braver than I will ever be."

We stepped out on the other side of the stream. "How much further?" I asked.

"Our clan lives deep within the forest. We still have some distance to cover."

"I suppose we should be lucky Everness is a fairly small country." Or this trip might have been impossible.

"If we can find some horses, then we'll make it there faster."

"I hate to break it to you, but I don't see any wild horses nearby just waiting to be ridden."

"Fool," she muttered, but I heard her clear enough.

"Excuse me?"

"We won't be taming any horses. We're going to steal them," she stated as a matter of fact and smirked, awaiting my reply. This was a way for her to test me. She would expect me to protest, judge or offer some form of disagreement. I wasn't very keen on stealing anyone's horses, but I doubted I would make it another hour if I had to walk.

"Very well," I said, and she eyed me thoughtfully for a moment.

We proceeded through the woods with the low light of a nearby village glowing in the distance. It wasn't long before we reached a campfire of what appeared to be sleeping merchants, no doubt stopping on the outskirts of the village — too small for an inn — on their way to trade.

Lara untied one of the horses before pulling herself up. As quietly as I could manage, I took the reins of the horse closest to me and untied the knot before mounting. Every part of me screamed in pain.

We quietly walked the horses away until we were at a safe distance. The men had been using their saddles as pillows, so I had to make an extra effort to stay on as we galloped away bareback. I wanted nothing more than for this to be over and all I could think about was the fact that my men were still back there and that I hadn't saved them.

We rode for a long time before Lara suddenly slowed her horse to a walking pace. "We're not too far now. Only a little while to go." I wasn't sure if she was saying this more to me or to herself. I heard something snap in the trees above and suddenly a body landed in front of us. Lara's horse spooked but she didn't seem to care.

"Ray, what are you doing here?"

"I was on night patrol," the young man replied, and something about his voice was eerily familiar. "The better question is, what are you doing here?" He pulled his hood away from his face and I immediately recognised him as one of the bandits who had attacked us near the Duke of Darwick's estate.

"You!" I said before I could stop myself and Ray's eyes flew to me before going back to Lara.

"What is he doing here?" he asked.

"It's a long story."

"You know this man?" I looked at Lara questioningly.

"Cai, this is Ray, my oldest friend, and, Ray, this is His Royal Highness, Prince Cai of Norrandale."

"Was that attack planned?" I asked Lara.

"No, that was purely coincidence." She chuckled uncomfortably. "We should hurry back to camp. We need Benette's help."

"Are you hurt?" Ray reached out a hand towards her in concern.

"I'll be fine." She gestured to me. "He needs help, though."

Ray didn't seem very keen on this, but we followed him back to where his horse was waiting before riding to the camp.

"You have a lot of explaining to do, you know," Ray said to Lara.

"People need to stop saying that," she replied in frustration.

"We all thought you were dead until I found you with him." His tone had a hint of disgust when he said the word *him*.

"I wasn't dead, I was busy working."

"What sort of business required you to dress up like a princess and ride around the kingdom with a prince?"

"That's none of your business."

Ray shrugged. "All I'm saying is that Arthur isn't going to be happy about this."

"I don't care what makes Arthur happy."

"If you knew who she was, why did you steal from us?" I asked Ray.

"I know Lara," he replied with a curt tone. "I could tell that she didn't want you to know something. I mean clearly you didn't know she was a bandit, which said enough. Plus I couldn't pass up the opportunity to make a prince beg." He smirked and I clenched my teeth.

We reached a small rock-strewn hill and made our way to an opening between the rocks. The tunnel was narrow and my legs almost scraped against the walls. There were small beams of moonlight leaking in through the rock formation but it was still very dark. However, Lara and Ray seemed to know the way very well.

We exited on the other side and made our way along a fairly quiet river before merging back into the thick of the woods. I heard voices and saw the light of campfires and small cabins and tents. So this was how the clan had managed to stay hidden from King Magnus for so long.

We entered the camp and my eyes fell on the scrawny bodies of small children running about. There were men and women in all manner of clothes, but some of them appeared to be dressed like warriors.

"Welcome to Fairfrith," Lara said over her shoulder.

"Are they all bandits?"

"Most of them are peasants, outlaws and rogues exiled or running from the monarchy because they couldn't pay taxes or had to steal or kill for survival. My uncle offers them protection in return for their alliance with the rebellion."

No one seemed to pay us much attention, which was a small comfort considering I was in a camp full of murderers. We dismounted and I stared in awe at the small society they had created.

"Take him to Benette," Lara ordered Ray, who didn't seem very keen on the task,

We left the horses in a paddock and I followed Ray to a small wooden cabin. There was very little candlelight inside and it smelled strongly of herbs and ointments. A large wooden table took up most of the space, with shelves containing all manner of jars lining the far wall. There was a small pallet bed in the corner but no one was inside the cabin.

"I'll go look for her," Ray mumbled. "Stay here, Prince." He slammed the door shut. I didn't mind the disrespect as much as I had a feeling my trials were very far from over.

Chapter 17

Clan Fairfrith Camp

Lara

My cabin was just as I had left it. I opened the trunk at the foot of my bed and pulled on some clean clothes. The cut on my leg was starting to bleed through the cloth I had tied around it. I flinched in pain and decided that putting on a skirt would be best for now. I would have to do something about that soon.

I made my way to Benette's cabin on the other side of the camp. Inside I found Cai, sitting with hands folded on her table, but no Benette.

"Where is she?" I asked, closing the door behind me.

"Don't know." He shrugged.

"Always missing when you need her." My eyes landed on all the supplies that were laid neatly on her small tables and shelves. "Take off your shirt," I ordered Cai, lifting a nearby pitcher and pouring the water into a bowl. There were a few strips of cloth on her table, so I dipped one of them into the water.

"What?"

I rolled my eyes. "Take off your shirt. Your wounds need to be looked at." I started picking through all of Benette's little bottles of tonics and ointments. Luckily, they were all labelled.

"I can do it myself, it's fine," he replied. I took a bottle that would help with the pain and another that would prevent his cuts from getting infected.

"I'm trying to help you."

"Yes, well, if it's out of pity or guilt, I'd rather you wouldn't."

After everything I'd been through, he had managed to tug my last nerve. I didn't feel guilty yet, but I wasn't going to have him die on me either.

"Cai, take off your damn shirt or I swear I will strap you to that table and do it myself."

"I'd like to see you try," he mumbled, but I heard clothes being removed as I wrung out the piece of cloth.

Cai's body was covered in cuts and bruises, from his face to below his ribs. There was one particularly bad cut on his ribs and another above his eyebrow.

"When did you get that?" I asked, referring to the one on his torso.

"One of the guards after Lance took you away."

I bent down and placed my hand near the wound for better inspection. It looked painful and uncomfortable. Something tugged in my stomach at the thought of Lance's guards beating Cai after Lance dragged me away. Cai had risked himself for me. My finger ran along the ridges of his defined stomach, and he suddenly sucked in a breath. The action cleared my mind and I pulled away from him, realising the intimacy of the gesture.

I pulled over a chair and began cleaning the cuts with the damp cloth. Cai winced, but didn't say anything. I took some of the medicine and attempted to pour it over the worst of the cuts. Cai's hands were wrapped around the edge of the table and his grip was so tight that it turned his knuckles snow-white. The strong muscles of his stomach contracted as if to pull away from my touch, but he didn't make any attempt to stop me. I mumbled half an apology and stood up to work on the cuts on his face, since he was so much taller than me.

"You're lucky your ribs don't appear to be broken, but they are severely bruised, so I would suggest minimal movement for some time."

"You seem to know a lot about this?"

"It's not my first time." And I didn't care to elaborate. I had cleaned more wounds than I could count, and some scars ... well, they never healed. I gently pressed my finger to his head, inspecting what I presumed was a hit from Lance's fist with his golden ring on, the one with the royal seal. I had thought more than a few times about attempting to steal it, but it would have been worth nothing as everyone would know it was stolen and I wouldn't easily be able to sell it. "It's not too bad, but you'll need some stitches," I said as a matter of fact.

He nodded wordlessly and I tried my best to keep my hand as steady as possible as I pulled the needle and thread through his skin. I dabbed the cloth over it once more to clean off the dried blood.

"How's your leg?" Cai asked as he stood up and pulled his shirt on again. My head spun a little and I pressed my palm flat on the table.

"It's fine," I said, trying to shake off the dizzy feeling.

"I thought you were a good liar." I refused to meet his eyes until I felt Cai's fingers grab my thigh and I yelped in pain as the world momentarily went black. My knees started to give and I grabbed for the edge of the table.

Cai cursed under his breath. "You're bleeding through your clothes, Lara. Why didn't you say anything?"

I watched the red slowly leak through the material of my dark skirt and sucked in a breath. The adrenaline from before had worn off completely and now the pain had set in.

"Lift up your skirt."

"Excuse me?"

Cai carried a slight smirk now. "I'm just trying to help you."

I scowled as he used my own words against me.

"If anyone is going to take care of my wound, it is going to be me," I insisted.

"You're hardly in the state."

But I wasn't going to agree with him. Before I knew it, he had his hands on my hips and had lifted me onto the table. I protested and pushed him away, but Cai wasn't exactly a weak opponent.

"Lift up your skirt or I swear I will strap you to this table and do it myself."

"Unbelievable." But I had stopped fighting him.

"With all due respect, that's very ironic coming from you." He sat on the chair, still wincing slightly, and lifted my leg onto his lap, the other one still dangling. I pulled up the skirt to where the wound had been wrapped and held it there firmly.

Cai started to unwrap the torn piece of cloth and I clenched my teeth as some of the dried blood pulled on the skin. His hands were pleasantly warm, allowing heat to spread up my thigh that had nothing to do with the wound. He cleaned it with a cloth, same as I had done with his wounds, and poured on some ointment. It wasn't so deep that it would prevent my movement, but it still hurt more than enough.

He picked up the needle and thread and I grabbed his wrist with my free hand. "What do you think you're doing?"

"You need a few stitches."

"Have you ever put in stitches before?"

"Once. Do you remember the friend I told you about? The one I used to get in trouble with when I was younger?"

"Thatcher? Yes, I remember."

"As we got older, Thatcher got involved in some gambling here and there. Most of the time he ended up drinking too much and they cheated him out of his money, but, once, he figured it out and got into a huge fight. I had to help him with some of the stitches so his parents wouldn't find out."

Before I could reply, the needle had already pierced my skin. I forced myself to be strong.

"I wonder where Benette is?" Talking helped to distract my mind from the wound, that and the feeling of Cai's hands on me.

"Ray said he was going to get her," Cai replied and didn't give me time to answer before asking, "So, are you two lovers, then?"

If I hadn't been so firmly planted on the table, I might have fallen off. "What? No, of course not. Ray is like my brother."

"It's certainly not how he sees it."

I frowned at Cai. "Whatever gave you that impression?"

"I see the way he looks at you, it's rather obvious." He cut the excess thread and unrolled a bandage.

I shook my head as he wrapped the material around my leg.

"What am I really doing here, Lara?" Cai asked, his hand coming to rest on my thigh after tying the bandage. Did he sense that all of my focus was now drawn to the burning contact?

"I—" He looked at me as if he could find the answer in my eyes.

I didn't get a chance to reply before the door burst open and Ray stood on the threshold. He looked surprised for a moment at the state of us, but quickly composed himself. Cai pulled away and my leg suddenly felt cold where his hand had been. I immediately pulled my skirt back down.

"Get dressed," he said to Cai, tossing him a pile of clothes, which he caught without effort. "Can't have people knowing there's a prince in the camp." Ray was right. There was enough tension as it was. Cai would have to keep his identity secret for the most part.

"Arthur wants to see you," Ray told me and then looked Cai up and down again with an expression of distaste. "Both of you."

I waited outside for Cai to get dressed, digging my bare feet into the ground.

It was one of the warmer summer nights and though it must have been the early hours of the morning, some people were still outside around the fires.

The way Cai looked surprised me for a moment as he exited the cabin.

His ruffled blond hair looked like he'd run some water through it and gone were the royal shirt and breeches, replaced with plain hunting trousers and a white linen shirt and some old boots. He almost looked like a bandit.

"Come along." I walked to Uncle Arthur's cabin with Cai following. The wooden door of the cabin creaked open. My uncle was seated at his table, looking at a map of Everness. Like all the other cabins, it was a single room. His worktable, where he spent most of his time, stood in the centre of the space. A few odd chairs, old and none of them matching, stood about the room, with a small bed in the corner. There was a trunk near his bed and I'd wondered since childhood what Uncle kept in there. Presumably weapons or something personal. Either way, he'd never let me go near it.

"Take a seat." He motioned at the chairs on the opposite side of the table.

Cai and I each took a seat and watched as he poured us cups of wine.

"You have quite the tale to tell, Lara." My uncle was tall, with the figure of a man who had once been a soldier. His eyes were dark to match his hair, but this had turned greyer in recent years.

"You disappear one morning and we all thought you were dead until Ray found you gallivanting around with the Prince of Norrandale."

"It was a difficult job," I replied.

"You're not going to tell me much, are you?" My uncle knew me well enough.

"Unfortunately not everything went according to plan and now Prince Lance is after us, if he isn't dead."

"Lance has been after bandits for a long time, this is nothing new," Uncle Arthur replied. "But with the King sick and the prince in a weak position, this could present some opportunities for us. Except for the fact that you have managed to drag the future king of Norrandale into this."

"Lance was going to kill him," I said. "You and I both know he could prove to be useful to your cause. Cai has access to soldiers and weapons. The fall of the Evernean monarchy wouldn't exactly be a loss for Norrandale."

"I am right here," Cai interjected. "And as much as I appreciate you not leaving me for dead, I am going back to get my men and then I'm leaving Everness."

"And how exactly do you plan on getting to Norrandale? I stabbed the Prince of Everness and left him for dead before escaping and taking a hostage with me," I said, arms crossed.

"If that is the case and Lance is alive, he will have every armed man in the kingdom looking for you. There will most likely be a bounty on both of your heads tomorrow and there are people who would kill for that kind of money. You'd never make it to the border."

"So am I to be your prisoner, then?" Cai asked, and Uncle Arthur shook his head.

"You are to be our guest until it is safe for you to leave."

"I cannot offer help to the rebellion."

"Well, considering you won't be able to get word to Norrandale, no one is expecting you to."

My shoulders drooped in slight disappointment at Uncle's words. I would have felt better knowing my uncle stood some chance with help from the Norrandish army.

"You can stay in her cabin."

I almost choked on my wine. "What? Why?"

"You're the one who brought him here. Where else do you expect him to sleep?" Uncle chuckled.

"Outside," I mumbled. I hadn't put any thought into sleeping arrangements.

"You're very cruel," my uncle said jokingly, as if Cai wasn't in the room.

"So I've been told." I stood up and headed for the door.

"Lara," my uncle called, before Cai and I walked out.

"Yes?"

"It's good to have you back."

Cai and I entered my cabin and I suddenly felt self-conscious as he looked around the modest space with its few possessions. I looked at the little single bed, my cracked, old mirror and the shelf of folded clothes, the little cold stove against the back wall, and wondered how it compared to his room.

I closed the door before locking it.

"Should I be worried?" Cai asked in jest.

"Some folks around here have had more to drink than they can handle. It wouldn't be the first time someone stumbled into the wrong tent or cabin in the middle of the night. Scares the crap out of you. It's also how Frederick lost one of his eyes."

"You cut out a man's eye?"

"No," I said, grinning slightly. "I believe it was Woody whose reflexes were faster than his awakening eyes."

"We'll arrange somewhere for you to sleep soon, but for now, you should take the bed. Sleeping on the floor isn't going to do your upper body any favours." I tossed a blanket onto the floor next to the bed.

"I can't have you sleeping on the floor while I take the bed. It wouldn't be right." He protested, picking the blanket up again.

"Don't get all princely on me now," I joked. "Just earlier you insisted on lifting my skirt against my will. What would your mother have said about that?"

Cai gave me a disapproving look. "I wonder how I ever thought you were a princess. You're much too improper."

I pretended not to be offended and made to grab the blanket from him.

"I was suggesting we *don't* share the bed. How am I the one being improper?"

"Are you always this stubborn?" He wouldn't let me take the blanket.

"Fine. Just for tonight." I said.

Cai took a seat on the bed and started removing his boots. "Don't worry, I don't bite." There was a hint of a smile playing on his face.

"You've clearly suffered major blood loss if you think you're coming anywhere near me. I promise I will not hesitate to use my dagger."

"I believe you." He looked up at me innocently and the cabin fell into a heart-stopping silence as we stared at each other.

"Surely you're not afraid." He knew exactly what words to use to challenge me.

"Of course not." I scoffed. "I just told you I will use my dagger."

"That's not what I meant." Cai pulled off his shirt, pausing in pain when he had to lift his arms over his head.

For the mere sake of needing somewhere else to look other than Cai's bare and ridiculously toned chest, I sat on the other side of the bed and started taking off my shoes.

"Then what did you mean?"

"I think you're afraid you'll enjoy sleeping next to me a little too much."

I was relieved my back was facing him and Cai was unable to see my face.

"Very funny." The blankets shifted behind me as Cai made himself comfortable.

I laid next to him and pulled the blanket up to my chest.

The cabin and the bed suddenly felt too small, and I was increasingly aware of the achingly little space between me and the Prince of Norrandale.

My gaze remained glued to the ceiling. Any reminiscence of tiredness was long gone.

"My men are still there." I heard Cai's voice through the darkness of the cabin.

"I know, Cordelia as well." At least she had her brother to look out for her. There was no telling what Lance would do to Cai's guards.

"I shouldn't have left them there. I should have helped them."

"We didn't have a choice." If we didn't make a run for it, Lance might have gone as far as to kill Cai, consequences be damned. "But we have a chance of saving them now."

"You seem very confident that we'll be able to."

"I can't promise my uncle's help. He's not the sort of man to hand out favours for nothing in return. But he's capable of a lot more than you think."

Cai shifted his arm, and I felt his bare shoulder graze mine, the heat of his body warming me. The only sound in the room was our breathing, and if I listened carefully, I could hear the insects outside. It must have been the summer night, but my body suddenly felt very hot. What was Cai thinking about? Did he also notice how close we were?

My leg was still partially in pain, and I moved in an attempt to evade the discomfort.

"Are you alright?"

"It's just my leg." I replied softly.

"Are you pain?"

"It will go away soon." I wasn't sure who I was trying to convince more.

Finally, I decided to roll onto my side, facing away from Cai.

"Goodnight, Your Highness." I whispered in a playful tone. He might have smiled at that. I would never know.

I closed my eyes and felt the blanket being pulled over my shoulder.

"Goodnight, fair bandit."

Chapter 18

Clan Fairfrith Camp

Cai

I woke up to unfamiliar sounds of chatter and rustling outside the cabin. As expected, my ribs ached in protest as I sat up from Lara's bed, while purposely ignoring the fact that it smelled like her hair. I searched for her, but apart from me the room was empty of human life.

After proceeding to get dressed, I washed my face in the bowl using the vase of water on one of the small tables. There wasn't much in the form of decoration in the cabin. Not that I would have expected it from Lara. Apart from a few objects lying around the room, there was nothing personal, nothing to tell you that anyone lived here. I listened carefully for the possibility of someone approaching the cabin, before I started looking through everything. Knowing what I did of Lara, it was impossible for her not to have a weapon lying around here somewhere. Even if I didn't want to admit it, I was in enemy territory and I was completely unarmed. I reached under the mattress and my hand wrapped around the hilt of a knife. Good. I slid it into my pocket.

The smell of burnt-out fires filled the air as I stepped out of the cabin. Most of the activity seemed to be at the centre of the camp. Between the firepits were wooden tables and I spotted Ray seated at one. I sat down opposite him and he nodded in greeting. "So you're still alive? Not bad."

"Good morning to you as well."

"Word of advice." He tore off a piece of bread from a loaf that was in the middle of the table and placed it on a plate, which he pushed to me. "If you want to survive here, you're going to have to stop talking and acting all royal. People here don't appreciate it. I wouldn't tell them I was a prince either. The less they know, the better."

I took a bite from the bread. "Thank you." It was practically stale, but I didn't say anything. My eyes caught Lara prancing over, and she fell into the seat next to Ray.

"Good morning, boys." She reached for bread herself.

"Good morning, Your Highness," Ray teased her and she smiled, spreading some of the questionable-looking jam on her bread.

"What happens today?" I dared to ask and Lara looked up at me in surprise.

"You should be resting, with your wounds."

"So should you."

Lara bit her lip in the way she did when she got annoyed.

"Some of us are going hunting — we need meat for tonight's feast," Ray said.

"Feast?"

"Tonight is the summer solstice." Lara took a big bite of the bread. "Around here, we usually celebrate it with a feast."

"I hadn't realised it was here already. Has it truly been that long since I arrived in Everness?"

"Afraid so."

"When are you leaving?" Lara asked Ray.

"You probably shouldn't come." Ray chuckled. "You're not a very good hunter. Even a kid could beat you with a bow and arrow."

"Oh, so that wasn't a lie?"

Lara met my eyes with a half-guilty expression.

"I am capable of telling the truth, you know," she retorted.

"Really?" I lifted my cup of water to my lips. "I had no idea."

She angrily took another bite of her bread and I couldn't help but smile then.

"What? Why are you looking at me like that?"

"You've got some jam on your face." I grinned and she wiped it away in embarrassment. "Definitely not a princess." She threw a berry at my face in response, which I dodged.

"You brute," she muttered, but she was grinning all the same.

I remained quiet and observant as the hunting party gathered and we left camp. Drawing attention to myself would lead people to ask questions. This part of the forest was dense and humid and I wondered how these bandits didn't more often get lost. Though I supposed it was different having grown up in such an environment. Same as I knew every corner and nook of my palace back home. We stepped quietly, causing us to move forwards more slowly, quite different to the horseback hunting I was used to.

Our group consisted of about ten, spreading out further the deeper we went into the forest. Apart from the sound of chirping birds, it was quiet enough that I heard my own breathing, and I suddenly found myself feeling sort of inexperienced, though I'd been hunting with my father since I was a child.

It wasn't long before I felt the skin of a somewhat delicate hand, pressing the back of its palm against my own.

I met Lara's eyes and she nodded left, gesturing for us to move that way. I frowned, but followed her nonetheless and we moved away from the group. Ray joined us as Lara pulled me further and further away.

"Where are we going?" I whispered.

"You'll see." She gave me a devious smile, suggesting that I wasn't going to like any of what was about to happen. I followed her and Ray away from the hunting trail, stepping over roots and ducking small branches. I glanced at Lara in confusion when we were about to step out into a road but she pressed a hand to my chest.

The three of us were dead quiet and I realised she and Ray were listening for something. "They're coming," Ray said, and I sent a frown Lara's way.

"Who's coming?"

Ray started climbing one of the nearby trees and a sickening feeling developed in my stomach. Lara pulled me towards another tree trunk and I let out a gasp as my ribs protested at the movement.

"Ray caught news at a nearby village that the Earl of Pearson would travel the road this morning. I have to admit, however, that our timing is impeccable."

"Impeccable for what?"

Ray had disappeared into the overgrown branches above the road.

"For robbing him, of course." She reached out for the tree trunk and I pulled her back.

"You cannot be serious."

"Of course I'm serious." Lara pulled out a large bag from the satchel she had been carrying. "Here, hold this and hide in the bushes."

"I'm not helping you commit a crime."

She turned to face me, her eyes lit like fire, and I thought, perhaps for the first time, I was truly seeing the real her. The person who hid under her skin. The bandit who was whispered about, like a breeze through tall grass, standing in front of me, with her dark hair and devious smile.

"I'm not asking you to commit a crime. I'm asking you to hold the bag."

"This is wrong, Lara."

"So is the money the earl carries for selling orphans into slavery. An eye for an eye, right?" She wouldn't say anything else and pulled herself up into the tree. I watched her squirm as her injured leg didn't appreciate the action. I cursed internally, knowing full well I could do nothing to stop her and somehow angry with myself that I had so quickly forgotten the truth — forgotten who and what she really was.

After taking a few steps back, I was safely covered by the brush next to the road, though my eyes didn't waver from Lara as she perched on a tree branch in her black cloak with her hood over her head. I heard the hoofbeats from a distance as the carriage wheels rolled all the closer.

Just as the carriage was about to pass, Ray dropped from the trees in front of it. The horses caught fright and stopped abruptly, letting out wild cries. The carriage driver himself looked flabbergasted as Ray held up a bow and arrow towards him. "Move and I shoot." Needless to say he didn't move. Lara swung herself down until she was on top of the carriage and gave me a wink between the leaves, before she put on her mask and swung herself inside.

I heard people scream — my gut twisted. There was nothing I could do — I was too injured to stop them. The carriage door flew open and Lara jumped out. Ray moved out of the way and Lara slapped the rear of one of the horses, sending him running off down the road, and the carriage along with him.

She emerged from behind the trees, taking off her mask and cloak, grinning in a way that made me slightly uncomfortable. "You should have seen their faces." She tossed me a bag, which I barely caught. But to my surprise it wasn't filled with any coins or jewellery. Instead, it was full of food … bread and fruit. I looked up at Lara in confusion.

"I thought it was money?"

"No, I said he stole money, which is why I didn't feel bad for taking his lunch. One thing the earl is very famous for is his love for overindulging in eating."

I didn't know what to reply, though I hated the smug look on Ray's face for some reason.

"Come on." Lara put everything in the bag I was holding and I wordlessly followed the two of them back to camp. Upon our arrival, we found out that the hunters had in fact caught something for tonight's feast. One of the children noticed Lara and ran up to her.

Lara bent down to the small boy's height and told him to close his eyes, which he did obediently, a smile evident on his dirty little face. I watched Lara pull out an apple and hold it before the boy, telling him to open his eyes again, which lit up upon seeing the apple. He greedily grabbed it with a mumbled *thank you* and ran away.

Of course, this caught the attention of all the other small children as well, and soon Lara was handing out the food to them, one by one. It made my stomach twist to see the hunger in the children's eyes. The only time I thought I might die of hunger was during the war. And I would never wish that upon any child.

A thought crossed my mind while I watched the satisfaction in Lara's eyes as she gave the skinny children something to eat. I realised that maybe she was more than a bandit.

Chapter 19

The Evernean Forest

Lara

I gazed into the small mirror above the little dresser in my cabin. It was old and cracked, allowing my reflection to become a blurry kaleidoscope.

Nonetheless, one had to get by with what one had.

The summer solstice called for very specific celebration. It was the one day of the year when all of us, no matter how poor, made an effort to dress up. Black was the colour of choice and patterns and swirls were painted on our bodies and faces. The top half of my hair had been braided out of my face and I was surprised by how much my reflection had changed in the mirror compared to the year before, despite dressing exactly the same.

It was supposed to be a joyous occasion, but I didn't seem to have much to celebrate, except perhaps for the fact that I was alive. I clasped a necklace, which I had stolen some time ago, around my neck and the amber contrasted with the light tone of my skin. I thought about how much nicer Cai's necklace would look but discounted the thought as foolish. It wouldn't be safe to be seen with it in the camp. Giving one last grin in the mirror, I turned to leave. The sound of chatter grew louder above the folk music as I opened the door of my cabin. My vision was filled with firelight coating the earth and the group of faces all made up similar to mine. I made my way between the trees and grassy patches towards the centre of the commotion.

The smell of fire-cooked food danced in the air and I ignored the rumble of my stomach. I hadn't seen Ray or Cai since this afternoon and I had a goal of finding at least one of them. I was still walking when something that felt like a berry fell on my head. I looked up instinctively and found a pair of mischievous eyes staring back at me. It was difficult not to smile. "What exactly do you think you're doing?" I asked Ray as he fell backwards and swung down from the branch. He had always been a better tree climber than I was.

Ray's face had also been decorated with the dark swirling patterns and for a moment he reminded me of his father. They had the same eyes. When we were much younger, I spent a lot of time with Ray and his family. But then Ray's mother got sick and nobody could do anything to save her. It took such a toll on his father that a few months later, in the village, he nearly beat a guard to death for mistreating an older woman. And he paid for it with his life. At least I had never known my parents. I couldn't miss someone I'd never met.

"I'm looking for you." He tilted his head slightly and I smiled at my childhood friend. "Come on, I'm starving," he said.

We walked to tables laid with more food than we could usually afford. Most of the time every scrap was stretched out or saved for as long as possible. But not on the summer solstice.

"Have you seen Cai?" I asked Ray, who shook his head.

I bit my lip. "I'm supposed to be keeping an eye on him. Uncle doesn't trust him at all."

"He's probably around here somewhere. I don't think he'd actually be stupid enough to run."

"Still, Arthur's already upset with me as it is. I don't have any intention of getting myself into more trouble."

Ray let out a chuckle and I scowled at him. "It's not funny."

"I don't know what's more amusing, the fact that you mind getting into trouble or that you think Arthur's capable of punishing you somehow. I mean, what's he going to do? Exile you when this is over?"

Wouldn't that be ironic? We walked through the commotion and I nodded in greeting at the faces that had become familiar to me in camp.

"I missed this," Ray commented.

"Yes, it's been a long time since we've really had something to celebrate around here."

"No, I meant, I miss this." He gestured between the two of us. "We were practically inseparable and then a few months ago you started acting all rogue, refusing to be part of this family."

I stopped, turning to face him. "I told you, I didn't want to be part of this rebellion. I know that things aren't run fairly in this kingdom — believe me, I do. But killing people? Seeing the people in our clan get killed? Ray, I don't think I can survive that. If anything were to happen to my uncle or you …"

"Hey, it's okay." Ray wrapped his arms around me and I had a flashback to when we were really young. Ray and I used to share a cabin with Uncle, and one night my uncle went out without saying where he was going. He didn't return until the late hours of the morning — I was up the whole night, terrified that he would never come back. I started to cry and Ray, as always, was there to comfort me.

"I know this isn't ideal. If life were, we would have had a fair king on the throne and we wouldn't have to steal and kill in order to survive. But we need you on this. You've given us a lever we've been waiting for, for years. Even if it wasn't intentional. Promise you'll try to cooperate at least until we've figured out a plan?"

His eyes were so pleading that I couldn't help but nod. "Okay, I promise."

I gazed around and caught sight of blond hair weaving through the small crowd. Cai looked left and right, as if checking whether someone was following him, and then proceeded towards the outskirts of the camp.

"I have to go." I didn't even give Ray an explanation or a chance to reply before running off after the prince. There wasn't time. At least Cai wasn't running, which made it easier for me to catch up with him.

"Where do you think you're going?"

He jumped a little upon hearing my voice behind him.

"I was going for a walk."

My brows furrowed and I wasn't sure if I believed him.

"All right, then I'll come with you." When he made no objection of any kind, I suspected he might have been telling the truth. "So." I made a little foolish twirl, holding my dress. "What do you think?"

Cai didn't seem to be in a very cheerful mood. He simply said, "You look different."

"What's that supposed to mean?" I looked down at the dress that stopped just below my ankles. The black material was just about as dark as the night. A belt hung low around my hips and the bodice was laced up in the front instead of the back like most of Princess Eloisa's dresses.

"You look like you're pretending to be something you're not." Before

I could say anything in return, Cai stepped in front of me. "I don't say that to be rude. I just mean that you looked more comfortable before. More like yourself."

I closed my mouth, trying to process his words and somehow finding it hard to do so. Maybe because I thought he could be right. I didn't really fit in with this family anymore. At least, it didn't feel like it. It didn't quite feel like I belonged anywhere. Maybe that was a blessing in disguise.

We continued walking below the high branches of the trees and I heard the hoot of an owl in the distance.

"I need to ask you something." Cai sounded breathless. The walking must not have been doing his body any good, considering he hadn't had time to heal properly. I was worried about his injuries when he joined us on the hunting trip. But he didn't appear to be in any pain.

We slowed down and I replied, "Fire away." I picked a blade of grass and played with it between my fingers as I leaned against an old tree trunk.

"Where is the necklace?"

Not the question I was expecting.

Not the question I had planned to answer.

"It's buried where no one will ever find it." At my words, Cai looked up and there was genuine concern in his eyes.

"I'm going to need it back."

I shook my head. "That necklace almost caused a war. It's better if no one has it, then no one can abuse its power."

"First of all, the whole story about the necklace being magical is ridiculous. These tales have been around for centuries and as the Prince of Norrandale, I can assure you, they are not true. Secondly, that necklace belongs to my family. It is my rightful property and you know it."

I wasn't sure if I liked the stern tone in his voice.

"You could be lying about the jewel not being magical. If that's the case, and that necklace falls into the wrong hands again, it could be worse than a war. Everyone is safer as long as no one ever finds it and *you* know that."

Cai snorted and I laid my head back against the tree trunk. The evening slowly started to set in as the longest day of the year came to its end.

"Should have known never to trust a thief."

It was strange how I actually felt a pang in my chest as Cai said that. I didn't meet his eyes. Couldn't, perhaps, because of my guilt and knowing I had never apologised to him for my betrayal.

"And what do you plan to do with it? Take over Everness? Eliminate your enemy for good?"

"I just want to give it back to whom it belongs to."

To whom it belongs to? Did he mean Eloisa? Was he still planning to marry her? I was curious. But I wouldn't ask. "I'm not giving you that necklace, Cai."

A jolt of nerves went through my body when Cai's hands wrapped around my upper arms and held me against the tree. I couldn't look away now. His eyes were greener than they had ever been before and, without meaning to, I could hear both of us breathing.

"Where is the necklace?" He didn't shout. Didn't try to hurt me. His voice was soft and serious, making me think about the night in the maze at Woodsbrook Manor. And how I kissed Cai in his rooms before running away.

He's still a prince, the voice in my head reminded me.

I was quick to knock Cai's hands away. "Do you have a hearing problem?" Even though he was no longer touching me, Cai didn't step away. "I told you it's gone and buried. The best thing is to just forget about it."

"I am the future king of Norrandale." As if I needed reminding. "It would be in your best interest to give me what I want, Lara."

"Of course, now you want to abuse your power." There was a twitch in his expression, and I wondered if my words might have hurt his feelings. Good. He did call me a scheming thief.

He looked away for a moment. "You really think the worst of my kind, don't you?"

"Your kind has given me very little reason to think otherwise," I spat out, contemplating shoving him so I could walk away from this conversation.

"That piece of jewellery is part of my family legacy. I need it back." Cai's voice rose slightly, with an edge of desperation to it.

"If it's so damn important, then why did you give it away in the first place?" I worried for a moment that someone would hear us, but the music would conceal the sound of my yelling.

"Because I was going to marry Eloisa and she was going to come and live in Norrandale, and it wouldn't have mattered."

"Well, I'm sorry to have ruined it for you." I threw my arms up in a slightly dramatic fashion.

It was only then that Cai seemed to notice our proximity, the fact that we were now so close that our breaths mingled in the night air.

The prince's face softened and the tension between us shifted into something that was no longer fuelled by anger.

"Yes," he breathed out. "How very ill-mannered of you."

Before I found myself getting caught up in his gaze again, I quickly looked away.

"I'm sorry." Any confidence my voice possessed before was now gone. "I can't tell you where it is."

Defeated, Cai let it go and took a step back. "Very well, then." He headed towards the camp and I stood back for a moment, watching him walk away and deciding I didn't like it. Nor the fact that I felt as if I disappointed him. Shaking my head, I caught up, and in silence, we made our way back to the firelight and music.

"So what usually happens at these events?" he asked, as if the conversation that had just passed between us had never happened.

"Well, as you can see, there is plenty to eat and drink, which is pretty much the highlight of the evening." Meat was being roasted on the nearby fires, while the tables were loaded with breads and fruits. All of which had been baked and gathered today. "That and the dancing. It gives us something to think about so we can forget the hardships, even if it's just for the night. We're not really ones for pretty speeches and ceremonies."

We stood at the edge of the party, like outsiders looking in. Like neither of us really belonged there with the rest of them. "What do you usually do on the summer solstice?" I asked.

"Those who can, go to the beaches. We usually have a garden party during the day and then at night we celebrate in the ballroom. It's a lot like this only …"

"Only completely different?" I finished his sentence and he smiled as he replied, "Yeah." The moment of peace didn't last very long before Ray came out of the crowd and jogged towards us.

"Where have you been? Everyone's looking for you," he said, and his demeanour had changed completely since the last time I saw him, not too long ago.

"Why? What's going on?"

"Arthur wants to talk to you. Both of you." He glanced towards Cai, who looked just as surprised and confused as I was, but we followed him nonetheless.

The door to Uncle Arthur's cabin was open and Ray closed it behind us as we stepped inside. Cai and I stopped in our tracks. The last person I'd thought I would see again was standing there in his uniform, looking like he'd seen a ghost. Rhen breathed heavily, as if he had just run all the way here.

"What are you doing here?"

"Sit down," Uncle said before Rhen could reply.

We both took a seat. I had no idea what to expect.

"Your friend here—" Uncle gestured to Rhen — "has brought us some rather important news."

"What is it? What happened?" A million bad thoughts were going through my mind.

"The King of Everness is dead."

Chapter 20

The Evernean Forest

Cai

The cabin was stuffy from heat that slipped inside from the summer day and I pulled my shirt away from my skin in some useless effort to cool myself down.

"You said you wanted to talk?" Arthur asked, while comfortably seated in one of the chairs. He was tall and built like someone who used to be a soldier but in recent years had given himself over to ale and age.

"I want to know what your plan is. If I'm to participate in any way, I don't want to be left in the dark."

Arthur put his hands together. "I thought you said you couldn't help." He carried the expression of a man who'd distrusted everyone all his life, and I started to understand where Lara got it from.

"Not from here. Not alone. If you want Norrandale's aid in your rebellion, we're going to have to rescue my men."

"I cannot guarantee we'll get them out alive," Arthur replied with little sympathy.

"I know it would be a very big risk. But there is no way I'm leaving my men behind."

"All right then."

I wasn't fond of the thought of siding with someone I didn't believe I could trust, but desperate times called for desperate measures.

I crossed my arms. "Everything that happens from here can have an effect on Norrandale. Especially considering the plans you have in mind. When exactly do you intend to tell Lara the truth?"

He stood up then, though his expression remained emotionless. "Which is?"

"This isn't about the end of the monarchy or poverty. This is about placing yourself on the throne of Everness."

"You're wrong. I have no intention of placing myself on the throne of Everness. I simply want a just ruler."

I stared at him from across the table. "So, what? You kill the royal family and end the monarchy? You and I both know the people cannot rule themselves or there will be chaos."

He smirked. "And you think I plan to place myself in that position of leadership?"

"I think it's a very convenient opportunity."

"It's a convenient opportunity for many people."

"Still, you already lead these people. It would be easier for them to trust you, than someone else."

He folded his hands together, observing me for a moment. "You're not entirely as dense as they make you out to be." I wasn't sure it was a compliment or who *they* were. "But you're still wrong."

"Free my men and I'll help you on the day of the rebellion. What you choose to do after that is not my concern, so long as there are peaceful relations between Norrandale and Everness."

His grin was back. "You have yourself a deal, Prince of Norrandale."

Lara paced back and forth outside her uncle's cabin, cutting into an apple as if she were angry at it. I didn't tell her about my earlier conversation with Arthur. Didn't plan to. "You're going to walk a path through the grass," I commented, leaning back against the cabin wall and crossing my arms.

"I don't know what to do," she said, looking up at me, worry in her eyes. She tossed the apple core. "We barely stand a chance, even with Rhen as our inside man."

"You're afraid of dying?"

"I'm afraid of innocent people dying." That was two answers within itself. "I'm afraid of being forced to take a life."

"Don't tell me you've grown a conscience?"

She stopped pacing. "I'm a thief, not a murderer."

"Fair enough."

A group of men arrived at Arthur's cabin and Lara motioned towards the door. "Come on, the meeting is going to start."

There was a large structural drawing of Levernia palace on the table in the middle of the room. Lara and I occupied one of the corners of the cabin.

"Who are these men?" I whispered, nodding towards the faces around the table. Ray and Rhen were there too.

"They are the masters of the clan."

"The what?"

"The masters. Before all of this, before there were so many of us, it was just my uncle and his little band of thieves. Each of them with a specific skill, who wanted to fight the Crown, like Arthur."

I glanced at the sunburnt, slightly wrinkled faces.

"Of course, that was practically twenty years ago," Lara continued. "That's Donald." She pointed to the scrawny man. "He is the master of weaponry. He used to be part of the Crown's arsenal team. Now he's in charge of collecting our swords, getting silver and persuading blacksmiths to join the cause."

I nodded in understanding.

"That's Murtag, he's the master of disguise." Murtag looked a little older than Arthur. "If you want to go somewhere undetected, that's your guy. He can help you blend in anywhere or disguise yourself as anyone."

I gestured with my head to the man with hair as white as snow. "And him?"

"That's Erwin, master of deception. He was orphaned as a child and used to perform in the castle as a jester when he was a little boy. He worked with a man who was famous for creating illusions. Next to him is Brosby, master of distraction. They believe that any good trick requires a good distraction, and back in their palace days, they made a good team."

"Most of them have a connection to the Crown in one way or another."

"If you want to bring down a house, you start with its enemies. These people of the clan have been wronged and they want revenge."

I watched the men argue about entrances to the palace. "Revenge is never a good strategy for war."

Lara let out a sigh. "You tell them that."

"And Ray, what is he the master of?"

"Terrain. He knows the forest like the back of his hand and is your best chance of escape."

"And you?" I raised a curious brow. "Or are you allowed to listen in because you're family?"

A devilish smirk crossed her lips and she gave a small bow. "Master of mischief at your service."

"Mischief?"

"It started as a joke when I was a child but …" She shrugged.

Rhen spoke up. "I say the coronation is your best bet."

"How so?" replied the scrawny man, Donald.

"It's when the palace guards will be most distracted with the public and the celebrations. It's the easiest way to sneak into the palace unnoticed."

"Murtag will be in charge of that," Ray piped up and Murtag nodded in agreement.

"Rhen's right." I stepped towards the table. "I think it's our best way in with the least amount of force." I didn't miss Ray rolling his eyes.

"What do we do once inside?" Erwin asked.

"The first step is getting out Cai's men, who have been moved from Woodsbrook to Levernia. Then we dispatch our own to infiltrate the palace," Arthur replied.

"Hold on," Ray chipped in. "I thought this would be our first strike at the Crown — and now it's a rescue mission?"

"We can't do anything violent on the day of the coronation. There will be civilians in the way," I retorted.

"Once Cai's men are rescued, he will send word to Norrandale in support of our cause," Arthur said. "In return, there will be an alliance between the kingdoms once it's over."

Lara and I had entered her cabin when she swerved to face me. "You struck up a deal with my uncle?" she asked in what appeared to be mocking surprise.

"Yes I did," I said sternly. "Those aren't just my soldiers out there, those are my friends, and I am not leaving them to be slaughtered."

"You didn't think to at least tell me about it?"

"Oh." I barked out a laugh. "So now we're telling each other everything all of a sudden?"

"I'm sorry!" She raised her voice. "Is that what you want to hear? Get over it, we've got bigger problems on our hands."

"Yes, like what exactly Arthur is going to do when this is over."

"What are you talking about?"

"What do you think is going to happen once he's killed the whole royal family?" I could feel my heart rate increase as I got closer to her, but I ignored it.

"My uncle will take care of it. It's not my concern. As far as I care, I should have been long gone and across the border already. At this point, I'm just hoping we all make it out alive."

"Did you ever stop and think that maybe this is about more than helping the poor?"

"Don't you dare talk about him like that! This isn't some kind of power grab!"

"Isn't it? Do you really believe your uncle wouldn't do something like that?" The question was earnest.

"Get out," she said, with a fierce look in her eyes.

"With pleasure."

I closed the door on my way out.

Chapter 21

Levernia

Lara

It was a cold day in Levernia, as if the weather could predict what was about to come. I fiddled with the laces of my dress, reminding myself that breathing was important, even though I was in the last place I ought to have been. I was supposed to be in another city — even better, another kingdom. I wasn't supposed to get caught. I wasn't supposed to get blackmailed into pretending to be a princess. I wasn't supposed to go back to the clan. I wasn't supposed to start developing questionable emotions towards a prince.

The throne room looked just as I remembered. Vast and elegant and yet even on this day of celebration, there was something dreary and cold about it. Something just melancholic enough to suit the weather.

My facial muscles twitched under the mask I was wearing. Lance must have had an appreciation for irony by making the theme of his coronation a masquerade. I stood among the masked faces of the aristocrats, all dressed to perfection, with no details spared on their lavish costumes.

My dress had been made by an old woman in the village, who apparently had to burn the midnight oil for it to be ready in time. At least that was her excuse when she charged us a fortune for it. I couldn't exactly blame her for being greedy. She was thin and frail, the lines across her face a thousand tales of the hardships she'd had to endure in her life. And then there was the little girl I suspected was her granddaughter, who hid behind her skirts.

The dress was heavy, but perhaps the most beautiful thing I had seen for a very long time. It looked like it had been washed by an ocean storm, a combination of dark blue and slightly tinted green. Little golden stars spiralled up the skirts to my bodice. My mask, draped in shimmer, had a crescent moon at the corner of my left eye. I looked like I belonged there, among all those strangers with their masks.

Trumpets sounded almost proudly and all the chatter quieted as faces turned towards the entrance of the new king of Everness. I felt a pang in my stomach as Lance approached the throne, white fur cloak hanging from his shoulders, no crown on his head ... yet. It was as if the word *bandit* were above my head, floating in big bold letters, and even though I knew there would be no way for Lance to recognise me from there, I was afraid that if I stared just a moment too long, he would catch my eye and call on his guards and our whole plan would be at its end.

We had barely slept in the past three days in preparation for this event. Every last detail had been planned and orchestrated and we could only trust that our sources were correct — that we wouldn't have to rely on any of our backup plans.

Lance reached the priest, who made a long speech about the responsibility and honour of being king.

He took a staff and the crown was lowered slowly to his head. It looked exactly like the one he had worn before, decorated with so many beautiful jewels that I could not even begin to imagine what it had to be worth. I got lost in my train of thought, thinking about everything else that was happening in the dungeons and empty hallways of the palace, while no one in this room had even half a suspicion, but I was brought back to reality when the crowd cheered and the sound of a choir erupted from the upper levels of the throne room.

I didn't want to, but I knew I had to smile. I couldn't risk standing out. The people of Everness always did love a good celebration. They would not think about their dead king. They would not worry about what the new king would do for them, what his reign might change. They didn't have to.

The only thing on their minds would be the alcohol they would consume in the next few hours. They would only concern themselves with the food they were about to eat, the music they were about to dance to and the lavish attire they would brag with. That was all they ever needed to care about. Little did they know that if all went according to the wishes of Uncle Arthur, it would not be like this for long.

"Let the celebrations begin!" Lance's voice rang out and the audience cheered once more. He gestured towards the great hall and guards opened the large doors so that the people could enter.

Lance began making his way from the throne, and the crowd parted to let him pass. Unfortunately for me, I found myself exactly where I didn't want to be, in front of all the people. Lance was going to walk right by me. I tried to step back and see if I could disappear into the crowd but everyone stood so close together to get a glimpse of their new king that it was impossible. The people bowed as he walked past them, chanting, "Long live the King." By the time he reached me, I was in a deep curtsey, keeping my eyes glued to the floor. Once more I was thankful for the masquerade theme that kept my identity hidden.

The party quickly filled up the great hall, where large tables had been decorated and laden with expensive cutlery, delicacies and cups of wine. I would even admit that I was impressed by the glamour of it all. If there was one thing I would give to Lance, it was that he knew how to throw a party. There was no question about that.

Musicians started playing their stringed instruments and the great hall was filled with a jolly melody. Of course, these were not the musicians that the festivities coordinator had originally hired. They were "most unfortunately" attacked by bandits in the woods and all the uniforms and instruments were stolen. Instead, it was our men who produced the happy music, weapons most conveniently hidden within their instruments. Lucky for them, they didn't sound too unprofessional.

My eyes scanned the crowd for Cai, who was undercover too. Nobody had asked him to be here. Yet he'd insisted he wanted to help. There could be no question as to how important his men were to him. Guards were stationed around the room, most of whom had been bought off or blackmailed, or were our men undercover. Soon they would change shifts with the guards stationed throughout the palace and should reach the prisons without too much trouble as Rhen would be waiting there for them.

I hadn't spotted Damon yet, which concerned me. Cai made his way across the floor and, once he reached me, held out his hand, silently asking me to dance. I followed, my eyes going back to Lance every few seconds, but he appeared much too occupied with his own party.

Cai pulled me closer into the formal dancing position and we swayed to the music, both of us constantly scanning the room and me falling over my feet a few times.

"You weren't lying about not being able to dance, that's for certain."

I purposely stepped on his foot. "This isn't dancing. You nobles have no idea how to actually dance."

He shrugged off my rude comment. Cai was in charge of getting his men out and my responsibility was finding Cordelia. Rhen could tell us where Jack and the rest of them were, but he hadn't seen Cordelia around the palace recently, which meant that she could be anywhere, or dead, for all I knew.

"We don't have a lot of time," I murmured, just loud enough for him to hear.

"As soon as the song ends, we have to move."

We hadn't spoken since our fight, but both of us knew we had bigger things to worry about than our bickering. This was about the mission, not about our feelings, whatever they might have been.

We danced until the song stopped and the next one began, signalling to the guards to change shift. It gave Arthur's men the opportunity to stand guard on the route to the prison while Lance's guards kept an eye on the guests at the party.

I started pulling away, ready to do my part, when Cai pulled me close by the waist. "Please be careful," he whispered softly as I met his pleading eyes. They trailed down to my lips momentarily before shooting back up to meet my gaze and then he let me go. Before slipping out of the ballroom, I cast a glance at Lance, who was seated at the head table at the far end of the room. His eyes were focused on the people, not a hint of concern on his face. But the almost empty cup of wine hinted he wouldn't be concerned about much tonight.

The skirts of my dress swished as I ran down the mostly empty hallways, a few people talking and guards standing here and there, but no one spared me a second glance. I tried to focus on where exactly I was, remembering against my will the path I had walked to the prison, and then to Lance's chambers the last time I was here. There was a nauseating feeling in my stomach. But I couldn't think about that. I had to think about Cordelia.

She wasn't in the prison. This Rhen could confirm. She had travelled back to the palace with her brother and the palace guards but Rhen hadn't seen much of her since arriving in Levernia. When he asked Lance about his sister, the prince shrugged it off. But Rhen mentioned seeing her once in the company of a few noblewomen when he looked out of the window into the gardens.

I made my way back to the bedroom where I had stayed the night that I was captured, and Lance blackmailed me into working for him. One turn at a time, the halls became more familiar. I doubted I would find Cordelia in a room, but this at least would be a starting point. Because of the celebration, the guards were stationed far away from the rooms of the palace. I started running faster, lifting up my skirts higher to avoid tripping. I turned another corner before running smack into another body, causing me to stumble backwards.

Cordelia's eyes widened abruptly. "What ... how?"

I didn't allow her to find her words before grabbing her arm and pulling her in the direction of the kitchens. We sprinted down the stairs and slowed down only when passing guests, politely nodding.

I swerved around a corner into the servants' quarters, as Rhen had directed me very specifically to do. Stopping in a small empty hallway, I caught my breath and took a second to inspect Cordelia, but she didn't appear to be harmed in any way. "Go through the passages. The others are waiting outside. We're getting Cai's guards out," I told her.

"And you came for me?" She was heaving a little herself, clearly not used to all the running.

"Of course I came back for you." I smiled. "I can't get anything done without my lady-in-waiting."

She returned a warm smile. "It's happening, isn't it? The rebellion?"

I met her gaze. "How did you know?"

"Rhen told me this would happened eventually."

I didn't have time to process Cordelia's words.

"Help me with my dress."

She untied the laces of my bodice and I dropped the dress onto the floor, leaving me in the shirt and breeches I was wearing underneath. I removed my mask and pulled the pin out of my hair, allowing it to drape over my shoulders. "Go ahead. I'll catch up."

She nodded and hurried around the corner.

I let out a sigh of relief. At least Cordelia was safe. Brushing a hand through my hair, I looked around me. Now, I needed to find Cai and then we could get out of this place.

I hurried down the carpeted hallways, the music of the party soft and distant. Cai would be close to the prison by now, which meant I needed to find a way to the lower floors below ground. If I went right at the next corner, I believed it would lead me in the direction of the kitchens.

I passed a parlour room and was about to reach the end of the hallway when a door suddenly opened, and I was yanked inside.

I didn't have time to scream before Lance closed the library door behind us.

"Did you really think I wouldn't recognise you?"

Drat, so he had seen me back there, despite my efforts. Hopefully,

Cai had managed to get his men out safely. I clenched my hands into fists, trying not to imagine all the ways Lance was going to get back at me. I would be lucky if I saw daylight tomorrow morning. Lance walked to one of the tables and poured himself a cup of wine.

"Come to finish what you started?" he said, and my eyes went to his torso, even though I couldn't see the stab wound under his shirt.

"Maybe I just like a good party."

My response made Lance snort, and fear hung over me like a heavy cloak as I anticipated what he would do next.

"Nice costume you had back there." He lifted his cup towards me before taking a sip. "You certainly aren't to be underestimated — I'll give you that, dear sister."

"I'm not pretending to be your sister anymore. There's no need to keep up the act, Lance."

"Oh, am I Lance now? Not Your Majesty?"

"You don't deserve to be king."

He took another sip before setting down his cup. "Oh, I know that. But please inform me as to why this is your opinion as well."

Not the answer I was expecting. He must have been lying again. Must have been trying to distract me from what I actually came for.

"Because look at *you*." I pointed to his crown and outfit. "You don't care about your people. You only care about the luxury and parties the position has to offer."

"True as that may be, out of the two of us, I'm still the one wearing the crown."

"How could I forget?" He hadn't mentioned the necklace and I wondered if he would bring it up. Either he had figured out he'd been left with a fake this entire time or he thought he was wrong about everything and too embarrassed to admit he'd been delusional.

"I thought you'd be smarter than risking your life like this. I mean, did you honestly expect you wouldn't get caught?"

Lance took a seat, leaning back comfortably in one of the expensive chairs.

"Maybe I'd come back to apologise. To beg you to pardon my idiocy."

That made him bark out a laugh. "If only that were the case. You and I might have made a good team."

"I would never be on your side," I spat out.

He stared at me intently like he knew something I didn't. An awkward silence fell over the room.

"So, are you going to kill me?" I had a dagger on me that I could use to defend myself and Lance definitely wasn't sober. But who was to say there weren't guards outside the door, waiting for me? I looked at the window over his shoulder. There would be guards outside on this side of the palace as well.

"I've told you from the start, my intention was never to kill you."

"Then what do you want with me?" I asked earnestly.

"I wanted your partnership, and I wanted you to steal me a necklace."

"Which I did. And then I got myself out of there before things got messy."

Lance tilted his head to the side. "Yes, how unfortunate that you were right, and the necklace is nothing more than a fancy piece of jewellery." So, he hadn't figured out it was a fake, or was he just lying again? His eyes dared me to reveal if I was hiding something. "Doesn't explain why you left so suddenly in the middle of the night. With the prince, no less."

"You tortured us for information. Did you really think I was going to stick around to see it all play out? I got out to save myself."

He took another sip of his wine and mumbled, "Load of good that did you."

I frowned at his response.

"You think I don't know about your little escape back at Woodsbrook? I know exactly how you got out." He slowly stood up. "You think I have no idea why you came back today, that it was to save Cai's men and get your little lady-in-waiting out?"

My eyes widened and I took a step back. "How ... how did you ... ?"

He tilted his head again, grinning. "You think I don't know that at some point my best guard decided to betray me and take your side, and is now aiding you and your clan of bandits on your little mission in the palace?"

My throat had gone completely dry.

"You think I don't know about your little friend Rhen and how he has been helping you?"

I started walking backwards to the door, but Lance made no advance towards me.

"I will have to make an example of him, so that people know what happens when you betray your new king."

My hand found the door handle. "What are you going to do?"

"I'm letting all of you rogues walk free today. I know Cai and his men are outside and that you're going to meet them there and go back to whatever miserable dark hole you crept out of. But as we speak, Rhen has been arrested for treason and is sentenced to death tomorrow afternoon."

I shook my head, feeling my hands shake and knowing that for the first time in a long time, I had absolutely no idea what to do. No power to fight. I could kill him right here, right now, but it wouldn't stop the execution — it would only make me a murderer and make escaping Everness so much more difficult.

"You're a monster," I breathed, slowly opening the door behind me.

"I'm doing what's necessary to protect my family. You — better than anyone — should be able to understand that."

I didn't understand. This had nothing to do with family and everything to do with Lance's horrible nature.

"I'm going to let you all walk free," he said, "because killing the heir of Norrandale is only going to make things more complicated for me right now. And because Arthur isn't even man enough to face me. If he wants a fight then I can promise you I'll bring a fight. But he will never get my throne."

Not wanting to hear another word from his mouth, I ran out. Wiping tears from my eyes, I slipped around hallway corners.

I couldn't get out fast enough. Couldn't get the picture of Rhen dying out of my head. And all because of me. All because he helped my family and me. My vision blurred and my eyes filled with tears.

I stumbled on until I saw Cai running down one of the hallways. Like he was looking for something. Like he was looking for me. He had come back to look for me.

"What happened?" Cai wrapped his arms around my sobbing self and I knew there was no use in holding back now.

"He's going to kill him," I murmured. "He's going to kill him."

Cai's arms tightened around me. "Shhhh." He pressed his lips against my head, holding me tight against him. The weight was comforting. "I'm here. It's okay. I'm here."

I shook my head almost violently, letting out silent sobs. "No, he's going to kill Rhen. He's going to kill Rhen because of me."

"I'm sorry," he whispered. "I'm so sorry." And he just held me for a moment. "We have to go. I'm sorry, but if we don't leave now ..."

If we didn't leave right then, we might never leave. Lance wasn't exactly a man of his word. My hands shook. The only way I was going to make it back to camp was if I didn't think about it. Cai led me through the empty hallways until we were finally outside. Our group was hiding in the brush just beyond the stables. There were no guests in sight, to our luck.

"You will ride with me," Cai said as we walked to his mare. I didn't see any point in arguing. Perhaps he knew that if I didn't cling to someone or something, I wasn't going to make it back home.

"What's wrong?" Ray asked as we mounted.

Cai only replied, "Not now." Our party rode steadily away. Cordelia and Cai's men were finally safe. All as it should be. Except the only thing I could think about was Rhen sitting somewhere in a dark cell, cursing the day he met me.

I held on to Cai as the horse proceeded to canter. The sky above was still tinted with grey, but rain refused to fall and wipe away the blood I felt I carried on my hands. Blood of the man who'd saved my life. The ride back to camp felt long and dreary. I should have been relieved that the people we went to save were here with us now and completely unharmed. It could have been so much worse. But Rhen's fate haunted me.

"I never thanked you." Cai broke the silence between us as we fell behind the rest of the group.

"For what?"

"For not leaving me behind in that cell at Woodsbrook Manor."

"Cai—" I started.

"I know you say you have your reasons. And true as that may

be, who knows what would have happened if you hadn't come back for me. So thank you."

"You're welcome. I suppose."

We arrived back at camp, tired and hungry. I dismounted and watched for a moment as Cai led his mare back to the paddock. Then I turned around and stormed off to my uncle's cabin. Ray was nowhere in sight.

The wooden door slammed open at my hands, cold air rushing in as I stood on the threshold.

He didn't look up at me, not a trace of shock or surprise on his face. Arthur wasn't the kind of man to be shocked or surprised. "Well, how did it go, then?"

"He's going to kill Rhen."

"Who?" The table in front of him was filled with papers and coins — he had been counting money.

"Lance!" I cried out. "Who else?"

"So he's figured out who's been giving us information. Not too bad for a petty prince."

"Did you hear what I just said? He's going to kill him tomorrow."

"Shame, really — though we have all the information we need, so I doubt we would've had much use for him after today."

"How can you say that?" I spat out. "If it weren't for him, I probably wouldn't be alive right now."

"He's a means to an end, Lara." Uncle finally looked up from his work. "You've been around these people for too long. They've made you sentimental and we know that sentiment is only a weakness."

I knew that regardless of any words or insults I spat at my uncle, the results would remain the same, so I stormed out and ran back to my cabin, not having the courage or guts to face anyone.

I didn't make it to the cabin door before hurling the contents of my stomach out onto the grass. Guilt. So much built-up guilt. Lance was going to kill Rhen because he had helped my family. Rhen was going to die because of me. I placed my hand on the wall of the cabin and breathed deeply. I was being irrational. I was being emotional. I closed my eyes — breathed in and breathed out. My emotions weren't going to change anything. This was a war, and war wouldn't be war without casualties. I was part of it now, even though I didn't want to be. Even though I still wanted to run.

In the days that followed, Cordelia remained silent and pale, refusing to eat or talk about what had happened in Levernia. I couldn't judge any of her actions — she was mourning the loss of her brother. Though some small part of me was thankful that she didn't show any form of hostility against me. But it pricked at my gut, seeing her like that, seeing my friend in pain. And that dark part of my soul that stomached stealing from the rich, the part that boiled with hatred for the monarchy who forced innocent people to become criminals, that awful part of me wanted — perhaps even needed — some form of revenge.

Chapter 22

The Evernean Forest

Cai

Alastor swung his sword towards my torso and I ducked away, rolling over to block his next swing, which would be for my neck. Over the years we had become familiar with each other's fighting patterns and it had become a betting game, of when one of us would break the routine and surprise the other.

I pressed forwards, forcing Alastor to take a step back and give me a slight advantage, which only lasted a moment before he jumped at me, dodging my sword as he knocked the air out of my stomach with his fist.

I let out a slight huff and the crowd, which had formed around us from the camp, clapped at his advantage. Alastor gave me a moment to catch my breath before advancing on me with full force, his jabs swift and precise, and the muscles in my arms started to protest as I defended myself.

Our dance went back and forth until the sweat trickled from

our foreheads, though no winner was apparent and the audience seemed to enjoy our banter. We agreed to call it a tie in the end and shake hands.

I quenched my thirst with a cup of water as I heard the small crowd start to murmur once more. My eyes followed their whispers until I saw Lara step into the ring. The sight of her made my stomach twist. I knew just what was about to happen.

"My turn." She raised a brow teasingly.

"I'm done for today," I replied, still attempting to catch my breath.

"Are you scared of losing?" It was more than a challenge.

"No." I took another sip of water. "Just trying to save you from embarrassment." My words lit a fire in her eyes and I knew I had awakened a sleeping beast.

"Winner gets a favour from the loser. Any favour." She pulled a sword from its sheath. It was sharp and dainty, just like her. I wiped my forehead with my shirt and stood up, grabbing my sword from on top of the rock next to me.

"Deal," I agreed, though only heaven knows why, as there was no reason this was a good idea.

"And lastly—" she flicked her wrist, swinging the sword around — "there are no rules."

I snorted. "Then you're lucky I'm a gentleman." The crowd had been forgotten and there was only her. I watched her approach me. She wore tight-fitting leather breeches and a short-sleeved shirt.

The air had become dense and silent and she didn't give me time to gather myself before jumping forwards and jabbing straight for my stomach. I jumped back a little, quickly blocking her, but she smiled, knowing that I had already been thrown off somewhat.

What she didn't know was that the element of surprise was a

dangerous game to be playing. We started going back and forth and I quickly realised why she was so fond of daggers. Not only were they easy to hide but also she had much better control over the smaller weapons, as her balance was slightly off with the sword. It wouldn't take too long to get her empty-handed, but I was enjoying myself almost too much to want it to end.

She turned, putting all her energy into the next swing, but she had too much momentum and too little steadiness in her footing. I struck back hard and her sword fell to the ground, causing panic to rush into her eyes.

I held my sword up to her throat with arrogance and smirked. "Surrender?"

She met my expression with equal playful ferocity. "Never." I wasn't prepared for her to dodge my sword and jump at me. She kicked me off balance and I fell. When I rolled to get up, Lara was ready to attack again. She went for my shoulders and I used her body weight against her, by turning us around so that I could pin her to the ground.

She fought against my grip, but I held her down by her upper arms.

"You're not playing fair," she said, trying to kick at me.

"You said there were no rules."

"You said you were a gentleman!" She placed her feet on my thighs and pushed back with all her might. I was forced to pull myself back into a standing position and she pulled out a dagger — which I should have seen coming.

She lunged at me. Her only mistake was forgetting she wasn't the first person to swing a knife at my throat and thus I knew exactly how to disarm her.

I grabbed her wrist and yanked her closer. Forcing the dagger out of her hand, I pinned her hands behind her back. She squirmed, and with her pressed up against me, I could feel every heavy breath she took. For a moment, I forgot we were surrounded by watching eyes. She tried to twist away but I held firm. "Face it, Princess. You've lost." I couldn't help but inhale the sweet scent of her, like she'd recently lain in a field of wild thyme.

Lara surprised me by kicking my shin. "Ow!" My body jerked with the pain, allowing her to push herself away from me.

"No rules, right?"

I shook my head at her. Oh, it was on now.

She picked up the sword, which had been lying in the sand, and held it up.

"On your guard, Prince."

I refrained from smiling and moved into a defensive position. Lara was quick to attack but I could tell she was still not entirely comfortable with the choice of weapon. It was too heavy and not made for her.

I countered her strikes one after the other, but Lara was determined, and I found myself taking a few steps back.

"Don't hold out on me now," Lara challenged.

"If I don't, you'll be too injured to come through on that favour for me."

She opened her mouth to say something, but someone else called her name. Lara and I looked at Ray, who stepped into the circle. "Arthur wants to see you," he said and Lara pulled herself free.

"This isn't over," she threw over her shoulder as she walked away.

"I think you're right about not trusting Arthur," Jack said later as we had a quick lunch. "He's definitely up to something."

"The problem is figuring out exactly what," I replied. "The

important thing is remembering that all of this affects Norrandale. And no matter what you do, somewhere, somebody is going to be angry."

Alastor shoved a piece of bread into his mouth.

"What's your father going to say?" Conner asked.

"Magnus's death isn't exactly a loss for Norrandale and neither would Lance's imprisonment be. However, if Everness no longer has a monarchy, we have no idea what that could mean for its relations with Norrandale. If Arthur decides to rule, there is a chance of a peace treaty, but he could always decide to turn against us. Everness has a much larger army than Norrandale. It was part of the whole reason for our alliance."

"But the people of Everness are starving," Alastor said. "They need the farming lands of Norrandale. They need the grains and to be able to trade across the border."

"Another war isn't worth getting thousands of people killed."

"What about Lara?" Jack asked.

"What *about* Lara?" I repeated.

"You and I both know all of us could be out of here tonight. We could sneak across the border and be back in Norrandale within a couple of days. But you won't, because you've taken a liking to her."

"It's not that." I tried to ignore Conner smiling like a child behind his food. "I suspect something and if it's true we cannot leave Lara behind."

"Suspect what?" Jack asked.

I sighed. "I can't tell you." They all looked at me in confusion. Even though I trusted these men with my life, I only had a suspicion and little to nothing to back it up. I could be very wrong about it all.

"Look, for now we stick with Arthur, at least pretend we're aiding them in this rebellion. Until I can find out the truth, for certain. Then we'll make a plan. There are dangers both in leaving and staying."

"Just be careful," Jack warned. "She betrayed you once. She might not hesitate to do it again, if her life should be in danger."

Chapter 23

The Evernean Forest

Lara

I was carrying a bucket of water from the river when Ray came running up to me. "I need to talk to you," he said. I hadn't seen Ray so serious in quite some time.

I grunted as my arm ached from the heavy bucket. "Ray, I'm not exactly in the mood for talking." It had been a long couple of days and I was looking forward to eating and falling asleep.

"This is important," Ray persisted. "I wouldn't be telling you if it wasn't. You clearly haven't slept or properly eaten in days and you look half dead."

I managed half a smile. "Thanks for the honesty," I muttered sarcastically. "What is this about?"

Ray looked rueful. "It's about Cai."

I rolled my eyes. "Seriously, Ray? I know you don't like him, and at this moment, I'm not exactly fond of him either but—"

Ray wouldn't let me finish. "This has nothing to do with me." He stepped in front of me, forcing me to stop walking. "Look, you and Arthur seemed quite eager to strike up a deal with the guy and I don't trust him, so I did a little digging."

"You've been spying on the Prince of Norrandale?"

"No, of course not. Last night his soldiers had quite a lot more than their share to drink. Not that I could blame them. I would probably overindulge myself as well, had I been imprisoned by Lance. But the one who's second-in-charge, Jack, we started talking and I asked him questions about how he managed to get such a high position with the prince. Long story short, he told me more than he probably should have, though I don't think he remembers any of it today."

"What's your point?" I started walking again, dodging past him.

"My point is, I found out something that I think you should know about him. About the kind of person he is."

"I have a feeling you're going to tell me, regardless of whether or not I want to hear it."

I was practically marching back to my cabin and Ray almost had to jog to keep up with me. "We talked about war. Mostly about all its gruesomeness. He started mentioning the Norrandish war against Argon some time ago."

"Yes, Cai mentioned something about it."

"Did he tell you how he managed to win that final battle?"

I didn't say anything. Of course I didn't know the answer. Hadn't given the Norrandish war against Argon much thought. After all, the past was in the past.

Ray stepped in front of me again and held my shoulders to make me stop. "Cai was leading the army just north of the Argonian coast. It was far from the cities of Argon and mostly surrounded by woods and small villages, where the Argonian soldiers were from. They were to march on the battlefield the next morning. But Cai ordered the nearby villages to be burned and plundered, killing the wives and children of the soldiers in the hopes they wouldn't fight the battle the following day. He murdered innocent people, Lara."

The world had gone silent enough to hear the bucket drop onto the forest floor, water spilling beneath the grassy stems and trickling past my boots. "He did what?"

"I'm sorry. But Cai isn't the person we thought he was. He's no better than Lance or any of his lackeys. The royals are all the same. And if his morality might be worse than ours, I just don't think they can be trusted. We've let them into our home and they have the perfect opportunity to conquer Everness."

I pushed past Ray without a word. I could hear him calling after me, but I would not be stopped. My feet carried me past the burnt-out firepits and cabins. My eyes would not focus on any movement other than where I was going, who I was looking for.

He wasn't in my cabin, or by the horses or the fighting ring. I stumbled past rocks and roots until my eyes finally landed on the head of blond hair. He was kneeling next to the river, washing his face.

Cai's shirt hung on a nearby branch, but I paid this no attention as I marched towards him with brutal anger in my veins.

"How could you?" I shouted, ready to push him into the river.

Cai turned abruptly and his eyes darted to his shirt after landing upon me.

"All this time I was under the impression that you were this kind and caring person. That *I* was the one who lied. And that *I* was the one who deceived."

"I don't understand — what happened?"

"What happened is that I finally found out the truth about

Norrandale's 'perfect and charming' prince. Who turned out to be just like the rest of them." My voice cracked at the end, against my will.

Concern filled Cai's eyes. "Lara, what's going on?" He reached towards me, but I slapped his hand away.

"Don't touch me! You walk around here in judgement of all of us, like you don't carry any blood on your hands."

His expression was that of someone who really hadn't the slightest idea what I meant. "What are you talking about?"

"I'm talking about the final battle against Argon."

Cai's face fell into a look that I had never seen him show before. "Who told you?"

"It doesn't matter who told me, it matters what you did."

"I did what I had to do."

"You murdered innocent women and children and you're telling me it was because you had to do it?" My tone was one of disbelief.

"My soldiers were starved, wounded and near dead. We had been losing ground against the Argonian soldiers for weeks. My father was in Norrandale trying to gather more forces and help for our soldiers. I was leading the army alone and the next day they would march upon us in battle at full force — we would be slaughtered."

"So you decided to slaughter their families instead?" I clenched my teeth at the pain in Cai's eyes but grew more determined from the emotions it evoked inside me.

"I sent out scouts. I didn't give them orders to kill any women or children."

"How do I know that's not another lie?"

"I was a child!" he shouted, breathing heavily. "And I was terrified. I didn't know what to do. I didn't know how to save the men that were dying next to me. I made a decision, and if you think that it doesn't haunt me to this day, then you're wrong."

I wanted to believe him. Wanted to believe the desperate, pleading look on his face.

"I still dream about that battle, over and over again, and I see my hands covered in blood, knowing what I did and knowing that I will never be able to make up for it. Why do you think I am so adamant on avoiding war at all costs?"

And I knew that his words were true. Knew that he carried guilt in the same ways I did. Knew what it felt like to have a conscience that followed you like a shadow, despite how much you tried to run from it.

But I didn't know how to face him now. So I turned and walked away.

I walked until the soldier prince caught up to me. He grabbed me, turning my body towards him. There was something in Cai's eyes — a look I'd never seen from any man before as it lingered on the edge of certain carnality and spelled out only one word ... danger.

Not the danger you face from getting too close to a fire, not the danger of a knife or a wild animal. This was a feeling of danger that I had never experienced before.

"What do you want?" I stepped away from him. "To make some worthless kind of apology in the hopes that your reputation would be restored in my eyes? If that's the case, you can forget about it."

He took a step towards me. My breath hitched. I prayed he did not hear it. Cai and I had been alone before more than once, but I'd never actually wanted to murder him up until this point.

"I don't want to apologise."

Part of me wanted to flee once more. To flee the violation of his broad shoulders and muscled torso in my personal space. Part of me wanted to release hellfire and beat him until he spat blood. All this time, I had thought this man to be all that was good and honest. But now I somehow felt betrayed.

"Then what is it?" I said curtly.

"You can't just yell insults in my face and run away like that." His voice was deep but soft, and I took a step back.

"So, what, you want *me* to apologise?" We both knew there was no chance of that happening.

"No," he replied and I lost my nerve.

"Well then, what do you want?" I cried out.

"I want you," he blurted. Instead of being surprised, it only caused me to be angrier with him.

"Well, you can't have me!" I said sternly, placing my hands on my hips and squaring my shoulders.

"Oh yes, I can," he retorted, and I could feel my blood boiling.

"And what exactly gave you that impression?"

"Because you want me too."

I gasped. "I do not!"

"Yes, you do, Lara. I know you do."

"I don't want you. I don't want anything to do with you right now." I was starting to grow unsure of what exactly I would gain by winning this argument.

Cai let out a huff of frustration. "You know, sometimes I think you're the most annoying woman I've ever met."

"You think I'm annoying? Well, take a good, lasting look in the mirror, sir, because you're the most infuriating—" I jabbed my finger at his hard chest — "displeasing, exasperating human being in all of Everness." I was throwing out all the big words I could muster while knowing none of them were actually true, but in that moment I didn't care.

"You're one to talk," he threw back, taking another step closer. "You're all charming and sweet with your witty words and nifty tricks, but inside you're miserable with this life you live."

It wasn't anything other than perhaps the fact he was right that scared me so much. "Don't you dare say that. You know nothing about me." Another lie. Though I would hate to admit it, he knew more than most.

"Yes, I do." He was so close that I could practically feel his warm breath against my skin. The scent of him reminding me of the forest on an autumn morning. I shook my head, trying to regain focus.

"I know you, Lara."

"What is your problem?" I exclaimed, throwing my arms up in the air. I hardly knew the point of this conversation anymore.

"My problem?" he repeated, looking away for a moment with half a sneer as he traced a finger across his bottom lip, drawing my attention to it without meaning to. "You want to know what my problem is?"

"Damn right I do." Not wanting to grant him an advantage of any kind, I risked stepping closer. I wasn't going to back away any longer. I was not a deer to be hunted.

"My problem—" he swallowed, tone softening, eyes not meeting mine — "is this." As the words left his mouth, he picked up my hand from where it hung at my side.

"My hand?" I asked idiotically.

"Yes, your hands. Your hands that keep holding knives to my throat and your hair that smells like a field of wildflowers and that damned mouth that won't stop cursing at me."

He looked at me then, and I was frozen. "My problem, Lara, is that I cannot sleep or eat or do anything anymore without thinking about you and it is driving me positively mad."

I plucked my hand away from his. "Oh, so all of this is somehow my fault now?"

"Yes, of course it's your fault." His breathing became more rapid. "Because if you hadn't worked with Lance and I didn't meet you, then none of this would have happened and I would never have ..." He trailed off.

"You wouldn't have what?"

"It doesn't matter. I just want you to stop lying to yourself."

The anger in my voice had not yet disappeared and neither had the frustration in his.

"Everything about this is ridiculous. You are the future king of Norrandale and I am an outlaw."

"I don't care who or what you are," he admitted. "Do you honestly expect me to believe that after everything we've been through, you feel nothing for me at all?"

"That's exactly what I'm saying."

"You're lying," he replied. "I can tell when you're lying, remember?"

"Nothing could ever happen between us and you know that."

"You're unbelievable," he muttered.

"Me? I'm unbelievable?" I asked in disbelief.

"Yes, you're unbelievable. I just poured out my heart in front of you and you had no trouble ripping it to shreds, even though I know you feel the same!"

"What did you expect? That I would swoon and confess my love to you? Is that why you're so mad?"

"No, I'm mad because it's one thing to lie to a person, but it's another to lie to yourself."

"I am not lying to myself. Just accept the fact that I don't love you, Cai."

"You're lying and I can prove it."

"Well, I'd like to see you try. You're just a bastard who can't take no for an answer." I tried to push past him, but Cai grabbed me by the waist and pulled me back.

"Then tell me," he persisted. I tried to wrench free, but he wouldn't let me go. "Tell me to leave you alone. Tell me that you hate me and that you never want to see me again. Stab my heart a thousand times over if you like, but please don't lie to me." His hand drifted to my upper back.

I had forgotten how to breathe, with him so close. "I don't love you," I said softly, though I couldn't decide which one of us was actually the liar.

"Prove it," Cai challenged with a whisper, and then he kissed me.

My immediate reaction was to simultaneously push him away and grab anything my hands could get hold of. My eyes closed on their own account and my other senses were left to take over.

He had challenged me and I had no intention of being proven wrong, but then his lips pressed against mine with a sense of yearning that I hadn't experienced before, perhaps didn't even understand. It was intoxicating and I wanted more. No. My sense of reason threatened to kick in. I didn't want to give in to his hands that stroked my back. I didn't want to give in to his mouth that coaxed me closer to him. I didn't want to give in to him at all.

But Cai took me by the wrists and wrapped my arms around his neck. I may have underestimated him in more ways than one. That perhaps the Prince of Norrandale was in fact a force to be reckoned with, in his own unpredictable way. I allowed my fingers to rest where hints of blond hair made their appearance at the nape of his neck and Cai managed to pull me closer.

I was hot and cold all at once, goosebumps forming on my arms.

Being kissed by Cai wasn't what I expected … it was better. And despite my better judgement, I pulled him closer, allowing his mouth to claim mine as if some hidden part of me belonged to him, always had.

But I didn't think about that feeling. I pushed it away instead and concentrated on the warmth of his hands that traced my body like it was a work of art. Cai made a sound in the back of his throat and I sucked in a breath before pulling back and resting my forehead against his.

"This is a very good example of a very bad idea."

He gave me an unsatisfied glance.

"I'm serious. Once this is over, you'll go back to Norrandale and I'll still be a bandit."

"It doesn't have to be that way."

"You speak as if the truth is fiction, Cai. You and I both know you have to marry someone of noble blood and that I was made to be alone."

His mouth travelled to my cheek, where he pressed a butterfly of a kiss. "You still proved my point."

"So?" I attempted to ignore his lips and roll my eyes.

"So you owe me one."

"I saved your life back at Woodsbrook Manor. That makes us even."

His lips moved to my other cheek for another kiss. "You betrayed me and stole my personal property. That makes us uneven."

"You lied about your past."

"You lost a duel against me and you said the winner gets a favour from the loser."

"What exactly is it that you want?" A dangerous question.

"Everything will change once this is over, but we don't have to end this until then. All I'm asking for is your honesty."

He knew the way my heart twisted inside when he looked at me like that. Because he felt it too.

"No more lies?" I wasn't entirely convinced. No matter how much I wanted to grab his face and kiss him again.

"No more lies," he confirmed. "You will give me a chance until this is over and we can go our separate ways. That is if you can stay away from me."

"Don't flatter yourself," I said. "I still won't be in love with you by the end of this."

"You can try and tell yourself whatever you please." He smirked. "But you're already half in love with me." He took my hand and bent down, gently pressing a kiss to my knuckles. "Your Highness," he teased before turning away, and I watched his shoulders disappear into the leaves.

I shook off whatever unfamiliarity had overcome me. I needed to go to my uncle's cabin, where our next clan meeting would be held.

When I got there, everyone else seemed to be waiting inside, making small talk or engaging in light debate.

"Glad you decided to show up," my uncle remarked as I closed the door, but I fully ignored him. I hadn't forgiven Uncle Arthur for our previous conversation.

"What happens now?" I asked no one in particular, stepping up to the table and surveying the map of the kingdom. I spotted the border of Norrandale and lingered on it for a moment too long.

"The next step is the aristocrats."

Chapter 24

The Road to the Levington Estate

Cai

The carriage hit another rock on the dirt road and Lara let out a groan.

"You're a real ray of sunshine this morning," I teased.

She glared at me from the opposite bench. "If you're going to be annoying all the way there, tell me now, so that I can throw you out of the carriage."

I chuckled, watching the grassy fields pass by through the partially curtained window. "My, what could it possibly be that has caused you such misery?"

She sighed. "It's much too early to be awake, I haven't had breakfast and this dress is more uncomfortable than a torture chamber. I suggest you don't attempt messing with me if you wish to live."

I couldn't help but smile. "I promise to make no such attempts, then." She was hardly in the mood for any humour, though this was in no way going to stop me from saying or doing anything I pleased.

I moved from my seat, placing myself next to her, and she kept her arms crossed and stared through the window like a small child throwing a fit.

"For what it's worth," I whispered, "you look really pretty in that dress." I pressed a lingering kiss beneath her ear and she shivered slightly, though made no attempt to address me in response.

We said nothing more for the rest of the journey, but Levington Estate came into view and I caught Lara gazing at it somewhat in awe. We pulled up around the fountain and a servant opened the carriage door for us. I got out and helped Lara down the steps.

"Who should I tell my master is calling?" the servant asked.

"The Lord and Lady Attebury," I replied and the servant nodded, before running up the portico steps. Lara hooked her hand into the crook of my elbow and we made our way into the house of Levington Estate.

Lord Levington was a man well into his years, accompanied by a belly that told of decades of overeating. His face was a strange reddish colour and I felt Lara squirm slightly next to me as he approached us.

"Lord and Lady Attebury." He greeted us with open arms and I forced a smile. "To what do I owe this pleasure?"

"We're here to discuss business," I answered, and we followed him to a drawing room.

"I like the sound of that. A man can never have too much money, I always say." We sat down and he called for a servant to bring us refreshments. "I must admit, I was surprised to hear of your visit. We have never met before? Or have I forgotten? You must forgive me, age does not accord well with clarity of the mind."

"No, we haven't had the pleasure of meeting before," Lara said. "We were hoping to see you at court but since you haven't visited the palace in a while, we thought it best to come and see you here at your estate."

"Can't say I'm very fond of staying at court," Lord Levington admitted. "I much prefer the quiet of the country if possible."

"Did you spend much time with the royal family on your last visit?" I asked.

"I saw the King a few times in passing. He had to take on so much responsibility before his father passed." I could see Lara holding back from making a snide comment. "But her Highness I've not had the pleasure of meeting. It seems the princess and I share the same love of the country. From what I've heard, she spends most of her time at one of the royal estates."

The room fell silent for a moment while Lord Levington observed the two of us. "So what can I help you with today?" He rested in a large reading chair and started shoving cake into his mouth.

"Well, Lord Levington, I like to get straight down to business, so I'll tell you first-hand that we know about the money you stole from the Crown."

Lara flinched next to me as he choked on a cake and let out a few coughs before looking at us wide-eyed.

"Who told you?"

"It doesn't matter," I retorted. "What matters is that we know how you cheated the late King Magnus out of money and I am quite sure the royal family would not respond well, should they be made aware of your treason."

Lord Levington looked at a loss for words but finally managed to get out, "What do you want?"

"Your allegiance," Lara said before I could respond. "We know there has been some unrest amongst some of the aristocrats about the royal family. The truth is that soon the monarchy will fall, and once this happens, we need the security and support of the lords as well as their soldiers and knights."

"You plot against the King?" He sounded almost in agony. "And insult me? I shall alert the authorities immediately." He jumped up from his seat, but toppled back down again.

"I wouldn't do that if I were you," I said quickly. "Should King Lance find out about this, he will also immediately be notified of your own treason. In any case, we have the woods around the palace filled with armed bandits, so I can guarantee whatever messenger you send will not make it there."

The red-faced lord had gone as pale as a white linen sheet. "This is blackmail."

"No," Lara said, standing up. "This is your past catching up to you."

"Think of it this way — once the King is gone, the more power the lords of the land will have. The more money for you."

"Get the support of the other lords. Should the royal line fall, the royal council would stand together with whoever came into power. For the good of the kingdom, of course," Lara said. "Or else."

Lara rushed to her cabin when we arrived back at camp and I followed in the hope of dumping my uncomfortable jacket and meeting Alastor or Jack in the fighting ring. I could use a good swordfight or two. Maybe I could even have a go at Conner, see if he'd actually been taught anything.

"Damn it!" I heard Lara say as I grabbed my sword from where it lay at the door.

"What's the matter?"

"I can't find Cordelia. I looked for her on my way here, but she's gone as always. Where that girl runs to, heaven only knows."

If the Crown Fits

"And the company of your female confidante is important because ... ?" I ventured.

"I can't get out of the dress by myself. The strings are too difficult to reach from the front."

"Oh." The air around us became awkward with silence. "I can help," I offered, and then quickly added, "If you want."

She turned to me, hesitating for just a second. "If you don't mind."

Her back was towards me again and I walked over to inspect the dress. It was the first time I had actually paid attention to it. The bodice appeared to be decorated with the same material as the skirts, and it laced up at the back. Lara's shoulders were bare, so I assumed she wasn't wearing a shift underneath.

I stood awkwardly and stared at the laces, though there didn't appear to be an obvious place where they came to an end.

"What's wrong?" Lara asked.

"Nothing."

"Then what are you waiting for?"

"I'm trying to locate where to untie it."

I didn't expect her immediate chuckle.

"Come on, Cai, you don't seriously expect me to believe that."

"Believe what?" I still didn't know where to start pulling the laces free.

"That you never undid a lady's bodice before."

I let out a snort, which awkwardly turned into a cough, and started pulling at random parts of the laces, seeing if something would loosen.

"You'd be surprised."

"Oh ... I see."

"See what?" Nothing would give and I started to get slightly frustrated.

"There was no need."

I looked up and stared at the back of her head, the smell of wildflowers in her hair overwhelming me.

"No! It's not like that." I could feel myself getting slightly flustered, though I wasn't entirely sure why. "Just tell me how to unlace this damn thing!"

She remained laughing as she pulled out the end of the lace from the front of the bodice and unwrapped the part that encircled her waist. I hooked my fingers around the lace and, wanting to get out of there as soon as possible, started pulling it loose.

"You're going too fast for someone who's apparently never done this before."

"You would know?" My reply shut her up.

I finally loosened the last part and the back of the dress fell open.

I had meant to look away, had meant to be a gentleman. But something on Lara's back caught my eye. Scars covered her soft skin like pieces of a scattered puzzle, each varying in shape and size.

"What?" Lara must have noticed me tense behind her.

"Your back," was all I managed to idiotically murmur.

"Oh." She breathed deeply. "What about it?" she asked in a way that suggested nothing was wrong.

"All these scars." I reached out without thinking and lightly pressed my finger to one that skewed across her spine, the length of my forefinger.

"It's the life of a bandit," she replied.

"What happened?"

"That one was from a royal guard when I was fourteen. He caught me stealing bread and whipped my back."

I let my finger graze her skin down to another scar somewhat lower.

"That one was from a knife that one of the girls of the Baruk clan of bandits stabbed me with. Her name is Nora."

Another one on her left shoulder blade. "That was from a man I tried to pickpocket who caught me. He shoved me into a wall, but there was a nail sticking out."

I was at a loss for words then, my breath hitching in my throat. Lara had unknowingly fought more wars in all her life than I ever would.

She turned around to meet my eyes.

"I'm sorry." I breathed out. "You didn't deserve to go through all of that." Part of me wished I could somehow go back and undo all the pain of her past.

"My scars don't hurt any more, Cai." She held my gaze. "They're a part of who I am now."

The corner of my mouth lifted into a slight smile. "You're one of the strongest people I know." I took half a step towards her, so that there was almost no space between us.

"If by that you mean I can kick your ass, then damn right I am." Lara's mouth curved into a smirk before I closed the distance between us.

Her lips were soft against my own, hesitant at first as if she were unsure of herself. Being this close to her made me wonder how I was ever going to pull away. Everything about her was intoxicating.

I wrapped my hands around her back, fingers getting tangled in the laces of her dress.

My mouth moved slowly against hers, wanting to savour every moment as if we could have stayed in the cabin for ever.

Lara wrapped her arms around my neck, and I trailed small kisses from her jawline down her neck. I spotted it then, the faded small patch of darker skin close to her collarbone. "You have a birthmark," I noted.

"It used to be more noticeable, but it's almost impossible to see now." She breathed deeply.

I thought back to the portrait of Princess Eloisa in Woodsbrook Manor, about everything I suspected. Part of me wanted to confide in Lara but something told me that it would not go down well.

I stood back, leaving her to hold the front of her dress. "Well, I assume you can handle it from here."

"Yes." She looked a little confused, wondering why I'd pulled away from her.

I was already out the door when I heard her say, "Thanks for the help, Cai."

Chapter 25

The Evernean Forest

Lara

"What happened between you and Cai that I should know about?"

Cordelia gently dragged a comb through my hair. Somehow this had become one of my favourite things even though she no longer had to pretend to be my lady-in-waiting. In the days that had passed, Cordelia had turned into her old self again. She started smiling more, talking more, and though I knew everyone mourned differently, it was good to see her like that again.

"What are you talking about?" I played with my fingers, giving her a shrug.

"You may be a good liar, Lara, but I can see that something has happened between the two of you, and as your friend, I demand you tell me immediately."

"I don't know what you mean," I persisted.

"There is an undeniable tension between the two of you. It's better you are honest with me, because you and I both know you haven't the slightest idea of what you're doing when it comes to romantic relationships."

"What romantic relationship?" I scoffed. "You're off your head, Cordelia."

"You kissed him, didn't you?"

I flung myself around on the bed to look at her. "How did you know?"

"It's written all over your face." She smirked and I covered my face with my hands, falling into her lap.

"Oh, what have I done?"

Cordelia gently patted my head. "There, there. It's not so bad."

"Technically I didn't kiss him. He kissed me."

"Did you stop him?" she asked, and I took more than a moment to answer.

"No."

She took my shoulders and pushed me back into a sitting position. "Calm down. You're being overdramatic."

"He's a prince, Cordelia. And if this war doesn't us both, he will go back to Norrandale and marry a duchess or something and I will still be a thief."

"You don't know that." She turned me back around to start brushing my hair again, before braiding it. "My point is, that man has been besotted with you since the moment he met you and I don't think it would be kind of you to break his heart."

"He's not besotted," I tried to argue, but she hushed me.

"I would give this a chance if I were you. You have no way of knowing how it's going to turn out."

"You and I know exactly how it's going to turn out."

She tied the bottom of my braid and I turned to face her again. "I told him I wasn't in love with him. Right to his face."

"And what did he say?"

"That I was lying." I let out a breath. "He's given me the time until he has to go back to prove him wrong."

"So what are you going to do?"

I stood up and pulled on my jacket, giving myself a hard look in the cheap, dusty mirror.

"I'm going to try and make it out of this alive. And then I'll allow myself to think about Cai." Having him in the way I did was enough … for now.

We travelled for half a day to Baruk clan territory. *We* being my uncle, his masters, me, Ray and Cai. This part of the forest scared me as much as the members of the clan itself. It was dark and gloomy and smelled like a swamp.

Even my horse stirred as we reached the centre of their camp. Eyes stared at us from the tree branches above. We were greeted by Olwin and his most trusted men. My eyes quickly landed on Nora, who wasn't standing too far behind her father.

She stared at me in the same way she always did, with an evil glint in her eyes. Cai immediately placed himself next to me, in a somewhat protective manner. For the first time, I was half thankful.

"Don't you think the black paint around their eyes is a bit much?" he whispered.

"I've learnt it's better not to ask questions," I replied hastily.

"Arthur," Olwin huffed out.

"Olwin." My uncle greeted him with the same hostile tone.

"Let's talk business, shall we?" The two of them then walked off and left the rest of us glaring at each other.

Nora was the first to walk over to me. Her black hair hung over her shoulders in small braids and I imagined, for a moment, pulling that hair out of her head. The thought gave me a little bit of satisfaction. "So Arthur finally got his men and his weapons." The only reason this meeting was taking place was in the hope of an alliance between our two clans. They would not take kindly to my uncle gaining power and thus there would be a discussion of support, and what they would want.

Nora's eyes landed on Cai. "I don't know your face. And not a bad-looking one at that." She smirked, but Cai kept his face neutral. I stiffened, curling my hands into fists.

"This is Cai," Ray said, as if somebody asked.

"Mmmhhh." Nora looked Cai up and down like he was a piece of meat.

I clenched my teeth. "Don't worry about us. We'll stay out of your way."

But Nora wouldn't take my offer. "Let's go for a walk."

We all half unwillingly followed as Nora started making her way through the camp. I caught the face of the man who had pulled me onto the horse that night when Cordelia, the guards and I were attacked. He didn't recognise me, couldn't have, as I looked like a completely different person.

There was a big difference between Clan Baruk and Clan Fairfrith. We stole from the rich in an attempt to tilt the scales. We did it to feed ourselves and to gather weapons for a cause that a lot of us deemed noble. But they pillaged and murdered as they pleased. From the rich or the poor, it didn't matter. I wasn't convinced when Uncle had suggested we meet with them, but as he made clear, we had little choice.

Nora and I had been enemies since our first meeting when we

were thirteen years old. Two groups of us ran into each other one day while hunting in the forest and I did not take kindly to Nora shooting an arrow through my leg. We had met various times since then, and none of these meetings ended without at least a drop of blood being shed between us.

Nora kept asking Cai questions regarding who he was, and where he was from. The way he lied through his teeth with so little effort caused me some discomfort. The better I got to know Cai, the more I realised how much there was to him and how different he was from what I'd originally thought.

"What about you, Ray, haven't put a ring on anyone's finger yet?"

Nora talked to us as if we were all old friends and not like someone who had stabbed me with a dagger once … or twice.

"You know me, Nora, I'm not one for settling down."

"Well, if you ever get bored, you know where to find me. I've always wanted to marry. We'd make a good team you and I." She gave him a wink and I rolled my eyes, not caring about Nora and her killer-couple fantasies.

"I'm surprised you haven't found anyone to settle with, yet. You're not getting any younger, you know?" I said sarcastically, before I could stop myself. This was how I got myself stabbed. Truth be told, the bandit life wasn't guaranteed to be a long one, which is why many people got married at a younger age, if they did get married at all.

"You're one to talk. I don't see any stolen rings on your finger."

"I have no intention of getting married."

"Hey, if you want to die alone, that's on you. Let's be honest though — who would want to marry you anyways?"

The men remained quiet as if sensing that, if they interrupted, they might just lose their heads.

"I'd sleep with one eye open at night if I were you."

She laughed. "Like you would ever try to kill me."

"Not me. But someone is bound to get tired of your ugly face pretty soon."

She made an attempt to step towards me, but Ray and Cai quickly pulled us apart. We made it back to our horses and Uncle appeared, finished with his meeting with Olwin. He gave me a slight nod as we mounted. Whatever they had discussed, the deal was done.

Chapter 26

The Evernean Forest

Cai

The breeze was warm and her forehead creased with fierce concentration. She had an arrow aimed at a target, a painted hay-sack on the branch of a nearby tree. Breathing slowly, I watched her, the string of the bow pulled tight. I leaned forwards on the tree branch.

Before she could realise my intentions, I gently pressed my lips to her jaw as she let the bowstring go, sending the arrow flying into the leaves of the nearby trees.

"You scoundrel." She elbowed me in the ribs and I let out a laugh.

"You and I both know you cannot shoot should your life depend on it. This way I saved you the embarrassment of losing, as you get to blame it on me."

She pulled out another arrow. "If you think you're getting away with this, think again." She pulled the string tight once more.

"Here, let me show you." I covered her hands with my own. "Pull the string to your mouth and relax your shoulders." She followed my instructions. "Now breathe in and once you've let it out, in that moment when you're completely still, before breathing in again, you let the arrow go."

She breathed deeply against me, then stilled completely. This time the arrow actually managed to hit the target. "See?" She grinned. "I told you I could shoot."

"I wouldn't call the winner just yet." I chuckled and her eyes met mine with an unfamiliar look. "Have you given any thought to my proposition?" I asked. She looked back towards the target almost shyly, allowing me to smile. Beneath that cold exterior, Lara had a softness she didn't allow many to see.

"Are you referring to the proposition of me falling in love with you before we go to war against the Evernean monarchy and possibly die?"

"Something like that."

She pulled the bowstring tight with a new arrow. "Well, I'll tell you this, Your Highness — you can kiss my neck until it kills you, but I still won't be yours." She let go and the arrow hit the branch next to the target.

I let out a laugh, placing my hands on her waist. It caused her to jump, and we ended up losing balance and plummeting to the ground. Luckily the ground wasn't too far off, but it still felt like the air had been knocked out of my chest.

Lara giggled. Her landing was more comfortable, considering she was practically on top of me.

"You really are trying to kill me," I said, and she laughed even more. I had grown fond of the sound.

"Nah," she said, surprising me by grabbing my collar. "You'd be no fun if you were dead." She pressed her lips to mine in a swift kiss that was over too soon. Lara sat up, her legs falling on either side of mine. I pushed myself up into a sitting position.

"Do that again," I said shamelessly.

"Are you ordering me, Prince?"

"Maybe." I couldn't help but grin.

"If you think I'm going to start taking orders from you now, then you are very wrong."

I placed a hand on her waist and gently brushed her hair away from her neck before pressing my lips to her collarbone.

"Mmhh," I murmured against her soft skin.

"We should probably be getting back," Lara said but I felt her breath hitch.

"Not until you kiss me again." Our faces were inches apart now and it took every ounce of self-control that I possessed not to close the gap between us. Lara started leaning forwards but we both pulled apart quickly upon hearing laughter nearby.

"Who was that?" she asked.

"Don't know. Probably someone fetching water." We weren't too far from the river. "The laugh sounded female."

I helped her into a standing position, in silence, as we tried to locate exactly where the sound had come from.

"We can't let anyone see us."

"It's nice to be appreciated like this," I teased.

"Shut up." She hushed me. "I will not be known as the Evernean rebel who had an affair with the Prince of Norrandale."

"You say it like it's a bad thing."

"It is a bad thing," she replied.

"How am I not supposed to get offended by this?"

And then we heard it again, more distant this time, but it was there.

Almost instinctively and for no reason whatsoever, I grabbed Lara's hand and she interlaced her fingers with mine. Another laugh came and this time it was male. Lara pulled me in the direction of the camp. "Come on, let's go before someone sees us."

"No," I whispered. "I know that voice. That's Jack."

"So?"

"So he told me he was going pheasant hunting this morning."

"Maybe he got distracted by some female company," she suggested.

"Jack doesn't get distracted. He lied to me. And if my second-in-charge lies to me, I want to know why."

She rolled her eyes, but walked after me nonetheless.

They were in a small clearing in the trees — Jack and, in his arms, Cordelia.

"Cordelia?" Lara half scolded in surprise, and Cordelia and Jack sprang apart.

"We … we …" Cordelia was at a loss for words.

"This is what you call pheasant hunting?" I grinned at Jack, who looked more than flustered.

"So this is why I can't find you most of the time?" Lara asked Cordelia, and suddenly everything started to add up. I felt stupid for being oblivious to it all this time. Angry with myself that I had been too focused on my own problems to notice what was going on with my friends.

"What are you doing here?" Jack suddenly asked, turning the tables.

"We were discussing matters concerning our entrance to the palace on the day my uncle decides to attack."

"We were?" I frowned for a moment before catching on. "Right, we were." I cleared my throat.

"You see, I thought that it would be foolish just to storm the gates since all their forces will gather against us there. But if we used that as a distraction, it would be easier to enter the palace from a different position."

"Right," she confirmed.

Jack and Cordelia looked at us strangely. For a moment the four of us only stared at each other awkwardly.

"Best be on our way, then," I said uncomfortably and turned in the direction of the camp.

"Right," Lara said again.

"You'd think I'd see that coming," I said a moment later.

"Don't be too hard on yourself." She ruffled my hair playfully and I pulled away. "One can only expect so much from a prince."

I barked out a laugh and chased her back to camp.

The moon was high in the sky and the night was at its darkest, but we were all still sitting outside, gathered around a large fire. Someone started telling stories and soon a small crowd formed. Despite the fire, the air outside was cold, not that I minded this at all.

"Delaris and Valerie knew they couldn't be together with everyone watching them." The man was telling a story about a prince and princess from long ago and their forbidden love.

"So, in the middle of the night, Valerie escaped from her palace, and with a dove, she sent a letter to Delaris, telling him to meet her in the centre of the forest."

"But we're not supposed to go there," one of the small children piped up. "It's dangerous. You'll die in there."

"It is dangerous, yes," the man replied. "During the day there is a mist that is so dense, you will never find your way out. Only those with royal blood can find their way through the mist. So when Delaris got Valerie's letter, he got on his horse and rode there as fast as he could."

"Did he find her?" a little girl asked.

"He did. And they lived happily ever after, where no one would find them."

"So nothing could hurt them?"

"No, nothing could hurt them."

I met Lara's eyes on the other side of the fire and she managed a smile. The stories continued with tales of the magic forest and heroes who roamed the lands long ago. The lot of us listened intently and, for that time, we could forget about poverty and rebellions.

Chapter 27

The Evernean Forest

Lara

"That bastard!" I flinched a little as a cup went flying past my head and hit the wall behind me, shattering into a thousand shining specks. "He's going to ruin everything!" Uncle Arthur attempted to pull himself together, but his anger was all too evident by the undeniable flush on his cheeks.

"I don't see how Lance getting engaged is going to ruin everything," I said.

It had been announced that Lance was engaged to a rich heiress from a distant kingdom named Lady Maliah, which sounded perfect for Lance's spending habits.

"King Lance cannot get married and have an eligible heir. We do not need more obstacles when it comes to the royal family."

I still didn't truly understand what the big problem was, but I wasn't going to infuriate him by asking more questions.

Uncle breathed heavily in anger and Cai's eyes slowly turned to mine. "Now what?"

"Now we rain fire and hell down on him," he answered for me.

"All fair and well, Uncle." I plopped down on a chair. "But how exactly do we plan on doing that? The spies you sent for the Norrandish soldiers are dead, and even if we have the alliance of the Baruk clan, our numbers still might not be enough. Plus there is no guarantee they won't betray us later on."

"We have plenty of people here willing to fight."

"Farmers and blacksmiths, but few with experience. You would be sending them to their deaths against armed soldiers."

"I can't stop people if they are willing to die for their freedom," he retorted and I bit my lip.

"So your plan is to storm the palace?" Cai raised an eyebrow.

"I don't hear you giving any better suggestions, Your Highness."

"You don't exactly have a list of options, but if your plan is to attack, I suggest you do it strategically."

"Need I remind you that I served in the royal army, son? I will not just have my people running like hooligans."

"If I may interject?" I interrupted the two men, whose glares had become all the more deadly. "The main entrance of Levernia palace has steel gates, which lead to the front courtyard, followed by two heavy doors. It is heavily surrounded by guards, but the other sides of the palace less so." I turned to face Cai. "Cai had the idea of using the gates as a distraction to gather the soldiers there, while the rest of us sneak into the palace at other smaller entrances."

"My men know the entrance to the prison cells. They'll free the prisoners to cause more chaos," Cai added.

"All in, we only have to fight Lance and the royal guards, with most of the servants being replaced already by our men. What will you do with Lance, kill him?" I asked my uncle.

"Would you prefer the honour instead?" he grinned.

"I would prefer to see him rot in a cell for the rest of his life. Death would be too much of a mercy."

"What about Princess Eloisa?" Cai asked. "She hasn't been seen for a long time now. Not even one of my spies could track her down."

"Then she's probably no longer in the kingdom," Uncle Arthur replied. I hadn't thought about that. Hadn't thought about the princess for quite some time. But it would make sense for Eloisa to leave temporarily with all the growing tension in the kingdom. Or for all we knew, she'd gone to visit some distant cousin or friend somewhere far away. What this could mean for us, however, I didn't know.

"So we take over the palace, which will give us power in Levernia, and with the royal family out of the picture and the support of the council, things should fall into place?"

"Then a new era in the kingdom of Everness begins," Uncle replied with a smile. "We give the people time to adjust. We make peace with the aristocrats. We employ a council of leaders consisting of the people. We lower the tax rate. The list goes on."

"It seems ideal," Cai said, almost suspiciously.

"Yes, well, that is what we are fighting for, is it not?"

We left my uncle's cabin soon after. I was heading for my own when Cai took my wrist. "Can we go for a walk? I need to talk to you."

I followed him until we were alone in the forest.

"I need to ask you an important question," he said, and I looked at him queryingly. He sighed. "You said that before all this, you were going to take the necklace and leave."

"Yes," I said, almost hesitantly.

"If you had left, would you have been done with thieving for good?"

I thought about it. "Probably not for good. I was just going to cross the border to Norrandale and start a new life there. With the money I could have got for pieces of the necklace, I could have done more than just survive for a while. My uncle had talked about this rebellion for as long as I can remember, but it was only recently that things started falling into place, and I don't know … I was scared of dying, scared of losing the only people I ever really knew. So I decided running would be better, even if it was the more cowardly thing to do."

Cai stepped in front of me and we stopped walking. "I want you to leave. Tomorrow morning before first light, you're going to cross to Norrandale."

"Lance has the border on lockdown, and I don't know the way." I reminded him of the obvious.

"I'm sending Brutus and Conner with you. They'll help you get there safely. Now listen carefully, you're going to find my friend, Thatcher, and give him this letter with my seal." He handed me a piece of paper. "He will make sure you stay safe."

"What about you?"

"I made a promise that I would contribute my forces one way or another. And I don't break my promises. Besides, it's the best way to see how things play out. What this is going to mean for Norrandale."

"What if the people find out? They would see this as an attack from Norrandale and not an uprising of the peasants."

"My men and I know how to stay undetected. I'll help your uncle where I'm needed with strategy — no more."

I wasn't entirely convinced.

"You're getting your second chance, Lara. I suggest you take it."

I found Ray on my way back to the cabin. "Don't you think you can at least try to persuade Uncle to change his mind?"

Ray blinked slowly as if not comprehending what I had just said. "Why would I do that? Why would you even suggest I do that?"

"Ray, please, I can't watch any of you get hurt tomorrow, or even worse, die."

He stared at me in almost pure disbelief. "Lara, we've had to steal and lie and practically starve in a fight for survival for most of our lives. And we're not the only ones. This rebellion should have happened years ago. But we finally have our chance."

I grabbed his wrist. "I'm leaving tomorrow morning. You can come with me. We can live that life we used to talk about as children."

He pulled his hand free. "I'm not going anywhere."

"Ray, please, I don't want to fight about this."

He wouldn't let me finish. "I'm sorry, Lara, I thought you were braver than this." And then he walked away.

It was still dark the next morning when Conner, Brutus and I stood outside the horse paddock, saddling up. "Are you going to be all right?" Cai asked and I nodded. "The rest of us will meet up with you as soon as possible. I just prefer keeping an eye on what happens today, so that I know what to expect."

"It's better that way," I agreed.

"Then I'll see you soon ..."

I turned to face him, but I didn't know what to say. There were so many unspoken words between us.

"See you soon." I mounted and the three of us rode off into the dark forest. I followed Conner and Brutus, though my thoughts kept drifting back to the journey that lay ahead for our clan and to the palace, knowing what was to come. I could hear steel swords clashing with each other. I could see blood spilling over the marble floor, and I became sick to my stomach all of a sudden.

Cai and his men were about to walk into what could be a bloodbath, and here I was, running away like a coward. I had betrayed Cai and he was still trying to save my life.

I stopped my horse and glanced back in the direction of Levernia, and then towards the crossing to Norrandale. All I had wanted was freedom from this life, this place, and here it was, completely within my reach. But an unpleasant thought lingered in my mind — there would be little worth in it, if Cai met his end in this rebellion.

"I'm not going with you," I said before I could stop myself. Brutus and Conner looked back at me in confusion. "You go ahead. There is something I have to get." And without another word, I turned my horse and started galloping towards Levernia.

Chapter 28

The Palace of Levernia

Cai

Jack grunted uncomfortably next to me as we huddled in the brush near the east wall of the palace. The guards walked in their regular places up and down on top of the wall. We were waiting for Arthur's men to attack the front gate, leading the guards away from this wall.

"What's taking them so long?" Alastor tossed a pebble in his hands. It was a small ritual he did before battle to calm himself down. I prayed that this wouldn't be like the battles we had witnessed before. He looked bored, but I knew that, deep down inside, he was shivering like the rest of us. Death was no beautiful thing.

"It hasn't been that long," Jack said. "Every second just feels like an hour out here." Suddenly the guards swerved and we knew they'd heard the ruckus from the front gates, where a contingent of Arthur's men was attempting to break in. We watched them run in that direction and, knowing it was our only chance, we sprinted for the walls.

The walls in this section needed some attention, the mortar between the stone crumbling to allow for finger and toe holds. Even so, it was an arduous climb. Beads of sweat dripped down my back, and every second I expected a cry to be raised from above and arrows to rain down. But finally, my fingers gripped the top of the parapet, and I cautiously pulled myself up.

The walkway was clear. I found myself relieved at the lack of discipline in Lance's men. My father's guard would never have been so foolish as to leave such a large section unguarded. But Arthur's intelligence was correct — they had been ordered to secure the front gates at all costs.

Jack, Alastor and I gave Arthur's other men the signal, and while some of them broke through the south gate, others scaled the walls. Chaos wasn't far away. The rebels in front of me ran across the grass towards the large windows of the ballroom. Glass shattered as they broke in. Already people were running around screaming and I could only assume that Arthur's men had breached the front gates as well. This meant they were in the courtyard, but not inside the palace yet.

It didn't take long for some of the guards to storm upon us with their swords. The guard who came at me went straight for my stomach and I had to jump out of the way. I didn't plan on killing anyone today, so disarming him would take somewhat more effort. I kept my eyes on Jack and Alastor in the event they required me to have their backs, before I struck back at the guard's swing towards me.

It didn't take long for me to notice that he didn't protect his shoulders, so I quickly thrust my sword into his right one, just hard enough to draw blood and make him pull away. I dodged past him, deeper into the palace. The scenes before me were enough to make my stomach turn and I had to remind myself to keep moving forwards, despite the blood and the horrible smell. I stepped over dead palace guards and palace servants, as well as some of Arthur's rebels.

I entered the throne room and my heart stopped.

Lara stood there, in the middle of the room, dagger in hand and face as white as a sheet.

"Lara?" I called her name and she turned to face me. An expression, which I could only recognise as relief, crossed her face and she sighed. My eyes travelled to movement at the other entrance to the throne room. One of the guards raised a bow, aiming straight for her.

A picture entered my mind. In a moment I recognised the bow and Lara's silhouette. It was the image I saw in the pond on the day we entered Everness. The vision had been a warning. A chance for me to save her.

I ran faster than my legs had carried me before, yelling at her to watch out. She grunted in pain as I tackled her to the ground, but the arrow went flying past into a nearby pillar. My eyes searched for the guard who had tried to kill her, but Jack had already taken care of him and gave me a nod from across the room.

"What are you doing here?" She was supposed to be halfway to Norrandale now.

Lara had an odd smile on her face. "I had to come to protect you. We both know your spoiled princely behind would probably get yourself killed."

I couldn't refuse myself a smile as I pulled her up. "You came back?"

"Don't look at me like that."

She dusted off her breeches, tendrils of hair falling in front of her face.

"Is Ray still alive?" she asked with concern, and some wicked part of me didn't like it.

I shook my head. "Ray has been missing since this morning."

"What?"

"No one could find him at camp. The last time he was seen was last night. Maybe he decided that he didn't want to fight anymore."

"No, he wouldn't. I don't understand. Maybe he's in trouble."

We started making our way down one of the hallways. "He'll be all right," I assured her, even though I didn't believe it myself. "Ray knows how to take care of himself."

"I need to find Lance," she said, and I grabbed her hand.

"I'm coming with you."

We ran down the hallway and turned the corner before another of Lance's guards was upon us. He swung his sword at us. I didn't hesitate to move Lara out of the way as I held my weapon ready to fight. I resisted his blows and told Lara to run and that I would catch up with her. I watched her disappear down the hallway, hoping that she would be safe. The guard put up a good defence but in less than a few minutes I'd managed to disarm him. I gathered all of the strength I could manage in my fist to knock him unconscious.

I immediately got on the move again, looking for Lara. Most of the screaming had quieted down and, to my surprise, most of the people who were walking around were not palace guards, but rebels. I may have underestimated Arthur and his capabilities.

"Your Highness!" Jack was standing some distance away. His expression looked serious.

"What's going on?" I approached him.

"Word just arrived. Your father has sent for you." That couldn't be good.

"Why, what's happened?"

"It's your mother." Jack hesitated for a moment. "She's dying."

It felt as though I'd been punched in the gut. I put a hand on the wall to steady myself.

"Your father wants you to come home," Jack said.

I tried to take a steady breath, my mind running rampant. With everything else going on, I didn't think I had the courage to deal with this too.

"I know you're worried about Lara," Jack said, as if he could hear my thoughts. "But I think it's best if we leave first thing in the morning."

He was right. I knew he was right. But the thought of leaving Lara in this mess didn't sit well with me either.

"How can I just walk away?"

Jack placed a reassuring hand on my shoulder. "This isn't your kingdom or your mess to fix. Your family needs you now."

I nodded with understanding, still forcing myself to breathe properly.

"I need to find her first," I said, without waiting for a response, and went looking for Lara again.

Chapter 29

The Palace of Levernia

Lara

I shut the door behind me gently, but still loud enough for Lance to hear. He turned from where he stood at a desk, twirling a small knife between his fingers. Lance was wearing his crown.

The study was cold and there was a hint of dust in the air, enough to make my nose wrinkle. It had taken longer than I wanted to find Lance, but once I had established he was not already apprehended, I asked the captured servants to tell me where he was.

"Come to kill me, have you?" There was a menacing tone in his voice.

"No," I said earnestly. "Though I'm surprised no one else has." I didn't even have a weapon on me. My only dagger was in the leg of some poor guard I had to fight on the way here. Maybe I had lost my mind. "I have come to right the wrongs."

He barked out a laugh. "I was wrong about you. You're not like me — I understand what it takes to stay in power. Even if it requires sacrifice."

My hands clenched to fists at my sides. "You're wrong," I protested. "An uprising was bound to happen. If it wasn't Arthur, it would have been someone else."

"Arthur." He sighed. Then, jabbing the small knife into the desk, his smile was as sinister as I'd always known it to be, but that didn't exactly do anything to calm my frantic pulse. Though I don't quite know what unnerved me so when it came to Lance. After all, I had the upper hand now. Lance's family was dead or missing. His palace was overthrown and I had simply made an effort to have this conversation with him so there would be a reckoning. This was my little revenge. This was me telling him that he would spend the rest of his life in misery.

"Arthur," he said. "Our uncle did always have a more violent side, though he hid it well. But you would know better than I do, wouldn't you, Elara?"

Elara.

My birth name. The name no one knew except my uncle.

I thought I was going to be sick, felt the breakfast I didn't even have slowly rising up my throat. "How do you know my name? Why would you call Arthur your uncle?"

Lance smirked and I shivered. "I knew from the very moment I met you that you ... that you were very clever, and yet you hadn't managed to see the single most obvious thing in front of you."

"What are you talking about?"

"Exactly what you're thinking."

"You're drunk, Lance," I spat out. "You're lying."

"Drunk? Yes," he said. "Lying, no. I'm afraid your worst fears have come true, dear sister."

"I don't believe you." Lance was a maniac. He'd lost his mind.

"Look at the painting behind you and tell me I'm lying again."

Somehow I knew I would regret turning around. But at the same time, I had to know. I moved my eyes away from him, slowly turning to face the wall behind me. And there it was ... hanging above the door, a portrait of the prince and princess of Everness. A painting of Lance and Eloisa. Only Eloisa's face was practically the spitting image of my own.

It was as if I could feel my blood turn ice-cold inside my body.

"Mother had two daughters."

I shook my head. "No."

"One was stillborn. Not the youngest, but the eldest. And the second resulted in Mother's death."

"No."

"Only—"

"No!"

"She wasn't stillborn."

He looked me dead in the eye, and no matter how hard I searched for it, there wasn't a hint of a lie on his face.

"But that is what the kingdom was told. That the child died along with our mother. To hide the fact that the eldest princess had been kidnapped on the day of her birth."

I had forgotten how to breathe.

"Magnus's younger brother, Arthur, had kidnapped his niece in a desperate attempt to get at his brother."

I couldn't say anything. Could not and would not believe a word that left his mouth.

"The King searched for his eldest daughter and his brother for years, but they could not be found. Until my father placed me in charge of hunting the masked bandit who had been pestering our kingdom. I sent my most trusted guard, Rhen, to go and find her, only to have him report she looked exactly like Princess Eloisa."

He dropped into a reading chair and took the knife from the table. "I wanted to tell Father immediately, but it was too late. He was a sleeping corpse. And then I caught word of a rebellion. It took me some time to put all the pieces together but I finally figured it out. I assumed Uncle wouldn't tell you the truth about your heritage, because you not knowing would aid him in his rebellion. Arthur was only Magnus's half-brother and thus it was impossible for him to be king. But he'd always believed Magnus was never fit to rule the kingdom. And now he had an heir to the throne. Once he killed me and Father, he could rule through you and use you like his obedient little puppet."

"You're wrong," I continued protesting. "He knew that this kingdom needed a leader who understood the will of the people."

"You know why our army didn't come to our defence?"

I didn't answer.

"They're across the northern seas, fighting alongside our allies in their own wars. I'd told Father not to send so many of our men. They've been there for months now."

Uncle Arthur knew as much. It was one of the many reasons he chose to attack now.

"But everything you did?" I asked. "With Cai and the necklace?"

"It was a convenient way to meet you. We might be bound by blood but I had no knowledge of the kind of person you are or the relationship you have with Uncle. I figured in the worst-case scenario I could use the necklace against Arthur in some way." He sighed. "But I guess there is no point now."

"You're telling me you had it all planned from the start?"

He stopped twiddling the knife between his fingers.

"Cai was the unfortunate soul that got caught in the middle. The bad blood has always been between our fathers. I knew you would eventually find your way back to Arthur, counted on it, in fact. I wanted him to think he'd won. Arthur had done a good job of staying in the shadows for the past two decades. I wanted to lure him out here so I could finally get rid of him. This was never going to end without blood."

"He has won!" I shouted. "Look at you, your palace is overthrown, your crown is gone, you're as good as dead."

"I never wanted the crown," he admitted. "But I cannot have that man take over everything my family has fought so long to protect."

This was too much to take in. I didn't know what to do with all this information.

"You used me," I finally said. "You used me, and you hurt me and you killed people."

"If you're talking about the young guard who was punished for letting you get away, that was actually a scare tactic. I only had him on kitchen duty for a few days."

And what about Rhen? I couldn't get the words out.

"I never claimed to be a good man," he continued. "And we both know you would smile happily upon my grave." I couldn't argue with him there. "But as I've told you many times, this life requires sacrifice in order to survive, and sometimes, the sacrifice is your soul."

"Well, I want nothing to do with it or any of you. I never wanted this."

He tilted his head slightly, inspecting me. "You might no longer have a choice."

I wasn't sure what he meant but I didn't want to consider it. I wanted to be far away from this place and these people.

"For a while I thought Cai might have told you," Lance continued and it felt as though my heart had stopped beating.

"What?" I said softly.

He sucked his teeth. "Oh yes, Cai has known for a while now, actually. Didn't think he'd be smart enough to figure it out and I'm still not sure what gave it away."

I opened my mouth, but the library doors burst open and a few of Uncle's men stormed in. They grabbed Lance but he didn't fight back.

"What should we do with him?"

I was surprised they looked to me for an answer. I almost responded that we should ask Uncle Arthur but decided against it.

"Take him to the prison. Everness no longer has a king."

I sat with my back against one of the stone pillars in the throne room, head in my hands. Lance's words kept ringing inside my head, over and over like a nightmare that would not stop. He was a horrible person who'd done horrible things and yet ...

He was my brother and I'd been lied to my entire life by the one man I called my family.

"Lara?" I looked up at the sound of a voice that had haunted my dreams. He stood facing me in the throne room, with a somewhat confused expression.

"Rhen?" I wiped something from my face. I wasn't sure if it was tears, sweat or blood.

"Rhen, I thought you were dead." I wouldn't have put it past myself to start seeing ghosts at this point.

"No, who told you that?" He helped me into a standing position.

"Lance did. He said he was going to hang you." But Rhen was there, standing in front of me and very much alive.

"I don't know what you're talking about, but Lance only put me in prison." Why did Lance say he was going to kill Rhen if he didn't? And why did he appear to want to be my ally against Uncle? It didn't make sense at all. Nothing made sense anymore.

"I don't even know what's going on. I need to speak with my uncle."

I made for the entrance of the throne room, but Rhen held me by my shoulders.

"Didn't you hear?" he asked.

"Hear what?" I had a feeling I wasn't going to like the answer.

"Arthur's dead, Lara. I'm sorry, but he didn't make it past the courtyard."

I froze. "No, that can't be right. Look again." I went for the door, but Rhen held me.

"I'm sorry, Lara."

A tear rolled down my cheek. "He can't be gone. I need to talk to him."

"Did Lance tell you?"

"The truth? Yes."

Rhen looked me dead in the eye. "Lara, listen to me. Arthur's gone, Lance is in prison and likely to abdicate the throne, and Eloisa is still missing."

I dropped to the floor from exhaustion or shock, maybe both. Rhen bent down to my level. "You are the heir to the throne of Everness now."

I was lying on a bed in one of the rooms, my face streaked with tears. It could have been hours or minutes or days, I didn't care. I didn't want to talk to anyone, to look at anyone. I just wanted to lie on this bed while I wished the world would disappear. The rebels had taken charge of the palace, Lance was in a cell and Uncle was dead. More importantly, I was a princess, and I didn't know what to make of any of it.

There was a soft knock on the door and I groaned out, "Go away."

When the person knocked again, I turned my head away from the pillow so that I could call out. "Rhen, I said I didn't want to see any—"

The door opened and Cai stood there with a worried expression. I sat up quickly. In the chaos of everything I didn't have time to consider what this meant for his kingdom but, of all people, I wasn't particularly eager to see him at this moment. He stepped into the room and closed the door behind him.

"I came to see how you were doing. Rhen said you'd been in here for a couple of hours."

And I had no intention of leaving any time soon.

I wiped my palms across my wet cheeks.

"I thought you'd be gone by now." Cai frowned at my words. "I heard about your mother," I explained, part of me wanting to say I was sorry about the sad news, but I was overwhelmed by my anger and frustration.

"Yes." Cai let out a heavy sigh. "But I wasn't going to leave before making sure you're okay."

When I didn't respond, he walked over to the bed. "Did I do something? You look angry."

"Angry doesn't begin to cover it," I blurted out, standing up. "How long have you known, Cai?"

His skin was pale and his beautiful blond hair was covered in specks of blood and dirt. He wasn't having a much better day than I was but that didn't mean I was going to excuse him.

"What?"

"How long have you known?" I asked, louder this time. "How long have you been lying to me about my family?"

"Who told—"

"Lance told me, of course." I considered for a moment that Lance could have been lying but he had no good reason to lie about something like this. "How could you?" I asked with a hint of desperation. "How could you keep something like that from me? How did you even find out?"

"There is a painting, in Woodsbrook Manor, of the royal children when they were young. Because you and Eloisa look so much alike, I wouldn't have noticed the difference if it had not been for the lack of a birthmark on her portrait." He gestured to the place on my neck. "I considered that maybe the artist had done it on purpose, so I asked you questions about Eloisa, pretending that we'd corresponded, and I realised you were lying about who you are."

It made sense. He'd started acting strangely at Woodsbrook and practically interrogated me when we'd been on the hunt.

"And then I began to wonder why you would lie to me. But Lance confirmed it that night in the cellars. I thought you knew who you were and that you were just pretending to be your sister for whatever reason. But then we fled, and it became clear you had no idea you were related to the royal family. It's why I'd always been so suspicious of Arthur, knowing he must have had something to do with it."

"That doesn't explain why you didn't tell me." Especially if he'd suspected it since Woodsbrook.

"I didn't know if I could trust you, in the beginning. And once I did, there never seemed to be a good time."

"No, I don't think there's ever a good time to tell somebody something like that but it gave you no right to hide it from me," I said sternly.

"You would never have believed me!" Cai cried out. "And you hate the monarchy. You wanted nothing to do with this life."

I rubbed my eyes with my hands, trying to keep the tears at bay. "It doesn't matter now, what I wanted." Turning my back to Cai, to face the window, I asked him, "Do you have any idea what it's like to be told your entire life has been a lie?"

"I'm sorry, Lara—"

"Just go, Cai," I said quickly, before I started crying again. "Go to your mother and your kingdom. They need you now."

He sighed. "I hope you can forgive me."

I heard the door close behind him.

The following morning, I was up bright and early, having not slept much the night before. There was a half-empty vase and ceramic basin in the room I'd occupied. I splashed my face with some cold water, hoping to scrub away the dirt and blood from the day before.

Cordelia walked into the room as I was retying my hair. She must have come to the palace once the commotion had died down. I could only imagine how overjoyed she was upon finding out her brother was unharmed.

"How are you doing?" she asked carefully.

"You know, I've been better."

"His Highness and his soldiers are leaving."

It was as if my heart skipped a beat. Cai was actually leaving. Of course, I knew he had to and I was still too furious to talk to him. But after spending every day in each other's presence for so long, it wasn't easy to imagine him being in a different kingdom again.

"I know what he did wasn't right. But I think you should say goodbye to him."

"I should," I agreed. Or at the very least see him off. I headed for the door but Cordelia stepped in my way.

"There's one more thing." She hesitated for a moment. "I'm going with them."

"What?"

"I'm going to Norrandale with Jack."

I shouldn't have been so surprised. Jack and Cordelia had been infatuated with each other long before any of us had the brains to figure it out.

"What does your brother say about this?"

"He's not overly fond of the idea but he knows it will make me happy."

The past few weeks had been a whirlwind. It felt as though Cordelia and I had barely had time to talk to each other. She had been there for me in many more ways than I deserved.

"I'm going to miss you," I admitted. "You were a good lady-in-waiting, but more than that, you're a good friend."

She gave me a tight hug. "I'm going to miss you too." Cordelia pulled back and held me at arm's length. "Promise me we'll write to each other?"

"Promise."

"Very well," she said with a sad smile. "Come and see me off then."

We made our way to the front of the palace where a few horses had already been saddled, ready for their journey.

Cai and Jack made sure all their weapons were in place while Alastor checked one of the horse's reins.

Jack looked up with a smile when he saw Cordelia approach.

"Are you ready?" he asked her.

She nodded with a wide grin and after greeting her brother, Jack helped her onto one of the horses.

I remained standing at the bottom step, unsure of what to do with my hands.

Cai walked over and my chest tightened.

"Well, goodbye then."

I cleared my throat, unsure how to respond. There were too many things running through my head.

"Have a safe journey."

There was something like hurt in Cai's eyes, and I wanted to tell him it wasn't fair. He didn't get to be hurt or sad when he was the one who'd lied to me, regardless of what his reasoning might have been.

I'd been too overwhelmed the previous day to have a proper discussion and now it was too late.

"Thank you. Best of luck with—" He gestured with his head to the palace behind me and I suppressed a sigh, not wanting to be reminded of my predicament.

"Goodbye, Cai."

Once everyone had mounted, the party heading for Norrandale was off. Cordelia gave a little wave over her shoulder to which I waved back. I watched their horses walk further and further away until the prince of Norrandale disappeared from my sight.

Epilogue

The Palace of Levernia

Lara

I glanced in the mirror as my new lady-in-waiting, Anesta, stood behind me, pinning up my hair. She focused intensely on her task at hand and I shifted my gaze back to my reflection. There was something different about my eyes now. They used to be empty, hungry and cold. A different soul had taken its place behind my irises, and now there was a glimmer in them that had never been there before.

"What should you like to do today, Your Majesty?" Anesta asked and I gave her a simple shrug in reply.

"I'm not sure, yet."

"I only wish to know which dress you would like me to take out."

I shifted in my seat to face the wardrobe with heavy oak doors hanging wide open.

"Take out the riding dress, will you? And the green one for tea afterwards. The Duke of Dankershire is going to pay me a visit."

Anesta walked over to the wardrobe.

"Anesta …"

She turned to face me.

"You do have to stop calling me 'Your Majesty'." I didn't like feeling as if I thought myself above her.

A strange look appeared on her face.

"Is that a problem?"

"Not at all. It's only, I like calling you 'Your Majesty'. Very few people ever get to say that in their lives. It is the highest honour to be employed by the royal family of Everness."

I couldn't blame her for wanting to feel important. I had very quickly taken a liking to Anesta when Rhen showed up with her as one of his first tasks as my personal guard and royal advisor. I wouldn't exactly get very far without a lady-in-waiting. Anesta was open and confident and possessed a sense of freedom that was unfamiliar to me. Though she could scarcely be sixteen or seventeen, she was a quick learner.

I would miss Cordelia very dearly. But I was happy she'd gone with Jack. They did fit so well together. I was only sad to be distanced from a friend.

"Very well, then," I said. "As long as you understand that I want us to be more like friends."

"As you wish." She took out the dresses and carefully laid them on the bed. I had since moved to the queen's chambers and it was very different from the room I had slept in before. This was my mother's old room. As far as I understood, no one had slept in it after she died, and everything was mostly as she left it, apart from the room still being cleaned. I hadn't allowed myself to look through her things yet.

Anesta walked back to me and sprayed some perfume. "So, the Duke of Dankershire," she said with a slight smirk and I rolled my eyes.

"It's not like that. At least, it's not intended to be. I found a letter in the king's study that mentioned the duke was owed money. I had invited him over today to get it settled." I didn't want to owe anybody anything. I had tried settling a lot of things in the past week.

I still referred to my father as the old king only because I couldn't yet bear the idea of the man actually being my father. I had grown up hating him. Had been brought up to hate him. And I had learned that the truth wasn't a fine line after all, but a pile of shattered glass instead. We find the stories in the broken pieces that we pick up.

"So you don't intend to find a suitor soon?" Anesta asked.

"My coronation has just passed and it wasn't even a public one. I have no idea how the people of Everness will react. I have a lot of politics to sort out before I can even think about suitors." I didn't have much of a choice in saying *yes* or *no*.

"Well," she said, dabbing some more perfume on my neck. I let out a small cough and she put the bottle down, taking the hint. "If they get to know you like I have, I'm sure they will be pleased."

I hadn't allowed myself to think about Cai either.

About how we'd left things. About how I hadn't heard anything from him since. No letters, no visits, no messages. Nothing at all. I hadn't gone to see Lance in prison, either. He had placed me in this position and if I refused, Rhen warned me, the kingdom might fall into anarchy with Eloisa still missing. Either way, I lost. It didn't matter that I was the one technically in power. I still felt like a pawn in this wicked game, unable to make choices for myself.

I smiled at Anesta for the compliment, nonetheless.

She gently picked up the jewel necklace from my vanity and draped it around my neck. My reflection grinned as I allowed my fingertips to touch it, thinking about how much trouble this necklace had brought me.

I had been called many things in all my life — bandit, thief, rogue — and now I would be called "Queen".

THE END

Acknowledgements

When I wrote the first line of this book, "The prince's crown was too big for his head", I could never have imagined the road that led to this moment. The story has changed so much since that first draft in early 2020. It's been a long journey, and I wouldn't have made it to this point without so many amazing people.

First, I would like to thank my parents. When your teenager tells you they want to become a novelist, it would be easy to encourage them to do something more familiar and secure. But you never discouraged me from following my dreams. In fact, most of the time you believe in me much more than I believe in myself. You've been supportive every single step of the way and I owe you so much more than I can put into words.

Then, to all my closest friends (you know who you are). I can't tell you how much it means when you tell people that your best friend is a writer or that you know a writer, hyping me up way more than I deserve. You're always there for me, whether it's to listen to me ramble about edits for the book or helping me become a better version of myself. I wake up every day and think how lucky I am to have people like you in my life.

And then to my wonderful editor, Jasmine, and the team at Joffe Books. Thanks for taking a chance on a 22-year-old girl with big dreams of becoming a bestselling author. We've got a long way to go but I'm so excited to be working with you every step of way. Jas, your edits and notes are always so insightful, and your kindness makes you a pleasure to work with. You are the only person I've ever looked forward to having a Zoom meeting with.

Finally, to everyone who has read my stories in the past three years. Had it not been for your lovely comments and sharing Instagram stories, I might have given up on trying to get traditionally published a long time ago. You remind me what I love about books and why I fell in love with writing. I adore being part of the bookish community and I can't wait to share more stories with you.

The Joffe Books Story

We began in 2014 when Jasper agreed to publish his mum's much-rejected romance novel and it became a bestseller.

Since then we've grown into the largest independent publisher in the UK. We're extremely proud to publish some of the very best writers in the world, including Joy Ellis, Faith Martin, Caro Ramsay, Helen Forrester, Simon Brett and Robert Goddard. Everyone at Joffe Books loves reading and we never forget that it all begins with the magic of an author telling a story.

We are proud to publish talented first-time authors, as well as established writers whose books we love introducing to a new generation of readers.

We won Trade Publisher of the Year at the Independent Publishing Awards in 2023. We have been shortlisted for Independent Publisher of the Year at the British Book Awards for the last four years, and were shortlisted for the Diversity and Inclusivity Award at the 2022 Independent Publishing Awards. In 2023 we were shortlisted for Publisher of the Year at the RNA Industry Awards.

We built this company with your help, and we love to hear from you, so please email us about absolutely anything bookish at: feedback@joffebooks.com.

If you want to receive free books every Friday and hear about all our new releases, join our mailing list: www.joffebooks.com/freebooks.

And when you tell your friends about us, just remember: it's pronounced Joffe as in coffee or toffee!